BACK

DM SEARLE

Back by DM Searle published by Nightscape Press Limited.

ISBN number: 978-1-7384438-0-2

ABOUT THE AUTHOR

DM Searle has worked as a copywriter for some of the world's largest advertising agencies. He lives in the heart of vibrant Camden Town in north London, where he enjoys writing speculative thrillers and other stories.

Feel free to connect with him on social media or drop him a line at dm@dmsearle.com

In memory of my father.

PROLOGUE

(-25)

Mark Doyle rode the escalator out of Canary Wharf station with murder in his heart and adrenaline in his veins. He stared at his hand and discovered he was gripping the rubber rail so hard his fingers had turned white. It had started with the dreams. Fantasies, really, flaring up around 4 a.m., eventually snapping him awake with their vividness. The dreams all had one thing in common – him, doing some kind of kung fu shit on that smug bastard Rich while a crowd watched and cheered. The impressively choreographed fights took place in playgrounds, town shopping centres and, once, on the street in the pouring rain, like he'd seen in *The Matrix*. In some of the scenes, hot women spurred him on, amazed at his fighting prowess, gasping in admiration at his every chop and kick. *What the fuck is all this?* Mark had wondered as he'd sat up in bed. But he knew what it was. He'd been reading about Smug Rich in *The Times* the previous evening. His old childhood nemesis had been opining about the state of the economy since the arrival of AI. Mark had been surprised to see how successful Smug Rich had become since their shared schooldays. Surprised, but also deeply angry. It was just so fucking unfair. *Life* was unfair.

Another thing that was not fair: the slow pace of the escalator. It was taking forever. In front of him, people in business suits stood double-parked next to each other, blocking his way as the mechanical belt slowly ground its way up, infuriatingly keeping him stuck on his step, just standing still until, at last, thank God, he was spat out at the top. At the exit, the lemmings continued to impede his progress, bunching together to create bottlenecks at the turnstiles. Mark was filled with a rage he hadn't known in many years. Yet, even so, he had no desire to strike any of these commuters. No, he was saving it all for Smug Rich. He almost cracked his Oyster card as he slammed it on the reader and burst outside. He was in a business district plaza that was the same dull, monolithic grey as the clouds above him. The morning air tasted fresh, but it did little to clear his mind, which was still flooded with images of Smug Richard's beaten, broken body. Mark stopped for a moment, tried to get his breathing under control as bankers, fund managers and secretaries streamed past him with indifference. He counted to five, nice and slow, and let out a deep lungful of air until his ribs felt like a deflated balloon. Repeating the exercise, he listened to his heartbeat. The pace refused to abate. It was like his heart was beating a war drum. He looked again at his right hand, the one he'd used to clutch the escalator rail. It was shaking, as though it had developed its own Parkinson's habit separate from the rest of his body.

Don't mess with me, Rich, I know ju-jitsu.

Hours before, at home, he had lain in bed, replaying the fantasies over and over in his head. At 6 a.m., he could bear it no longer and forced himself to get up. Marched out of his house in Wimbledon and towards the nearest Tube. Knowing what he was going to do.

A light spit of water tapped his cheek. Summer rain. It wasn't coming down hard, but it would be any minute now. His legs were already carrying him towards the homogenous monoliths of steel and glass, where over 300,000 people were beginning their day, grinding the transcendent wheels of capitalism. He glanced down at his brogues, which stepped onto Cabot Square, marching him ever forward. Mark tried to get a hold of his thoughts, slow the tide of frenetic images of blood and gore.

You don't know who you're messing with, arsehole.

Both his hands bunched into fists.

This is your last chance.

Through the revolving glass doors now, into the cathedral-like lobby of Weller & Morgenstern, where the suits poured around him like gushing rivulets, keen to check on the markets and start trading. At the barriers, he paused, realising he had no employee ID pass. The batwing-like glass doors were waist high, easily jumpable. But as Mark contemplated it, he heard a voice behind him.

'Help you, sir?'

He turned around to stare at the security guard, one of many on duty in the enormous antechamber.

'It's best you stay out of this,' Mark said to the uniformed man, who he only now observed was approximately twice his body size.

'Sir, I will need to see your company ID. Or do you have an appointment? I can check you in with reception—'

'Please,' Mark whispered.

Only vaguely aware that he was causing a scene, Mark felt a surge of pity. He didn't want to hurt this guy. The man was just doing his job. He didn't deserve to be caught in the cross-fire. He spun around, vaulting over the barrier before he could stop himself.

'Sir!' the security guard shouted. 'Stop!'

Mark ignored him, running for the lifts. There were six in

total, three doors on each of the opposite walls. Lucky for him, there were bodies everywhere to blend into. A pinging sound and a yellow light told him which lift to head towards. Nobody said anything to him as he pushed his way aggressively through the crowd. Not even a dirty look. They simply acted like he wasn't there. Mark wondered if it was just the culture here, the me-first, dog-eat-dog attitude people expected you to adopt if you worked for an investment bank as big as this one. There were more shouts from the main lobby, and his heart quickened. The guard had managed to round up a couple of his colleagues, and now a squad was chasing after him. The lift doors finally opened and he nudged his way to the back of the car. Still absorbed in their own internal thoughts, his fellow lift travellers ignored the frantic calls from security to halt the doors. The steel frames banged shut, the cacophony soon fading below him as the cables wheeled the lift up. In the cramped space, nobody paid him any attention. So far, so fortuitous. Mark tried not to look at the mirrored panel, not wanting to see his reflection, or rather the other-worldly look he was afraid he would observe in his eyes. Small white buttons on the gold panel lit up with each floor they passed. He realised he had no idea where he was supposed to get off.

You weren't exactly a hard man to find.

He heard a loud ping and felt a gust of welcome oxygen rush in as some of the lift's occupants exited.

Surprised to see me? Yes, well, rumours of my death have been greatly exaggerated.

Except Smug Rich wouldn't be surprised if Mark couldn't find him. He cursed himself for not thinking this through. He studied the panel. Forty storeys to go. His enemy was hiding on one of them.

Come out, come out wherever you are.

The lift opened on an open-plan office on the ninth floor,

fronted by double glass doors. The divisions they housed were helpfully etched on them.

TREASURY SERVICES

TECHNOLOGY

RISK MANAGEMENT

No, none of those was where Smug Rich worked. Mark remembered reading posts from the school group someone had set up on Facebook.

Hey, anyone know what happened to Richard Wendell?

Oh, didn't you know? He's helping big companies avoid tax by funnelling their profits into banks in the Bahamas.

At the next floor, Mark discounted 'Operations' and 'Human Resources'. Step and repeat. The car was almost empty when it reached the twentieth floor, whose sign promised 'Corporate Clients & Specialist Funds'. That finally sounded promising. Mark marched out of the lift and through the glass doors, almost knocking over a young man on the other side, who barely held on to his pile of papers.

'Can I help you?'

Mark turned around to face an older woman who had exited the lift behind him. Her suit was as sharp as her stare.

'No,' he said, abruptly. 'I know where I'm going.'

Which was a lie, of course. He let her pass, watching as she swiped her ID card and then following in behind her, trying to appear confident as he made a beeline towards the middle of the floor. This level, like the others, was open plan, with three glass meeting rooms in the centre, surrounded by rows of cubicles fanning out in all directions. All three meeting rooms were occupied, earnest suited types gathered around board-room tables. Mark approached the nearest room, scanning it carefully. He started by singling out the men, trying to mentally subtract decades from some of the puffier faces. Nope. He tried again with the second room, pressing his face against the glass. Of course, Smug Rich could be anywhere. Mark had no idea whether this particular meeting had anything to do with the Bahamas, or was even linked to his nemesis. It was entirely plausible that he wouldn't find Smug Rich on this floor at all. Perhaps the bastard had business in one of the other departments. He could even be off sick. But Mark had to keep going. One of the meeting attendees spotted him. Curious, they pushed up from their chair. But before they could open the glass door and ask his business, Mark was already moving across to the third conference room. The suits in this one were fixated on a large TV screen mounted on the adjoining, semi-opaque glass wall. Mark studied the fresh set of faces. And then, at last, the gods smiled benevolently on him.

1995 had been over thirty years ago, but Mark would have recognised that arrogant, ruddy face anywhere. The shirt and tie could just as easily be swapped out for the old school uniform. Smug Rich was oblivious to him, his dark, beady eyes transfixed on the charts displayed on the presentation screen. He was absent-mindedly spinning a mobile phone around on the table with his index finger. Even the way he was twirling it projected self-importance.

Time's up, buddy.

Mark grabbed the handle of the door and yanked it open; everybody looked up sharply. The man at the head of the table, who was leading the presentation from his laptop, frowned at him.

'Yes?' he asked.

Smug Rich joined the throng of puzzled faces staring at Mark. Some people seemed as if they were trying to place him as a colleague. Smug Rich narrowed his eyes. Was that a flicker of recognition in those pupils? Mark wondered.

'Richard Wendell?' he said, trying to keep his voice calm.

'Yes?' replied the jowly, rouge face of his enemy.

It was a face that Mark guessed had enjoyed far too many lunches with Weller & Morgenstern's corporate clients.

So. We meet again at last.

Mark's fingers clenched, just like they had done on the escalator. They balled into fists so tight he felt like he was about to cut his circulation off from below the elbows.

'Do I know you?' Smug Rich asked.

The investment banker flipped his mobile up like a large tiddlywink from the edge of the table and caught it in his other hand. Then, unexpectedly, he flicked his eyes down at the screen, checking his messages, perhaps, or some stock alert. 'We're in the middle of a meeting here,' he said, dismissively.

It was like telling a homeless beggar you had no change and hoping that by not looking them in the eye, they'll just move along and leave you alone. Mark's guess was that Smug Rich had decided that he didn't know who he was after all.

But you will. Oh yes, you will.

'Prepare to die,' Mark whispered.

A woman let out an involuntary snigger at one corner of the table. She clearly thought this was some sort of prank.

'What?' said Presentation Man. 'I don't understand. Who are you?'

'Waaait,' Smug Rich said. 'Are you from GreenCo? I told you the petroleum market wasn't going to be stable. You can't come back at me now.' Still, he refused to look up from his phone.

'I don't think he's from GreenCo,' said someone else.

Mark stared at Smug Rich incredulously. He was being blanked, even after his threat had been heard. Like the threat had been nothing. Like he was nothing. He felt it all over again, just like he had when they had been at school. 'I hope you've made your peace,' Mark said.

'Are you for real?' somebody else muttered.

But instead of answering, Mark clambered onto the table. He ran towards the end, stooping to pick up Presentation Man's laptop. Before anyone had time to react, he brought the computer down hard against the side of Richard Wendell's temple. He heard a crunch, the sound of a magnesium alloy meeting calcified bone. Blood spurted from the side of the investment banker's skull, and from his left eye. The phone dropped from his hand. Mark pushed off the table and launched himself at him. The impact took both him and Richard through the glass partition behind, shattering it as the two men, one still in a swivel chair, tumbled onto the carpet. Mark experienced the episode in a bizarre kind of slow motion. It seemed to be playing out very differently from the dreams. Rather than the deft, calm martial arts expert whose techniques elicited admiring sighs from onlookers, his arms were flailing about clumsily as his fists pounded Richard's face. Their spasmodic movements reminded him of what it had been like three decades ago when his limbs had kicked and thrashed about underwater in the school pool. He felt the intensity of memory, the pressure on his lungs as they filled with acrid chlorine. He swore he could hear the muffled laughter from his PE class burbling through the water. He recalled the strong hands holding his head down, Mark's younger heart over-beating as he began to panic. How his oxygen-starved muscles burned and ached. The struggle against the weight bearing down on him as a young Richard Wendell held him down. Little Rich had been laughing with unadulterated, side-splitting enjoyment at the terror he was causing weak, nerdy young Mark Doyle. Mark remembered how he had gone limp as the darkness came for him. When he had eventually come to, his swimming teacher was standing over him, having dived in and pulled his semi-conscious body from the water. Mark vividly recollected how his heart had raced and how glad he was to still be alive. But most of all, how he'd continued to cough and splutter water as he struggled to breathe normally again. In much the same way as Smug Rich was coughing and spluttering blood now.

'How does it fucking feel, you fuck?' Mark said. 'Not nice to feel like you're drowning, is it?' His fists continued to fly free, just as his hysterical words did. 'You remember laughing at me? Do you? Well, who's laughing now?'

The answer – he was. He could hear himself cackling hysterically as the person who had once regularly bullied him stared up in disbelief and confusion as he coughed up more blood from his lungs. Mark's laugh became deeper and more hateful until, at last, his fists ceased their frenzy of brutal and Darwinian violence. Mark stared at the pale, bloodied face that looked back up at him and was abruptly struck by just how vulnerable and boyish Smug Rich now appeared. Like he was ten years old himself. It really could have been him in that pool, struggling to breathe. There was that same look of fear in his eyes. Fear that faded away as Richard became colder and colder until he was completely still. And then Mark Doyle stopped laughing.

PART ONE

ONE

(0)

Nick Winters was at home when his mobile rang, threatening to deliver the worst news of his life. He stared at the phone, his mind racing back to all the research he'd done to try to arm himself with as much information as possible. But, for once, it all eluded him. Instead, he thought about Evan Miller, who, like several of his friends over the years, had been touched by the Big C. Stomach, Evan's had been. By the time it was diagnosed, it was already too late. The poor guy spent a miserable two weeks in hospital visited by his wife and twelve-year-old son as they said goodbye. For Nick, the crisis had started with a bathroom mirror. Two weeks ago, after his morning shower, he had spotted a lump under his armpit. *You should get that checked out,* a voice in his head told him. *I'm sure it's nothing,* it added nervously. Nick summoned the courage to call his GP the next morning. It was a week before he could get an appointment, during which the inner voice changed its mind completely. *You know what this is,* it whispered. *You know exactly what this is.* He tried to ignore it.

It had taken all of his willpower to get to the appointment. He was on the side of the bed with his shirt off while his GP, one Doctor Miriam Bryant, examined the lump. Bryant was a warm soul in her early sixties, with a gentle bedside manner. But even she was not able to assuage his fears. 'It's probably harmless,' she said. 'But you need to see a specialist.' A heavy rock formed in his chest. *Specialist*. He knew what kind of *-ist* that was. The oncologist turned out to be a short, pleasant Pakistani gentleman called Doctor Abdul Ravani. Nick had sat in the man's tiny office at St Bart's Hospital as he had explained slowly, and very carefully, that there would need to be a biopsy. The good doctor's words seemed like a far-off warble, and Nick was having difficulty following them. He had to rely on the follow-up letter a couple of days later to fully comprehend what the next stage was. They were going to take a sample of the lump and examine it in a lab to determine whether it was malignant.

That operation had been last week. Nick had been discharged four days ago. Since then, he had barely slept or eaten while he waited for Doctor Bryant to call him. Of course, he hadn't helped himself. For one, he'd made the mistake of ignoring Bryant's advice to stay off the internet. Within minutes of searching, he had found plenty of diagnoses, including non-Hodgkin lymphoma. And that was only the start of the rabbit hole. The web offered a plethora of other possibilities, most of them terrifying, even if they had only been posted by armchair experts. It was fair to say this had been the most stressful experience of his life. No wonder, then, that the voice was urging him not to answer his phone, which still buzzed on the coffee table. *If you don't pick it up it can't be bad news*, the voice reasoned. He sighed. Deep down, he knew the voice was bullshitting him. However much he dreaded this, there was no point in putting it off any longer. If life had taught him anything, it was that the truth was always the thing that mattered most. Hesitantly, he forced himself off the sofa, scooped the phone up, held it tight and shut his eyes.

It felt like an eternity passed before he heard a familiar soft voice on the other end.

'Nick? It's Miriam Bryant. How are you doing?'

His throat dried up before he could answer.

'I'm sorry,' Bryant said, gently. 'Silly question.' She paused. 'I'll come straight to the good news, Nick. Your test results came back negative. The tissue sample is benign.'

He let out a long breath. A million hours of wasted tension unknotted in his body in one go as a wave of relief poured over him. He opened his mouth to speak but could only croak. 'I . . .'

'It's okay,' Bryant said, in her soothing voice. 'It's a shock. I know. But the good kind.'

'I'm not going to . . .?' he managed.

'Die? No. One day, unfortunately. But not today. And hopefully not for a while.'

He blew out a long breath.

'You can let go of the worry, Nick. You're going to be fine. We'll need to keep an eye on the growth, of course. But it should start to recede as the weeks go by.'

He closed his eyes again and waited for the whisper-voice to tell him that the doctor was lying to him. That maybe he'd fallen asleep and that this was a dream. But no. He could feel the trembling in his hand.

'Thank you, Doctor,' he said at last. 'I thought it was going to be bad news for sure.'

'Well, it's not. Take the day. Reflect on things. You know, for some people, something as horrible as this can turn out to be a positive thing.'

'It can?'

'Oh yes. For many, it's a chance to re-evaluate their lives.'

'Oh,' he said. 'Oh, I see.'

'Think of this as a gift,' she said. 'Ask yourself . . . what roses do you need to stop and smell?'

He backed up slowly to the sofa and sank down into the seat cushion. 'You're right,' he said, 'thanks for the advice, Doctor.'

'You're most welcome,' Bryant said. 'Oh, and Nick? Make the most of today, won't you?'

Finally, he could swallow. 'I will,' he promised.

TWO

(0)

He didn't. But only because he spent the rest of the day asleep. Sheer exhaustion had finally caught up with him. The next morning, however, he awoke completely refreshed. He felt like he was a new person. As he drank his morning coffee, Miriam Bryant's words came flooding back to him.

'Well, you can let go of the worry. You're going to be fine.'

Fine. Yes. He wasn't going to end up like poor Evan Miller. A flash of guilt followed that thought, but it was swiftly vanquished by intense gratitude towards whatever higher power held sway in the universe. He'd known a couple of people who'd had health scares. One had told him the initial sense of relief wore off pretty quickly once you knew you were going to be okay. Before too long, normal day-to-day life resumed and you could easily forget it had happened. The idea horrified him. He made himself a solemn promise that he would take Bryant's advice and use this awful trial to re-evaluate his life. There were, after all, a limited number of days on this earth. He was acutely aware of that now.

He started that afternoon by grabbing his laptop and sitting at his kitchen table. Where to begin with his bucket list? His browser was open on his email, where he already saw several rejections for the latest article he'd been trying to pitch. He was used to them by now. Did he regret being a journalist? Not for a minute. There was no other profession he would have wanted to do, both then and now. Which meant whatever else was on his list, it wasn't a change of career. So what, then, did he need to change? He looked around him at the cosy Kentish Town flat he had rented for the last ten years. Was this the life he had dreamed of? To live here alone? What did he not see himself still doing at his age? The first and most obvious answer was renting. Did he wish he had bought a property? Should a grown man still be paying rent at fifty? It was the norm in a lot of European countries, sure. Besides, wasn't having a mortgage too dull for a bucket list? He did, however, feel a pang of sadness associated with the thought, so he probed it further. Perhaps he lacked a sense of permanency. Not of a house, necessarily, but of home. So was it a family he had missed out on then? Children?

He turned his attention back to the laptop and opened up Facebook. His feed was half full of photos of other people's kids. He stared at a recent picture of his young niece and nephew. The two of them, looking cute in their school uniforms. Children would have been a blessing, sure, but they were too abstract a concept in and of themselves. You needed to have them with the right person. *Ah*, he thought. *There's the rub.* How had he fared on the romance front? All of his relationships had eventually failed, the most recent having fallen apart just three months ago. Never married, never settled. Peter fucking Pan, that was him. Had he ever truly been in love?

He clicked on his friends list and scrolled down, sifting through until he found her. A woman he had reconnected with on this site several years ago. A friend. But she hadn't always been a friend, had she? He scrolled through her profile pictures until he came across one that looked like a Polaroid that had been scanned in. He had to stop and remember to breathe. It was the same woman, much younger, dressed in her graduation robe, standing between her parents. The smile on her face was one he remembered well, even from all those years ago. They had talked congenially on Facebook and had even met for coffee once or twice. It was cordial. Pleasant even. But the crazy sparks that once flew had long been dormant. He clicked back to his own page, where he was confronted by a sponsored ad that had been intruding on his feed for weeks. He'd ignored it up until now but this time he decided to click the play button. The video featured a couple in their early sixties. They were rollerblading through a park, hand in hand, and grinning like idiots. Nick turned on the sound and listened to the cheerful voiceover that accompanied it.

'Remember being young and carefree? Remember when the world was new and it felt like anything was possible? Now you can feel that way again . . . with Nostal.'

The visual cut to a pack shot of a drug that had regularly been in the news over the past year before returning to the couple, who were now doing an ice-skaters' pirouette. The man held the woman as they spun around giddily, still chuckling as a super ran across the visual.

'Speak to your GP today about the benefits of Nostal as part of a balanced health and wellness regime.'

A long scroll of legal caveats ensued, starting with a warning not to copy the actors' antics at home, followed by a long list of possible side effects, until the final dissolve back to the drug's pack shot and logo. Nick leaned back in his chair, cupping his hands behind his head. It was slightly depressing to think the ad must have targeted him because of his age. But he couldn't say it didn't resonate.

You're still very much alive, Nick. Think of this as a gift. Ask yourself . . . what roses do you need to stop and smell?

Maybe it was not too late. For either of them. He allowed himself to entertain the idea. Could the drug really do what it promised? If so, this could be more than worthy of a bucket list. Assuming, of course, *she* would feel the same. But first things first. He needed to do a little research.

THREE

(0)

'What do you want to know?' Doctor Bryant asked.

Nick was sitting in her office, listening carefully and ready to jot notes on his phone. He wasn't sure whether this was an interview or a consultation, but he suspected a little of both. 'Do you prescribe it a lot?' he asked.

'More and more,' Bryant said. 'It's very popular, especially with patients over forty.'

He nodded. *A drug that makes you feel young again.* Nick recalled the hype back when Nostal had first been given its licence back in 2025. It had sounded almost too good to be true.

'But it's anti-depressant, right?' he said. 'So it should only be used if there's a clinical need?'

'It's classed in that category, yes,' Bryant said from behind her desk. 'But Nostal works differently. You don't have to take it all the time for it to work. In fact, it's supposed to be taken for short periods only. A temporary mood lifter. And that's good news in one sense, because you don't develop a dependency.'

He made a note. 'Uh-huh. So I read it works by temporarily reverting certain proteins in your brain chemistry, which in turn stimulate certain hormones?'

Bryant shrugged. 'It's a bit more complicated than that, but essentially, yes.'

'But you still keep your memories?' he said.

'That's right. You just feel younger. Emotionally and psychologically, it's like reawakening the younger you.'

'And is all that safe? In your view?'

'Oh yes,' Bryant said. 'It's passed all the usual clinical trials.'

Nick knew this, too, from the research he'd done, but it was good to have Bryant confirm it. He pressed her on the point, however. 'What about side effects, though?' he asked. 'I saw a whole list of them.'

'Sure,' Bryant said, 'there are side effects. All I'd say to that is check the leaflet in any box of paracetamol you have at home. Everything has some side effects. But Nostal is perfectly okay for the majority to take.'

Nick's ears pricked up at the word *majority*. 'So it's not safe for everyone?' he asked.

'The drug itself is safe,' Bryant clarified. 'But it can bring back a lot of old feelings. And that's not suitable for everyone. That's why it's a controlled medicine. There are safeguards.'

'Such as?'

'Well, if a patient asks for it, we'd first have to fill in a questionnaire together. To help determine whether it's an appropriate treatment. And it would need sign-off from a second GP. As I said, there are some people who Nostal is not suitable for.'

Nick considered this. 'I guess not everyone wants to feel like their younger self again.'

Miriam regarded him thoughtfully, a gentle twinkle in her

eyes. 'And what about you, Nick? What do you want to feel again?'

'How do you mean?' he asked, but he knew what she was getting at.

'Is this just a coincidence that you're in my office less than two days after getting the all-clear?'

He gave her a guilty smile. 'All right,' he admitted. 'I *have* been thinking. About the things I wish I'd done with my life. And there is something. Well, someone. We used to have something once. I think we were both happy. I wondered . . . well, I wondered if this drug could help us.'

Bryant nodded. 'All I can tell you is my patients report positive results,' she said. 'If you genuinely believe it can enhance your happiness or boost your mental wellbeing, then maybe it's the right thing for you. What does this other person think?'

He let out a long, slow breath and shrugged. 'I, er . . . I haven't exactly asked her.'

'Well, don't you think you should?' Bryant said.

That evening, Nick sat on the sofa in his living room, his laptop open, staring at his ex's profile page. It had been so long. So many years. Would she even want to? He supposed there was only one way to find out. Nick cracked his fingers together, breathed out, and sent a woman he had once been madly in love with a long and very personal message.

FOUR

(O)

Three weeks later, Heather Newton walked into the Brighton pub where they had arranged to meet. She looked around the place, no doubt letting the same memories flood back in that Nick himself had done. Her eyes met his and he smiled, pointing down at the glass of wine he had bought for her. He had chosen a table by the window, where the summer sunshine streamed into the once-familiar venue. He rose to greet her, planting a friendly kiss on her cheek.

'Do you know, I hardly recognise it here?' Heather said as they settled. 'It's changed so much.'

'Thirty years will do that,' he said.

She winced. 'Oh God. Please stop putting a number on it.'

Nick sympathised. Thirty years was a long time. Back then, Heather's hair had been naturally blonde, her eyes devoid of the crow's feet that marked them now. Not that he could talk. The years had not exactly been kind to him either. The increasing waistline, the almost universal greying of his once-auburn, once-thick hair. The Royal Oak wasn't alone in having undergone major changes.

'So,' he said, 'how was the train? You take it from Victoria?'

The conversation spilled into mundanities, starting with Heather's train ride (indeed from Victoria), to the weather (glorious), to how her job was going (busy). He asked after her son George, and how his first year at university was going. She asked him whether he was still liking his new motorbike. Nick suspected it was a relief for both of them to put off the main subject. They had, after all, spent many hours talking about it now. But eventually one of them would have to address the elephant in the room.

It was Heather who went first. 'You told anyone what we're trying?' she asked.

'Nope,' he said. 'Have you?'

'Thought about it. Maybe telling my friend Kate. But I know what she'd say. "University fling? Bad idea."'

'We were more than that,' Nick said. 'We were . . . I mean, we could have been so much more.'

She nodded but said nothing. They both knew why they were here.

'You nervous?' he asked.

'Yes,' she replied without hesitation.

She sipped her wine, sloshed it around in the glass and stared into it as though further thoughts were forming there.

'What if it doesn't work, Nick?' she said.

'We've been over this,' he said.

'Nothing ventured,' she said, quoting him.

'Exactly. I'm single. You're divorced. What's there to lose?'

She looked away. 'I know,' she said. 'It's just . . . now that we're actually here . . .'

He knew what she meant. He was fond of Heather, but the idea of doing what they were about to do seemed counter-intuitive. Even wrong. Like making a pass at a friend.

'Heather, it's okay if you want to back out,' he said. 'Just because we've got them doesn't mean we have to take them.'

She turned back to meet his gaze. 'We were just kids,' she said.

'Maybe we can be again,' he said.

She hesitated.

'Everyone deserves a second chance.'

'You really think so?'

Why not? he thought. After all, he had been given one, hadn't he? Heather stared intently at the stem of her glass as if continuing to have a conversation with herself. Nick reached inside his leather jacket and placed the small bottle on the table. It was a vibrant green colour. He assumed the branding was deliberate, chosen to symbolise spring, or rebirth. Heather leaned forward for a closer look.

'Minus thirty,' she said, reading the red roundel on the label.

'Same as yours, right?'

She nodded, reached across and squeezed his hand. 'Nick, this isn't a guarantee. I don't want you to get your hopes up.'

'I'm not,' he assured her. 'I promise.'

But that was a lie. Their respective GPs had both expressed confidence in the drug's potential. He gave her an imploring look. For a moment, he was worried she was actually going to back out. They had spent so long discussing the pros and cons that he was surprised she was still raising objections. But then he saw the lines on her brow relax.

'It'll only last three hours?'

'More or less,' Nick said.

She sighed. 'Nothing ventured,' she said.

She reached into her handbag, removing her own bottle of Nostal. They smiled nervously at each other as they each undid the childproof lids. Nick tipped his bottle until a single bright green pill fell onto his palm.

'To second chances,' he said.

He placed his pill on his tongue, watching as she did the same. He took a large gulp of lager, feeling the tablet slide down his throat. There was no backing out now. He was committed to the experiment. And from the determined way Heather swallowed her own pill, he saw that she was too. He was glad. Now, all they had to do was wait.

FIVE

(-30)

His first clue that it was working was the tingle he felt scurry down his spine. It was like seeing an old photo of yourself and getting a sudden rush of the exact same emotions you felt when it was taken. Or how the right song, played at the right moment, can magically transport you back in time. Across the table, his perception of Heather began to change. A memory formed, a vivid image of her, nineteen years young, standing in this very pub. Instead of her elegant floral dress, he pictured her in ripped denim jeans and a red lumberjack shirt over a *Nevermind* T-shirt. In place of the designer handbag she'd been carrying, she held a khaki satchel.

'You Nick?' she had asked him, slinging the bag down on the table.

He remembered it had been hard to hear her over the music the pub had been playing in the background. The song came back to him too. East Seventeen. A popular boy band at the time.

'God, this music is shit, isn't it?' she said, plonking herself on the stool next to him.

She lit up a cigarette and offered him the open pack. He shook his head.

'So, you got any ideas for the assignment?'

Nick squeezed his eyes shut and opened them again in the present. The chill he felt was the same one he'd experienced when he had first set eyes on Heather Newton. He noticed his hands were trembling too, just like they had back then.

'You all right? What's happening?'

Forty-nine-year-old Heather shot him a look of concern. He blinked at her. This mature, sophisticated woman was about as un-grungy as they came. Yet he felt as though it was the girl in green eyeliner and Caterpillar boots staring back at him. He remembered the old adage that you never get a second chance to make a first impression. But that was wrong. His first impression of Heather was returning with gusto.

'What's happening?' she asked. 'Is it working?'

He swallowed. 'I think so,' he said. 'I feel like I just jumped back in time.'

He tapped the table. 'I think we were in this exact spot,' he said. 'I tried to pick it as accurately as I could. I was by the window when you came in ...'

She bit her lip and her eyebrows shot up. 'Wait,' she cried. 'I think I feel something too.'

Her pupils were dilated, a sure sign the drug was working. She placed a palm over her heart. He sensed she was struggling to put it into words. He knew he was. How do you articulate what it's like to feel nineteen again? He was convinced that he was back at the *old* Royal Oak, the one from all those moons ago when it had been a popular student pub. Though Nick knew the drug did not cause hallucinations, he would not have been surprised if the decor around him suddenly reverted to its original shabby charm, complete with red carpet stained with lager and cigarette ash. He was almost convinced the air had changed too, becoming tinged once more with the musty sweat of the portly landlord that somehow always crept into every nook and cranny of the place.

'I remember they were playing some godawful boyband shit,' Heather said.

'Yes!'

'And you. You had that horrible green beanie on.'

'It was the nineties,' he said.

'I introduced myself,' Heather said. 'But you were acting all weird. I thought maybe you had a tic.'

He smiled. 'I was nervous,' he said. 'I feel nervous now.'

And he did. In all the few times they had met since reconnecting on Facebook, he had felt nothing but platonic warmth towards his old girlfriend. Now, her physical presence was erotically charged. The feeling was both comfortingly familiar and very strange.

They'd been put together by the university, where they'd both been studying journalism. The idea had been to form pairs that would collaborate on a local interest story. They had agreed to meet in the Royal Oak.

'I remember I wasn't sure about working with you,' Nick said. 'You seemed a bit full of yourself.'

She chuckled. 'I wasn't sure about you! You asked me whether my parents were upper middle class. Do you remember that?'

'No,' he admitted, feeling a little sheepish.

'You said everyone studying journalism must be from a posh background, apart from you.'

'You're kidding.'

'You were a bit of a wanker about it, to be honest.'

'I told you, I was nervous,' he said. 'I was probably just blabbing. Trying to impress you.'

Like I feel like I'm doing now, he thought.

'Well, lucky for you, I found you quite endearing.'

'God knows why,' he said.

'I do remember we talked for ages though. Eventually, I told you about my parents. How Dad was a builder and Mum worked in Tesco's. The look on your face was priceless.'

'I definitely misjudged you,' Nick said. 'You had that Nirvana T-shirt on and I guess I just assumed you were one of those middle-class kids with a trust fund. But I did fancy you. From the moment I saw you, actually.'

She blushed. 'I could tell,' she said. 'By the time I worked out you were acting weird because you were shy, I realised you were actually quite sweet.'

They went back to discussing that first night. Heather filled in some of his blanks, and he hers.

'You had so many ideas for our assignment,' she said.

'I remember,' Nick said. 'I wanted to change the world.'

'*Plus ça change*,' she said.

It was his turn to laugh. 'Yeah, well. We did an okay story in the end, I suppose. Our own little Watergate.'

He smiled. As they continued to go down memory lane, Nick offered to buy them both another drink. She readily accepted, and he trotted to the bar with nervous haste. It wasn't until he was back that he realised what he had done.

Heather curled her lips back. 'No! No way.'

'I . . . I just asked for them. I didn't even realise.'

'Oh my God, Nick. No!'

He laughed. 'The barman thought I was crazy.'

Nick placed the glass in front of her. 'One snakebite for the lady,' he said.

Half cider, half lager. They had gobbled up the putrid stuff back in their student days.

He clinked his glass with hers and smiled. 'Cheers,' he said.

She rolled her eyes. 'Happy days!'

It had been her stock phrase. She said it with exactly the

same snark Nick remembered from thirty years ago. He realised, with some degree of shock, that he was suddenly in love with her again. Just as easy and as simple as if someone had turned on a switch inside him. Her widened eyes met his and, in that gaze, two souls who had been apart for thirty years instantly reconnected.

SIX

(-30/0)

They spent the afternoon visiting old haunts. 'Stomping grounds', Heather called them. First up was the pier, where they had whiled away so many hours instead of attending lectures. Nick held her hand, just like he had when they were first going out. They weaved their way around fruit machines, coin pushers and arcade games. A cacophony of shrill alarms, bleeping jackpot jingles and other once-familiar sounds filled the air, prompting old memories as the chemistry in their brains changed. Nick insisted they go on one of the old rides. They picked the ghost train, which was still as ridiculously unthreatening as he remembered. As they exited, he stared up at the pier's roller coaster, thinking it was exactly how his stomach felt right now. Nearly fifty years old but as giddy as a teenager. Even his hand was clammy in hers. They took a stroll on the pebbled beach, where they bought ice creams and sat down near the pillars under the pier. Nick bit into his cone and watched the calm sea sparkle in the late August sunshine. He turned just in time to catch

Heather licking hers and realised he was looking at her lasciviously.

'You all right?' she asked.

'Sorry,' he said. 'This is just so . . . *weird*.'

'I know. It's weird for me too.'

'Good weird or bad weird?'

'Oh, definitely good,' she said.

She caught his eye, and he saw a playful flicker in her pupils. He grinned back at her.

They jumped on the number twenty-five bus. Sat together, fingers interwoven, oblivious to the other passengers. His stomach was still cartwheeling like crazy. It felt so all-encompassing that he almost missed the stop. But then they were in front of the old university admissions building, which was the same drab colour it had always been. She hooked her arm around his, resting her head on his shoulder.

'I wonder if the halls are still as shit,' she said.

'Probably not. The kids get Wi-Fi and everything now.'

He looked at her. 'Want to check out the old house?'

She squeezed his arm, which he interpreted as a *yes*. It wasn't far from the campus, just a ten-minute walk. An ordinary terraced house he'd once shared with two other boys. But it had also been special because Heather had stayed over at the weekends. He visited her in halls during the week, she came over on Saturdays. That had been their deal. Standing in front of the gate brought back a flood of new memories.

'I looked the place up online,' Nick said. 'Whoever owns it now rents it out as an airbnb.' He took out his phone and showed her a picture. 'They've done it up quite well,' he said. 'My room looks totally different.'

She took the phone and expanded the photo on the screen.

'I hardly recognise it without those five-pound throws you had pinned to the wall.'

'Yeah, but no Bob Marley poster,' he said. 'I wasn't your total student cliché.'

She pointed to the far corner of the room. 'That's where you kept your vinyl collection, remember? I loved that record player.'

'Vinyl. Who'd have thought the hipsters would have kept it alive, huh?'

He smiled. 'You know if this works, we could, you know. Stay there some time. If we wanted to, I mean.'

She grinned. 'What made you think I would agree to go that far on our first retro-date?'

'I didn't . . .' he began.

'Except I probably would,' she said.

Unable to deny his feelings any longer, he turned her around gently. She didn't resist, instead turning her face up towards him. Their lips found each other. Over the years, Nick had experienced his fair share of kisses, but this was easily the strangest of his life. It felt charged with urgency, as though an external force was pressing their faces together. He knew she felt it too, the way she clutched at him as their tongues mingled. He didn't know how long they stayed that way, but the spell was eventually broken by a gang of laughing teenagers passing by.

'They're probably repulsed at the sight of two old people snogging in broad daylight,' Nick joked.

'But I don't feel old,' she said, and her eyes sparkled again.

He nodded. 'Come on,' he said. 'We've probably only got an hour left.'

They visited the Churchill Square Shopping Centre, strolling along the surrounding streets, pointing out shops they remembered and those that were new, lamenting the demise of favourite pubs. They wandered through the Lanes, past all the jewellery stores and touristy eateries. At the seafront once more, Heather drew his attention to a familiar chip shop. Like many of its counterparts along the strip, the Jolly Fryer suffered from the constant onslaught of sea air. Its signage had faded and the blue paint around the front glass had chipped. But the logo was the same one from the nineties – an anthropomorphised cod standing on its tail fin, proudly holding a deep fat frying basket in one of its fins.

'There's our Watergate!' she said. 'It's still here!'

He smiled.

Their local interest story, the one they had eventually collaborated on, was about the Jolly Fryer. The owner had been in the habit of pouring his chip oil down the drain instead of asking the council to collect it, a fact Heather had only discovered because one of her housemates happened to work there part-time. After a bit of research, Nick had discovered this contravened Section 111 of the Environmental Protection Act. The pair had co-written the story and handed it in. As well as being marked by the university, the article had also been submitted to the *Brighton Gazette*. It was the first time either of them had seen their work in print.

'Let's not go in,' Nick said. 'I doubt they've ever forgiven us for that particular exposé.'

'Good idea!'

They about-turned and headed north, at which point Nick checked his watch again. The effects of the Nostal would wear off any minute now. He suggested they call it a day. They walked together in comfortable silence, both mulling over the experience they'd just shared. It was almost six o'clock when they approached the train station and the sun was starting to cool. Nick accompanied her to the platform. She was about to board when he touched her arm and she turned.

'I'd like to do this again sometime,' he said. 'If you would.'

'Of course I would,' she said.

He offered his hand and she took it. Their fingers touched, but it felt different now. There was none of the electricity that had been there just an hour ago. It felt like he was holding his sister's hand. They smiled awkwardly at each other.

'I'll call you,' he promised.

SEVEN

(O)

He retrieved his motorbike from the car park behind the station. He had only recently acquired the Honda. It had a more street racer-y feel than his old Triumph, which Nick had traded in a couple of weeks ago. He told himself at the time that he needed a change, but he suspected it might have been a subconscious move. He released his helmet from the seat's netting and slipped it on, giving the visor a quick wipe. Traffic was light on the A23 back to London, which meant he didn't have to concentrate as much, leaving his mind free to reflect on the day's grand experiment. Not that he needed much reflection. The results were in. The day had been phenomenal. Nostal had literally scrubbed away the time he and Heather had been apart. Feelings that had faded long ago were once again ignited. For the first time since his scare, Nick actually felt grateful for that lump.

Two hours later, he was back home in his London flat. As he heated a plate of chicken in the microwave, he heard the familiar sound of a WhatsApp message alert. Hoping it might be Heather, he hastily retrieved his phone from inside his leather jacket that he'd slung over the back of the sofa. But the message was from Sam Goddard. Sam was his old editor, back when respectable newspapers would still employ him. Before he had burned all his bridges. He hadn't spoken to Sam for years.

Hi Nick. Know it's been a while. And I know there's history. But I think I can make it up to you. I have a story for you. A pretty fucking big one too. Got time for lunch next week?

Nick stared at the text. Why would Sam be contacting him out of the blue? And since when did he want to throw him a bone? Over the last five years, Nick had had plenty of time to reflect on the way things had gone and had concluded long ago that it wasn't Sam's fault. The truth was, he had just been doing his job, just as Nick had been trying to do his. He didn't know if they were still friends, but as far as he was concerned, Sam was not his enemy. He considered asking what the story was about, but he figured if this was an olive branch, it was important he grab it unequivocally.

Sure thing, Sam. When and where?

A few moments later, Sam replied, suggesting meeting on Wednesday at Molto Penne, an Italian restaurant near Liverpool Street. The two of them had frequented it a lot when they had worked together and had shared more than a few liquid lunches at its white-clothed tables. *Just like old times,* Nick thought. It seemed revisiting old times was his thing this weekend. Still puzzling about Sam's agenda, he confirmed the meet and placed his phone down on the arm of his sofa. Wednesday was going to be an interesting day.

. . .

Later, just before he was about to take himself to bed, he heard another ping. This time, it was Heather.

> *Hey Nick. Good to go down memory lane. Let's do it again. What are you up to tomorrow night? Xx*

He smiled and set his thumbs to work.

> *Could visit some more stomping grounds. If you fancy.*

He waited as her typing dots danced around the screen. When they fell, they formed three simple words that instantly warmed his heart.

> *It's a date.*

EIGHT

(O)

The next morning, Nick checked his email, only to discover that his latest pitch had still not garnered any interest. No one wanted to commission him to write about glitches in the UK's new air traffic control system, which some insiders said put passengers at risk. Nick had been tipped off to the story by an anonymous subscriber to his website, where he published most of his articles nowadays. The source claimed to be a senior figure in the Civil Aviation Authority who had raised concerns with colleagues that had fallen on deaf ears. It was credible and had clear public interest, yet Nick still couldn't get anyone to bite. It wasn't that they didn't want to run it. They just didn't want *him* to write it. Nick's reputation continued to precede him, even years after writing the story that had changed his fortunes. It was nothing new, but the situation continued to put constraints on his finances. With his rent due soon, he knew he had to abandon the pitch and instead go in search of more likely sources of income, where his previous history wouldn't count against him. More recently, this had taken the form of reviewing tech products for consumer magazines and websites. It might not be Pulitzer-winning journalism, but work was work. And Nick could not afford to be proud. Plus, on a hobbyist level, he actually enjoyed learning about the latest gadgets.

Inspired by the morning's aviation theme, he spent the next hour putting together a proposal to review and rate the top ten drones on the market. Niche, but sellable. By lunchtime, he had sent the pitch off to the desks of several technology and aviation titles. Having done as much as he could, he rewarded himself with the afternoon off. The morning had been so productive that he'd barely had time to reflect on the day he'd spent with Heather. But after he'd made himself a sandwich and watched the lunchtime news, he found himself reliving some of the best moments they had experienced together. Nostal really was remarkable. Sunday was the first time in a long time he had felt alive again, renewed in purpose. And, most astonishing of all, deeply back in love.

NINE

They arranged to meet in Camden Town in an old pub they once used to see gigs in. Heather arrived exactly on time. He felt a slight shock when he saw her standing at the bar. This was grown-up Heather again. The chemistry they had both experienced in Brighton was completely gone. But he was glad she was back for more. He gave her a friendly kiss on the cheek. They started with water, each taking a dose and waiting until they saw the pupils in each other's eyes widen. One moment, it was like he was still talking to an old friend, and the next, his hormones were on fire. He watched her change too, the look in her eyes that went from platonic affection to something fierce and indescribable. Revived emotions swept back through them.

A band was playing on a small stage at the back. They weren't very good, but Nick didn't care.

'Remember when we used to go to gigs?' Heather was shouting in his ear.

'Were we really as young as all these kids?' he asked.

'Younger,' she confirmed.

Heather turned to face the band on stage, and he glanced at her side profile, feeling the erotic frisson that went with it. *My God,* he thought. *It's like I'm a teenager again.* Had he been this horny all the time at that age? What a nightmare that must have been. He tried to take his mind off it.

'Good day at the office?' he asked, shouting over the din.

'The usual,' she said. 'Chaos. Nice to be done.'

Since leaving journalism, Heather had been working as an in-house copywriter for an up-and-coming gin company.

She turned to him, gripping his arm. 'Let's not talk about work,' she said. 'Let's just get fucked up, okay? Like we used to.'

'Okay, but no more snakebite.'

He heard the same dirty laugh he remembered from her youth. She went to the bar, returning with vodka shots.

She handed him one. 'Happy days!' she said, downing her drink and winking at him.

TEN

(-30)

They ended up in Shoreditch in an industrial warehouse, electronica-cum-trap music rebounding off the red-brick walls. It was dark inside the nightclub, rainbow lights washing the revellers in colour. Nick's short-sleeved shirt was soaked in sweat. Heather danced in front of him with utter abandon, throwing her arms up in the air and her head back. She clearly couldn't care less about the looks the Zoomers were giving her. Neither could he. The hours that followed were a blur, but somehow they made it back to Nick's flat.

'Nice place,' Heather said, looking around.

'Not as nice as yours, I imagine,' he replied, referring to her house in Clapham.

'What can I say?' Heather said. 'Dave paid for half of it.'

Nick invited her to sit, and went to fetch them each a glass of water.

'And how is Dave?' he asked, running the kitchen tap.

'Same as ever,' she said. 'I think he's with another younger model now. I can't keep up. He's such a cliché, honestly. But at least we can be nice to each other, even if only for George's sake.'

Nick returned to the table and placed their glasses down.

'What do you think Dave would say if he knew about this?'

'That's a tricky one,' she said. 'I think he was always jealous of you.'

'Really?'

'Sure,' she said. 'He always knew that we had something special once.'

Nick sank into the chair opposite her. 'So how weird is this?' he said.

'Weird but wonderful.'

They sipped their water, a strange feeling permeating the air. Then Nick stood up, kicking over the chair. She rose too, and then they were on each other, like animals in heat. Somehow, they stumbled into the bedroom without knocking into any more furniture. Their lips met again, endorphins flowing through every part of him. The next thing he knew, they were naked. He became aware his whole body was trembling as they made love. Of sweat seeping off him. Of Heather, moaning, writhing. And then, something else that hadn't happened since those long-lost days. He climaxed . . . and cried.

'Hey, you okay?' she asked, rubbing his back gently.

'I . . .' He blinked hot tears. 'My God, I love you,' he whispered. 'I love you. I've always loved you.'

She stroked his back. 'Me too,' she said.

Later, Nick rolled onto his back. Heather propped herself up on her side, pinching his chest hairs affectionately.

'Well,' she said. 'Someone found their third wind.'

He checked his watch. It was 2 a.m. They'd been in bed for two solid hours, having both taken another pill. He rolled over, reached into the bedside drawer and withdrew a familiar object, holding it between his finger and thumb.

'Is that . . .?'

'Herbal refreshment,' he confirmed. He held the joint out to her and smiled.

'Where'd you get it?'

'One of the advantages of living close to Camden Lock,' he said. 'Remember how we used to smoke it and just listen to music? It was my favourite way to pass a Saturday.'

'Or any weekday we had no lectures. But I haven't touched that stuff in years.'

Her words slipped away as she stared at the joint. The look in her eyes seemed to Nick to be one of deep recollection.

'Yet you fancy a smoke, right? I do too.'

She nodded.

'Like old times,' he said, lighting the blunt and taking the first toke. He handed it over.

Heather took it cautiously between her fingers. 'Young times,' she said.

Later still, he stared at the ceiling, his mind full of wonder. He felt her palm run down his stomach, self-conscious at the flab that now permanently lived there. He glanced across at her, this grown woman, with all her beautiful realness, all the flaws of a human body starting to visibly age, her stretch marks. All these things were there before him, and yet they weren't. It was difficult to put into words, but it was as tangible as anything he had ever known. They held each other gently as they drifted off, the Nostal receding as sleep eventually came for them.

ELEVEN

(O)

He woke the next morning to the sound of the shower running. Five minutes later, the door opened and a stranger walked in, wrapped in a towel. For a confusing moment, Nick thought it was Heather's mother.

'Good morning,' Heather said.

He shut his eyes. With no small degree of shame, he realised his first reaction to seeing her was mild regret. There was no getting away from it, was there? In the cold light of day, they were two middle-aged people with bodies that were starting to fade. He sat slowly up in the bed and felt a tender itch under his arm. His fingers traced the line of his biopsy scar. Heather had discovered the lump in the heat of their passion last night, but had asked no questions. Just as he had not asked about the two new tattoos he had found on her. They had been apart for decades, after all, and they had a right to their own private stories.

'Last night was . . . special,' he began.

'Yes, it was,' Heather agreed.

Looking at her, rubbing her sleepy eyes, he felt as though she was little more than an old photograph. Familiar and evocative of memories, but distant. She regarded him coolly in the bright morning light and he suspected she was experiencing much the same. Heather flung the towel she'd borrowed onto the bed and started dressing, fishing out a compact mirror from her handbag. Nick watched her apply make-up haphazardly, increasingly aware of tinges of musty body odour. He felt vaguely ashamed, as though he had got drunk at an office party and embarrassed himself. He was sure Heather could feel something similar too, just from the hurried way she was getting ready.

'Are you all right?' he asked.

'I'm fine,' she said.

He ran his hands through his hair and exhaled. 'Regrets?'

'What? Oh no, no. Nothing like that. It's just that I feel different. Like I'm me again. That doesn't make any sense, I know.'

'No, I know exactly what you mean,' he assured her.

She stopped fiddling with her eyeliner and looked into his eyes. 'I'd forgotten how much I loved you.'

'Me too,' he said.

She nodded, attending to her face again. They sat in silence for a while until Heather picked up her bag and told him she had to go. Nick started from the bed, intending to show her out, but she waved him away dismissively.

'I'll call you, okay?'

He nodded and, moments later, heard the front door click shut. Nick moved to the window and flicked the blinds open, watching her clamber hastily into an Uber. Not so much as a goodbye kiss. But that was okay. He hadn't wanted to kiss her either. Today was the morning after the night before. And as far as his heart was concerned, it was the night before that counted.

Later that morning, he opened his laptop and was happy

to discover that *What Gadget?* was keen to commission him to write the UK's top ten drones story. Nick replied that he would be delighted to accept the job. He wasted no time cracking on with his research. By lunchtime, he had pulled together the newest models, and how their technical specs compared. It had been a good distraction, but now that he was taking a break, his thoughts returned to Sam Goddard and the lunch that awaited him the next day. Since they had parted company, Sam had been promoted to Editor-in-Chief at the *Sunday Record*. But Nick still found it hard to believe he wanted to commission him. What story could he possibly consider giving to a pariah like himself? He was itching to find out. Hoping to clear his head, he left the flat and was in the middle of a long walk when his mobile rang.

'Let's do it again,' Heather said. 'How about Friday?'

His stomach flipped. 'Are you sure?' he said. 'We're not going too fast?'

'Let's not overthink it. I'm free. I'd like to meet again. Would you?'

He didn't need any extra persuading. After they had agreed a place – yet another old haunt – Nick hung up. All he could think about was how strange it had been to listen to her voice. The sound of it had stirred nothing in him. But the memory of the previous night, how magical it had felt, that was a whole other story. And all it would take to get back there was a single green pill.

TWELVE

(O)

Nick arrived at the Molto Penne at 1 p.m. sharp on Wednesday. Sam Goddard was already waiting for him at a table by the window. He stood up as soon as he saw Nick approach and extended a hand.

'Hey,' he said.

Nick stared at the hand, then took it. The men nodded cursorily at one another and settled into their chairs. Sam ordered a glass of wine. Nick had his bike so asked for a lemonade. He stared at his old friend, whose salt-and-pepper hair had whitened in the five years since they had last been in contact, but who otherwise looked the same. When the waiter returned, Sam broke the silence.

'So . . . I guess we probably both have things to apologise for,' he said.

'I don't,' Nick said.

Sam shut his eyes and the vein in his neck throbbed like it always used to.

'No, of course you don't.' Sam sighed. 'You've never let anything get in the way of a good story. Even friendships.'

'If you had really been my friend, you'd have backed me up,' Nick said. The words were out before he could help himself, but it was too late now.

'I wasn't just your friend, Nick,' Sam shot back. 'I was your editor too.'

Nick felt his own throb of irritation. 'Then maybe you should have behaved like one and taken my side.'

Sam sighed. 'Look, let's not rehash it,' he said. 'It's been five years.'

'Five years in the wilderness for some of us,' Nick said.

Sam replied in a voice filled with exasperation. 'Christ, Nick. What did you expect? You bite the hand that feeds you, it's what you fucking get.'

Nick took a sip of lemonade. It was tart and bitter, much like how he was feeling right now. The hand that had once fed him was, of course, one Reginald Hastings. Proprietor of NewsAlliance and one of the richest men in UK media. Hastings owned two television channels as well as several newspapers, including the *Sunday Record*, where Sam and Nick had both been employed. Nick's story had been about a corruption scandal involving the then Home Secretary who just so happened to be Reginald's old school chum from Eton. Reginald had ordered Sam to kill the story, but that hadn't stopped Nick. He'd gone ahead and published the article on his website. Worse, he had mentioned Reginald Hastings by name, stating that the media mogul was complicit in wanting the scandal covered up. That was more than enough to get Nick fired. But that wasn't his cardinal sin. The fact he was willing to burn his own employer so readily meant few editors had wanted to hire him since, even those outlets with different politics to the *Sunday Record*. However good a journalist you were, nobody wanted the guy who was happy to set fire to his own house. Nick couldn't blame them. If given the chance to go back in time, he would have happily done what he did again. And he took the opportunity to tell Sam so. The other man just shook his head and sighed.

'Still the same old Nick, eh?' Sam said. 'Prepared to sacrifice all on the altar of truth. You haven't changed a bit!'

Nick put his glass down on the white tablecloth harder than he needed to.

Sam stared at him, then smiled. 'Which is exactly what I was hoping,' he said.

Nick frowned. 'What?'

'Look, I have a story,' Sam said. 'A really big one. One that needs a crusader like you.'

Anyone else might have been offended at this line, but Nick knew Sam well enough to know he hadn't meant it as an insult.

'What's the story?' he asked.

Sam looked around him. The restaurant was relatively quiet, the only other occupied table right at the back by the kitchen. But he still seemed worried.

'Big corporate cover-up,' he said, in a voice that was barely above a whisper. 'Big pharma cover-up, in actual fact. A drug that brings in at least three and a half billion pounds a year and is used by millions around the world. Except it turns out it might be dangerous.'

'Which pharma company?' Nick said.

'Lakefront Sciences. I don't know if you know them, but they're the guys who make—'

'I know who they are,' Nick finished.

He did too, thanks to his recent research. The hundred-and-fifty-billion-pound company that had created Nostal. He signalled a passing waiter.

'Hang on,' he told Sam. 'I think I might need a drink after all.'

THIRTEEN

(O)

Sam waited until the waiter had brought another glass of red before he began.

'You hear about that man who killed that investment banker at his workplace?' he asked.

Nick remembered the story. Some city banker type had been bludgeoned to death in his office in Canary Wharf. 'Yeah, I read about it a few weeks ago,' he said.

'Yes, well, there's a lot you wouldn't have read,' Sam said. 'The killer was a guy called Mark Doyle. Doyle had a history with Richard Wendell, the man he murdered. They went to school together, apparently. This Wendell character used to bully him relentlessly. For years.'

Nick raised an eyebrow. This detail had not been reported as far as he could recall.

'The thing is, when the police arrested Doyle, they also took some bloods. Negative for narcotics and alcohol. But the results showed he had a lot of Nostal in his bloodstream.'

Nick tensed at the mention of the drug. 'Really? How much is a lot?'

'According to my source, about two hundred milligrams.'

Nick did some quick mental maths. 'So . . . he would have been on minus twenty-five,' he said.

'Correct,' Sam said, looking impressed. 'You're familiar with how Nostal doses work?'

'A little,' Nick said.

He saw Sam's curious expression, but he didn't elaborate.

'Well, Doyle's thirty-nine,' Sam said. 'So . . .'

'So that would have put him emotionally at around fourteen years of age,' Nick said. 'Just on the tipping edge of legal.'

He recalled this fact from his chat with Doctor Miriam Bryant. It was against the law to regress further back than fourteen. Any younger was considered a medical risk to yourself and others.

'It would have returned him to the same mental state as he was as a schoolboy,' he said.

'Exactly,' Sam said. 'Enough to bring his old feelings back. And also, it seems, to induce a murderous rage.'

Nick took a moment, swallowing a gulp of wine. He remembered his own rivalries in the schoolyard, how intense they had felt. It always puzzled him when people said your schooldays were the best years of your life. It was like they deliberately forgot how awful they were.

'My God,' he said. 'How come I haven't heard about this?'

'Because no one has,' Sam said. 'At least no one outside the media. The trial is coming up in a few weeks. And, fearing negative publicity, Lakefront Sciences applied for a super-injunction. Which the High Court granted.'

Nick stared at him in disbelief. 'What? Why would they do that?'

Sam lowered his voice even further. 'Because they're covering their arses,' he said.

'No, I mean why would the court even consider it?'

Sam shrugged. 'Potential defamation. Lakefront Sciences argue that if the public were aware of the trial, it would unduly influence the outcome. And some High Court judge agrees with them.'

Nick shook his head. It was an involuntary reaction, indicative of how stunned he was. In his time as a journalist, he had run into injunctions before. Usually they were taken out by footballers or celebrities who wanted to keep their personal lives out of the public domain. But a super-injunction was a unique concept in British law, one that gagged the media from reporting that an injunction existed at all, even if the parties involved were not named. It had been more than a decade since a corporation had successfully applied for one. Nick couldn't believe it had been granted.

'It's absurd,' he said. 'If Nostal caused this Doyle guy to do what he did, that's Article 10 of the European Convention on Human Rights. It's public interest.'

'No doubt what the prosecution argued,' Sam said. 'But they still lost.'

Nick whistled. He leaned back, thinking about what could be inside a drug that could drive a man to commit murder inspired by events that had happened so long ago.

'So. Doyle's barrister going to argue this as a defence?'

'He probably hopes to get Doyle acquitted with it,' Sam said.

'This is crazy,' Nick said. 'Someone needs to run it.'

'Sure, if you like jail.'

'What about internet and social media? Hasn't it leaked?'

'Not yet,' Sam said. 'It's possible you could get away with publishing the story on a platform that's registered overseas.'

'Like my SubsNews account?' Nick said.

His subscription-only website, where he did most of his worthy journalism, had its headquarters in the United States. Then a corollary thought struck him. 'Except the story would be broken by a journalist based in England,' he said. 'So I could still be breaking the law.'

'Honestly? I don't know where you'd stand legally,' Sam warned. 'But make no mistake, they will come after you.'

'And you really think I should be the one to incur their wrath?' Nick said.

'I can't think of anyone else who'd have the balls to take them on,' Sam replied. 'I mean that as a compliment.'

Nick studied Sam's eyes and saw he was being sincere. Sam really was trying to do him a favour.

'This was your story originally?'

'It was,' Sam said. 'We had a source. Went to Lakefront Sciences for comment. Their lawyers told us to cease and desist.'

Nick nodded. 'Word got around about it?'

'In our circles, yes. Let's just say it's not exactly a well-kept secret.'

'But no one else wants to run it?' he asked.

'Everyone's too shit scared,' Sam said. 'Just as we are. Word from on high is that we're not to go anywhere near it.'

Neither man spoke for a moment.

'Well?' Sam finally asked. 'Do you want it or not?'

Nick bit his lip. Did he? He thought about Doyle battering Richard Wendell to death in front of all his co-workers, with Nostal swimming around his veins. He couldn't help but wonder what it might be doing inside his own system, and Heather's too. What if it was doing something to them right now? Screwing them up in some way? Should he be worried about where the truth might lead?

'It could have . . . implications for me,' he said.

'You're a big boy,' Sam said. 'You know the consequences of breaking a super-injunction.'

Nick was about to tell him that wasn't what he meant, but Sam continued.

'I thought you'd jump at it. This could be your chance to

remind the rest of us how it should be done. Like you always have. *Vincit omnia veritas.*'

Nick rolled his eyes. 'And for those of us without the benefits of a private education?'

'It means *truth conquers all.* Which I believe was your original point. It's a good story. One that deserves to come out.'

Nick agreed. It *was* a good story. In fact, it was the kind of story that might boost his subscriber levels by hundreds, if not thousands. It could even be big enough to catapult him back into the mainstream again. He imagined what it would be like to potentially reach millions of readers again. To get the stories that mattered out there once more. He had to admit, it felt pretty good. Pursuing this one, however, could lead him to discover things about Nostal he might wish he hadn't. It could have big consequences for him and Heather. But Sam was right about him. He was a believer in truth conquering all.

'I want it,' he said. 'One hundred per cent.'

FOURTEEN

(0)

'So, tell me about your source,' Nick said after their food arrived.

'She's a young employee of Lakefront Sciences,' Sam said. 'Works in their legal department. She contacted the paper a couple of weeks ago to say she was uncomfortable with what's been going on inside the company.'

Nick put his fork down. This was good news. A whistle-blower, especially an insider, could mean solid info.

'I've only met her in person once,' Sam continued. 'I explained to her we can't legally run the story. But that you might be willing to.'

'I'll need to investigate,' Nick said. 'Do due diligence on it.'

He didn't want to make any assumptions. This Doyle guy might have just been mentally unstable for all he knew. Lakefront Sciences might have overstepped in applying for a super-injunction, but that didn't mean their drug *was* dangerous. He had to gather the facts first. 'I'll need to dig into this Doyle's background a bit too,' he said, finishing his thoughts out loud.

'I wouldn't expect anything less,' Sam said. 'But there's actually more to it than just Doyle.'

'More?'

'I'll send you a copy of the super-injunction. Have a look on page six.'

'What's on page six?'

'I'll set up a meeting with my source,' Sam said. 'She can tell you herself.'

Nick looked at the dregs of his wine, wishing he wasn't riding so he could have another. This story was tantalising, to say the least.

'Listen, Sam. I appreciate you throwing me this bone.'

'You won't thank me when you're in jail.'

Nick smiled, despite knowing his old editor was only half-joking.

The ride back to Kentish Town passed by in a blur. His mind was spinning with everything Sam had told him. A big pharma company shutting down the press? A murder they could be held responsible for? The story was a gift. But he also couldn't stop thinking about the past few days. What would this mean for him and Heather? He would have to tell her about it. As soon as he got to the flat, he sent her a text, asking her if she could meet any earlier than Friday. He waited a while. There were no ticks by his message, so he assumed she must be busy at work. He slipped his phone back into the pocket of his leather jacket, which he'd draped over the kitchen chair.

He sat, opened the laptop and brought up his search history from three weeks ago. Scrolled down to a page he'd originally visited doing his initial research. It was an article from a popular science magazine. The story had been about Nostal's origins. About how the drug had been discovered completely by accident, sharing similarities with Viagra, which was originally developed as a heart medicine. He had been struck by the account. Nostal had started life as a promising Alzheimer's treatment but had produced equally unexpected results. One person in the Phase 1 trial reported feeling homesick for a house they spent their childhood in. Another said a friend they'd lost touch with decades ago was so vividly present in their mind it was like they'd seen them that morning. Someone else had described feeling intense excitement ordering a Starbucks, saying it tasted just like the first cup she ever tried. All different reactions, yet all a revival of past feelings. The article had explicitly made clear that no major side effects had been reported. Nick remembered reading it and feeling reassured. And that was before he had spoken with Doctor Bryant. He closed the browser window and did some more searching until he found an expert who might be able to verify the drug's safety. He emailed him a request for an interview.

Heather messaged him back around four to say she was having a friend over tonight and was working late on a new website launch on Thursday, so Friday was the soonest she would be free. She still sounded keen to meet up again. Half of him wondered whether he should call her, just tell her outright. But the more he considered it, the more it felt better discussed in person, especially considering the implications for their new relationship. Besides, it wasn't like either of them would ingest any more Nostal in the meantime. Plus, he needed time to get his facts straight. And where better to start than with Mark Doyle himself?

His first step was searching for Doyle's name. Within minutes, Nick had found the website of his employer, which was a chartered surveyor's firm. On the employee page, there was a small black and white photo that matched the picture of Doyle that Nick thought he remembered seeing in the news. There was a brief professional bio underneath that told him nothing. Next, he searched the man's social media and the public posts he'd made. Nothing severely alt-right or too political. Nothing that appeared to be directed against bankers or capitalism in general. No anti-bullying groups either, he noted. For all intents and purposes, Doyle's online presence depicted him as a normal, average guy with a relatively common job and fairly generic interests. If he wanted to know more, he would probably have to talk to the man himself. To this end, he searched the local courts until he found which Crown Court Doyle had been brought to for his initial hearing. From there, it would be a matter of public record where they had taken him on remand. It turned out the answer was Pentonville.

Nick visited the prison's official homepage, where he discovered the Ministry of Justice had rolled out a unique messaging service for contacting inmates, called InMeet. Nick emailed the governor as a first step, formally requesting direct contact with Mark Doyle through the service. There were usually strict criteria that needed to be met before a journalist would be allowed to visit a prisoner on remand. One of them was if there was sufficiently strong public interest in the case that made the interview necessary, which was the argument Nick made. Although he didn't reveal any details, he hinted there could be a potential miscarriage of justice and implored the governor to ask Doyle if he would be willing to be interviewed. There were no guarantees. And there was also the question of the super-injunction. The prison's media office would undoubtedly be aware of it but that wouldn't necessarily prevent Nick from speaking to Doyle. It was illegal to publish anything about the upcoming trial, but there was no reason a journalist couldn't gather facts or, indeed, write the story up in case the injunction was subsequently lifted. But there was no way of knowing whether the governor would concur. The next step was out of Nick's hands.

Just as he was about to close the laptop, an email arrived

in his inbox from Sam. The subject line read: PRIVATE AND CONFIDENTIAL. There was no note apart from the letters FYI. Nick knew what the single Word document attached was before he opened it. The super-injunction. He skimmed the first page, skipping to page six. There, he found a paragraph Sam had emboldened, which read:

'To the extent necessary to conceal the identity of the Applicant, any references, whether to persons or places or otherwise who could be considered related to matters in contention in the trial are expressly prohibited.'

Curious. It was dry legalese, but essentially seemed to hint that there might be something else that Lakefront Sciences did not want the press reporting that could lead back to them, and the trial. Nick was tempted to email back asking for more details, but Sam had already told him the source would fill him in. He would just have to be patient. That virtue was needed for little more than an hour, however, when his mobile emitted another chime. Nick fished his phone out of his jacket and discovered a text from an unknown number.

Hi, are you Nick? Sam said to get in touch and that I could trust you. Any chance you could meet me tomorrow morning in Hyde Park?

Nick replied immediately, saying he was free and asked for more details. He was amused by the choice of meeting point. *Hyde Park?* What were they, spies exchanging dossiers? This was all getting a bit cloak and dagger. But it was also hard to deny he wasn't deeply intrigued.

FIFTEEN

(O)

The next day, Julia Conway was exactly where she said she'd be, which was sitting on a bench by the Serpentine. The summer weather made trench coats impractical, but they were all that would have been needed to complete the spy movie scene. Julia was in her early to mid-twenties, with a shock of ruby-red hair that was obviously dyed. Even from this distance, she looked nervous and twitchy as hell. Nick half expected her to gallop off as he approached, but instead she eyed him up and down repeatedly.

'Hi, Julia. I'm Nick. Mind if I sit?'

She shook her head and he took his seat, making sure to keep far enough away so as not to encroach on her personal space. Luckily, they were alone, apart from a gathering of ducks swimming in the lake.

'Sam said you don't work for him,' Julia said.

'That's right. I'm a freelancer.'

'So where will the story appear then?'

He didn't see the point in lying to her. 'If it's published, it'll be my own website,' he said. 'At least, at first.'

'You won't mention my name, will you?' she blurted.

Her eyes looked borderline misty. Nick felt for her. It was obvious she was scared. It wasn't easy being a corporate whistle-blower. Especially if you were the only one.

'I promise you'll remain anonymous,' he said. 'Though I will have to say I have a source on the inside. It'll give the story more credibility. You understand?'

She nodded, apparently thinking this over. 'Lakefront Sciences is a massive company,' she said. 'If you don't use my real name, maybe they won't know. I keep my opinions to myself when I'm at work.'

'That's wise,' Nick said, taking out his phone. 'Mind if I record this? It's just for the transcribing later.'

Julia Conway looked uncertain, so much so that Nick told her it was okay, he wasn't going to. He replaced the phone inside his jacket pocket and was relieved to see her visibly relax.

'It's just that I can't lose my job,' she said. 'It pays better than anything else I could get at my level.'

'You're a lawyer?'

'A paralegal,' she corrected.

She briefly outlined the differences. Nick made a point of showing interest, asking her a couple of questions to get her talking about herself a little more to help ease her in. It was working too. As she described her average day and her responsibilities, her voice slowly lost its quaver.

'So you're not in the office today?' he asked gently when she had finished.

'Called in sick,' she said. 'I thought it was safer to meet somewhere else.'

'Smart,' he said.

He waited a moment before diving in. 'So, Sam told me you don't agree with what the company's been up to?'

Julia latched on to the sentence as if she'd been waiting to be asked. 'It's just not right what they're doing,' she said. 'The public have a right to know.'

'You mean about Mark Doyle?'

'They're not doing themselves any favours by trying to hide it! It makes them look bad.'

Nick nodded sympathetically, then asked her to tell him about what she knew. Slowly, Julia recounted the story she'd given Sam. Shortly after Richard Wendell's murder, she had heard rumours in her department about an application for a super-injunction. She was too junior to attend the meetings with the lawyers from the big city firm Lakefront Sciences had hired, but she had picked up some of the details from more senior colleagues.

'Everyone worked day and night on it,' Julia said. 'Getting it as tight as possible.'

'Were you copied in on any emails?' Nick asked.

'A few,' she said.

'Any from senior management specifically mentioning the super-injunction?' he asked. 'Or anyone who's on the board?'

'I don't think so,' Julia said. 'I'd have to check. There were a lot of emails flying around.' She paused, staring down at her hands. 'Then I was copied in a trail where they were talking about widening the criteria.'

Nick wasn't sure what she meant, but it made him think of page six of the super-injunction and its legalese paragraph. This sounded like the additional piece of the puzzle that he was still missing.

'It was the final straw for me,' she said. 'That's when I knew I had to go to the press.'

'What was the straw?' Nick asked.

'They added extra language to the injunction to include the others.'

'Others?'

'It's not just Mark Doyle,' Julia said. 'Twenty-three other

people in the UK are trying to sue Lakefront Sciences right now, claiming Nostal negatively affected them.'

Nick leaned back, taking a moment to absorb this. Twenty-three sounded significant. 'Any of them fly into a homicidal rage?' he asked.

Julia shook her head. 'Each case is different. But they all claim Nostal made them do stuff they didn't want to. Damaged them in some way.'

'So the company is facing multiple lawsuits?'

'The lawsuits are only half of it,' Julia said. 'Our lawyers think there's a good chance some of these claimants might be called as witnesses by Doyle's barrister when his case goes to trial. Which means their testimony will only strengthen Doyle's claim that the Nostal drove him to kill Richard Wendell.'

Nick nodded, encouraging Julia to continue.

'The company is worried a jury will believe them,' she said. 'So they made sure to stipulate no reporting on anything related that might prejudice the outcome. They're hoping they can keep the public in the dark about these other cases, at least until the trial's over.'

Nick whistled. It sounded like Lakefront Sciences was in a lot of trouble. The kind of trouble he sensed he was only just starting to get a handle on.

SIXTEEN

(0)

Julia reached into the small black handbag she'd been resting on her lap and extracted a USB stick. She handed it to Nick.

'You can't tell anyone about this,' she said. 'And you didn't get it from me, okay? Promise me.'

Her voice was starting to waver again. Nick tucked the data stick into his jeans pocket and nodded solemnly back at her.

'What am I going to find on there?' he asked.

'The details of the claimants,' Julia said. 'Names, addresses. And a brief description of the case they're bringing.'

Nick reached out and gently placed a hand on the girl's shoulder. 'Julia, tell me you were careful. If anyone knew about this . . .'

'I was *super* careful,' she said. 'I'm more worried you're going to expose me.'

'Never,' he said. 'I have never given up a source and I never will.'

She studied his face. 'Sam told me you had buckets of integrity,' she said.

He smiled, his admiration for the girl growing with every minute that passed. 'Actually, I think you're the one with the integrity,' he said. 'You're jeopardising your career over this. That takes bravery. Believe me, I know.'

Julia blushed. 'I didn't know what else to do,' she said. 'It isn't right to keep this quiet. People have a right to know what they're putting into their bodies.'

'Yes,' he said. 'Has anyone in the company specifically mentioned anything about Nostal being unsafe?'

Julia bit her lip as she mulled it over. 'No, not that I can recall.'

'What about you?' he asked. 'Do you think it made Mark Doyle kill that guy?'

'I don't know,' she said. 'Nostal's passed all the clinical trials. They wouldn't be able to put it on the market if it was dangerous, would they?'

Nick shrugged. 'You'd think so.'

'But they must be worried about *something*.'

Nick found it hard to disagree.

'So, what are you going to do?' Julia asked.

'First things first,' he said. 'I'll investigate. When I'm sure I have all the facts, I'll write the story up.'

They sat in silence for a while, watching a pair of geese skim across the water.

'Will you go to jail for this?' she asked.

'Maybe,' he said. 'But Sam probably told you that wouldn't stop me.'

'Yes,' she said, laughing. 'He did.'

Her shoulders fell, and for the first time, she looked to Nick like she felt comfortable in his presence.

He handed her his business card. 'If you remember anything else you think I should know, give me a call. Any time.'

She nodded.

As Nick got up to leave, he turned back to her one last time. 'And make sure you keep your ears open, but your head down, okay?'

She promised she would.

The ride back to his flat was mercifully free of traffic, and he was back at his kitchen table by lunchtime. He wolfed down a cheese sandwich and texted Sam to let him know the meeting with Julia had gone okay. He received a message back straight away.

They're desperate to keep this from getting out. You're going to make a powerful enemy, you know.

Nick texted back: *You'll visit me in prison, right?*

A moment later, Sam replied: *Of course. Seeing as we're friends again.*

Nick smiled. It felt good to let bygones be bygones. He was grateful for the story. And now it was time to dig even deeper into it. He dipped a hand into his jeans pocket and pulled out the black USB.

'Okay,' he said. 'What have you guys got to say?'

SEVENTEEN

(O)

The next morning, Nick cruised slowly along the leafy streets of Putney, west London. He found the road he was after and parked the Honda next to a pay-and-display machine. He secured his helmet with cargo netting and made his way towards a terraced house with a small driveway and pressed the buzzer. The door was eventually answered by a man in a wheelchair. Nick knew from the file that he was eighty years old, but he didn't dress like it. He wore a casual white linen suit and a loose T-shirt. Shock-white hair fell around his shoulders and his skin had a red, leathery texture that suggested overexposure to the sun. He stared up at Nick over librarian glasses perched on the end of his nose.

'Mr Charles Mills?' Nick asked.

'Yes?'

'I'm Nick. We spoke on the phone?'

"Why yes, hello,' Charles said, warmly. 'Please come in.'

Nick followed behind as Charles wheeled himself past the staircase and into the living room. A plethora of photographs on the walls depicted exotic destinations, from Shanghai to New Orleans. Charles invited Nick to sit on a long L-shaped sofa as he wheeled himself nearer to the window.

'Thank you for agreeing to see me.'

'I'm happy to help,' Charles said.

On the phone, the old man had initially been hesitant about being interviewed, but once Nick told him about the murder trial and Lakefront's legal injunction, he had changed his mind immediately. As Nick removed his phone, he asked Charles if he minded being recorded. The old man shook his head.

'Let's talk about the Nostal, if that's okay,' Nick said. 'I understand you were in New Zealand when you took it?'

'Christchurch,' Charles confirmed.

'Right. And how much did you take?'

'A minus sixty, just before we set out. It was about five in the morning. I had booked a tour of the Southern Lakes, you see.'

'This was a walking tour, correct?' Nick asked.

'Uh-huh,' Charles said. 'We were supposed to do a five-day hike, camping in between.'

'And are you usually quite active?'

'For my age you mean? Yes. I try to walk for at least an hour every day.' He looked down sadly at the wheelchair. 'At least, I used to,' he said.

'And you believed you could endure hiking for five days?'

'Yes, I did,' Charles said. 'I booked it ages in advance and didn't think anything of it. But I had no idea the effect those pills were having on me.'

Nick nodded. 'May I ask what made you take Nostal in the first place?' he asked, softening his voice.

Charles's eyes glistened. 'Have you ever known what it's like to feel regret, Mr Winters?'

'A little, yes,' Nick said. 'I guess you could say I've been thinking about it a lot more recently.'

'Well, I became a qualified accountant at the age of nineteen,' Charles said. 'My wife Lily and I enjoyed fifty wonderful years of marriage, forty of them in this very house. We had two wonderful children too, who now have children of their own. In other words, I did all the things you are supposed to in life. But sometimes, you can be so busy doing what society expects of you that you forget to do what *you* want.'

'And what is it you want?' Nick asked.

Charles wheeled himself over to the mantelpiece and reached up for one of the smaller picture frames placed there. Nick leaned forward as he moved across and handed him the picture.

'Thailand,' he said. 'My daughter first went when she finished university. She said the beaches there were beautiful.'

Nick stared at the photo. It was of Charles, standing on a beach with a fisherman, both of them holding up a marlin fish at least their own body length. It looked like the photo was taken recently, except that Charles was different, and not just because the wheelchair was absent. His face looked decades younger. A joyful smile spread across his lips, and there was a twinkle in his eye.

'All my life, I wanted to travel. But we only took one holiday every year. A week in a little village in Cornwall. We never went abroad. Ever.'

He sighed. 'Then, when my Lily died, I wondered what the point was of going on. Apart from visits from my children and grandchildren, there really wasn't anything to live for.'

Nick handed the frame back.

'Then they invented Nostal. And I found myself wondering what it would be like to feel young again. So I asked my doctor for a prescription.'

Charles wheeled himself back towards the window. 'From then on, I didn't look back. I've been travelling the whole wide world since. Somewhere new each time.'

He picked up a statue on the windowsill, a genderless figurine that Nick thought looked African, but might have come from anywhere.

'It's been worth it,' Charles said, turning the object over. 'These last few months have been nothing short of amazing. Like I'm living a second life, all over again.'

'May I ask you something?'

'Please.'

'Why the Nostal? You say you never travelled. I get that. But why not just see the world as you are now?'

He grinned. 'Have you ever heard the expression about travel broadening the mind? Well, that effect is amplified a hundred times on a mind that is still young. Me, as I am? I'm jaded. But on Nostal . . . I don't know. For example, whenever you meet the locals, it's like you're meeting future friends for the very first time. I don't know how to describe it. You just trust people more. Open up to them. It changes how you see everything too. Sights, smells . . . food. The world is a more exciting place, Mr Winters. I think without the Nostal I would feel less . . . adventurous. I worry I would be more concerned about staying in a nice hotel with clean sheets than sharing a beach hut with total strangers. I don't know if I'm making much sense . . .'

Nick shifted, reclining further back in his seat. 'I think I understand. Travelling with the outlook of a Gen Zer.'

'I suppose. I don't know much about their generation. But I feel like I'm closer to understanding them than I have ever been. Or at least I was.'

He tapped one hand on his knees. 'The doctors say I'll probably never go anywhere off-grid again. No more sleeping in the desert under the stars. No more cycling across the Fijian islands. My legs will never recover.'

'You dived off a cliff halfway through your hike,' Nick said. 'Is that correct?'

'I did. A few of my group were doing it. I thought it looked . . . fun.'

'You thought plunging your body sixty feet into the ocean looked fun?'

'I know how it sounds,' Charles said. 'And that is my point in a way. I don't believe that's something I would have done if I was in my right mind.'

'By right mind, you mean the mind of an eighty-year-old, not a twenty-year-old?'

'Correct.'

'And the group you were with were a lot younger than yourself?'

'Oh, considerably. But that's part of the effect. That drug made me believe I was akin to them. That because I felt like them, I could do whatever they did, without consequence. It's why I decided to jump in the first place. Thank God for that helicopter ambulance, really.'

'And you're sure it was the Nostal that impaired your judgement?' Nick asked.

Charles didn't skip a beat. 'I've never been more certain of anything,' he said. 'It made me think all things were possible, even at my age. Here I am, an eighty-year-old man, fooled by that drug into doing something utterly stupid.'

His eyes fell back down to his lap, where his hands lay folded on legs that could no longer work. The old man snapped his head up and stared into Nick's eyes. 'You'll tell everyone, won't you?' he said, with bitterness in his voice. 'What they've done to me?'

Nick swallowed, feeling a deep stab of pity in his stomach. 'I promise I'll write the truth,' he said.

EIGHTEEN

(0)

Later, on the ride back to Kentish Town, Nick mulled over his conversation with Charles. It seemed that Mark Doyle's legal team had not yet reached out to him or asked him to be a witness in the trial. Perhaps they didn't know about him, or maybe they had other witnesses they could call on. Charles's story would certainly tug at a juror's heartstrings.

Nick felt sorry for the guy. It was clear he had done what he'd done because he'd taken Nostal. But the million-dollar question was how much it had impeded his judgement. When he and Heather had slept together for the first time in thirty years, had the Nostal made them do it? Sure, it had messed with their brain chemistry and caused them to feel young and in love again. But how much of their actions had been down to free will and how much was the overt influence of the chemical changes in the body? He needed hard proof, something forensic. Like a secret document on some hard drive with incriminating trial data that only the top executives at Lakefront Sciences had access to. If such a proof did exist, however, his only hope of getting to it was probably Julia. And so far, she didn't seem to be senior enough to be privy to secrets like that. In other words, he had no smoking gun. Yet, when he pictured poor Charles Mills sitting in that wheelchair, that feeling in his gut returned. Something felt amiss.

Once he was back in his flat, he made a brief bathroom visit and checked his email on his phone. He was surprised to discover Pentonville prison had been back in touch. The governor's office had granted him permission to join the prison's official visitor list. The governor must have accepted his potential miscarriage of justice argument, perhaps especially in light of the super-injunction. But the email didn't say any more than he'd been given the green light to make contact. It remained to be seen whether Mark Doyle would agree to an interview, but at least Nick could now find out. The first step was registering online for the prisoner messaging service and downloading the InMeet app. Once the app was installed, Nick selected Doyle's name from the contacts list and dialled.

'Hello, this is a message for Mark Doyle. You don't know me, but my name is Nick Winters. I'm a freelance journalist. Your lawyer probably told you no one's allowed to report on your case, but I'd like to meet you if possible and maybe tell your side of the story. If you could be so kind as to contact me—'

The Wi-Fi call cut off, a notification informing Nick that he could only leave an initial message of thirty seconds. *Oh well,* he thought. He would just have to wait and see if Doyle wanted to talk. He was about to put his phone away again when he felt it vibrate. It was Heather.

Hey, how are you? I've been missing our retro-dates already. Can't wait for Friday. Xxxx

He stared at the text dumbly. Maybe he should call her. But if he was being honest, he liked the fact she was clearly getting keener on him. Was it the Nostal that was doing it? Residual traces in her bloodstream perhaps? He didn't know. But it was still a conversation that was better face to face. He sent her as diplomatic a reply as he could.

Can't wait either. See you there. X

He tried to not think about what they'd have to discuss when they met.

NINETEEN

(O)

After a quick shower, Nick changed into a fresh polo shirt and jeans and left the flat once more. He had prioritised the names on Julia's list in order of proximity, and was now on his way to the only other person who also lived in London. This address was close enough to reach on foot. The afternoon sun was hot on his face, but there was a light breeze to counteract it. Just after five, he arrived at the driveway of an imposing detached house in Hampstead. The woman who answered the door adjusted her dreadlocks. Dressed in blue dungarees and a white T-shirt, she didn't seem as glamorous as the photo he remembered from five years ago when she had collected Best R&B Newcomer at the Brit Awards.

She beamed. 'Mr Winters! So good of you to come all the way here.'

'So good of you to invite me,' he said.

Nick had been surprised, actually. There had been no contact details for Lenora Cox on the file, and when he had searched online, he found only her agent's details on her website. Nick had called her, telling her he was investigating Nostal and about the upcoming Doyle trial. The agent had listened with much interest. She informed Nick that Lenora's life frequently attracted a lot of interest from the tabloids and gossip columnists, so her original advice to her client had been to keep the lawsuit on the down-low.

'But in light of what you've told me, it might actually be good for her to speak out,' the agent said. 'Let me see if I can reach her.'

From there, it had taken less than an hour to contact Lenora and confirm that the star was more than happy to be interviewed. And now Nick was standing on her doorstep.

'Do come in, Mr Winters,' Lenora said.

'Nick, please.'

He stepped into a hallway that was easily as big as his kitchen. He followed her into an even more capacious living room, which looked out onto a private garden surrounded by high walls. Lenora offered him a drink, which he politely declined. She slid open the glass door and beckoned him through. He was led across a square lawn to a wooden structure that resembled a cabin. They both went inside into what Nick realised was a working studio.

'I hope you don't mind,' Lenora said. 'I'm in the middle of recording.'

'Of course,' Nick said. 'I'm not interrupting you, am I?'

'God, no,' Lenora said. 'I don't mind stopping for this. It's just that I like to inhabit this space. If we were in the house, it would kind of screw with my mojo, you know?'

Nick nodded though, of course, he didn't know. He had no idea what it was like to be a young musician, barely twenty-two, and to sell over twenty million copies of your debut album.

'So this is where the magic happens?' he asked.

The studio was divided in two. One half was the recording booth, shut off by a rectangular glass window through which he could see a boom mike overhanging a single chair. The two of them were in the other half, which housed the mixing desk. Lenora gestured for him to sit on one of two guest sofas.

'I had this built shortly after *Life's Aces* came out,' she said, taking the main seat behind the audio console. 'This is my space, where I come to express who I really am.'

'I'm honoured to be invited into it,' Nick said, taking out his phone.

He asked permission to record their conversation, which Lenora granted. Nick pressed the red button, leaning back and offering a friendly smile.

'You know I bought *Life's Aces*,' he said. 'I thought it was a great album, actually.'

'Thank you,' she said.

'Did you always want to be a singer?'

Lenora frowned. 'Music was just a hobby to me when I was a teenager. I never actually thought that I would take it anywhere.'

She told him a little about her background. How her emotionally absent father often made her feel like she was worthless. How she felt her mother resented and envied her talent, even though she professed to hate all forms of music. Lenora confessed that she had been a rebel at school, kicking back against authoritarian structures and finding refuge in her songwriting, until a record label had finally taken an interest in her music. She paused, fished a hand into the front pocket of her denim dungarees, and pulled out a roll-up cigarette.

'You mind?'

Nick shook his head, and Lenora retrieved a lighter and sparked up the end of the roll. There was a puff of whitish smoke. She leaned back in her chair and exhaled.

'That first album did crazy well,' she said.

Nick nodded. That much was obvious from the house she

lived in. Of all the claimants lining up to sue Lakefront Sciences, Lenora was by far the wealthiest and most high profile.

He moved the conversation on delicately. 'I understand your claim against Lakefront has to do with the, um, second album? Which has had mixed reviews?'

'My follow-up,' she confirmed, smiling. 'And *mixed reviews* is putting it kindly.' She sighed. 'The thing about talent is that it's a gift from God,' she said. 'I thought I'd have no problems giving that gift back to the people. But the truth was I struggled. A lot. It took me four years to do the second album. The label almost dropped me. That's when I realised it was a different me that received the original gift.'

'Can you explain what you mean?'

'Sure. Let's say your parents gave you a birthday present when you were six. A bike, say. So the bike's perfect because it fits you. It's the right size, it's got trainer wheels, the right number of gears, whatever. The point is that gift is good for the time you got it, but it's not so great if you were to try and ride it, say, five years later.'

'Right.'

'So what happened is I tried to get on that same bike a few years later and it didn't fit me.'

Nick thought he was following her logic. 'Uh-huh. Because you've outgrown it?' he said.

'You got it,' she said. 'I was a different person by then. I was monied, for one. I could pay off my parents' mortgage, buy nice cars and holidays. People recognised me in the street. I became, I dunno, different, I guess. Nothing changes you like success.'

Nick gave her another encouraging nod.

'The reason *Aces* worked so well was that it was from the heart. As all good music should be. I was hungry for it back then. But in trying to emulate that, I was being fake, you know? I was trying to share a gift I had outgrown. That former me, raw and hungry me? She was gone. And you could tell that in the music. There was none of that original fire.'

'So is that when you decided to take Nostal?' he asked.

She shut her eyes. 'I thought it would make me feel the way I did when I first started to write songs. Bring back that innocent self-belief, you know?'

'Like your six-year-old self was back on the bike?'

She looked at him, nodding. 'Exactly! You have no idea the pressure you are under to make a follow-up album when your first achieves platinum sales. I couldn't sleep some nights. I really had no choice. I had to try the Nostal and hope it would make me creative again in exactly the same way.'

'But ultimately it didn't work?'

She laughed drily and sucked on her cigarette. 'That's why I'm suing those bastards. Their drug fucked me up, Nick. Feel free to quote me on that.'

Nick gave her a sympathetic look. Like Charles Mills, Lenora had not been contacted about testifying at Mark Doyle's trial. But he was pretty sure she would be champing at the bit if she was asked.

'I'm guessing the Nostal didn't change you back to the person you once were, then?' he said.

'Actually, it did,' Lenora replied. 'It made me *too much* like her. Young, stupid, naive. Making all the wrong choices.'

She blew smoke out and Nick caught a whiff of it. He realised it was nothing like cigarette smoke. And it wasn't marijuana either. This was crack. Lenora was smoking crack.

'Only this time I couldn't control it,' she said. 'And the music suffered. I couldn't tell what was good anymore.'

TWENTY

(O)

After leaving the musician's house, he took a longer, more scenic route back through Primrose Hill. He'd known from the file that Lenora was claiming Nostal had compromised her artistic judgement. And there had been a brief reference to using drugs. Yet the crack had still taken him by surprise. It shouldn't have, given the telltale signs. The slightly sinewy look around the face. The constant, furtive glancing all around her. It was all quite obvious if you knew what to look for. Nick reached the entrance on the north side of the park and was soon following a footpath bustling with dog walkers, families and joggers.

During the rest of their interview, Lenora had told him the full story. When she was younger, drugs had played a minor role in her life, but not enough to stop her making great music. She was, to quote her own words, a recreational user. Following the success of *Life's Aces*, she had even managed to stop altogether, all by herself, and with no difficulty. After that, she'd been clean for years. Since taking the Nostal, however, her younger self had resurfaced and, with it, all of her old vices. Only this time, she wasn't as good at managing it. The crack, in particular, had been difficult to control. As soon as she realised there was a problem, she had stopped taking the green pills. But by then it was already too late. Cue Lenora suing Lakefront Sciences for a terrible quality second album. Nick saw what Julia meant when she had said that each case was different. People were taking Nostal for their own reasons, and discovering that it almost worked too well, and not always to good effect. A couple approached him, struggling with an especially difficult boxer who was straining at his lead. Nick smiled politely at them as they passed, and arrived on the crest of Primrose Hill, where the London skyline was like a mirage beneath the azure sky. He sat on a nearby bench, popped in his wireless ear pods, and played the interview back to himself. He stopped at the part where Lenora lit her crack cigarette. Listened to the sound of the air exiting her lungs. He still didn't have any forensic evidence that Nostal had overridden her free will somehow, forcing her to make bad choices. But there was no denying that it had still done her damage. His gaze settled on the cityscape again, and he thought about the millions of people going about their business. He wondered how many of them were also taking Nostal. About what harm it was doing to them. And to him.

TWENTY-ONE

(O)

He slept badly, troubled by odd dreams. In one of them, he was drowning in a river of flowing blood, streaming through giant tunnels that in dream logic he knew to be veins, all leading to a pumping heart the size of a house. He welcomed the reprieve of his early morning alarm. After a strong mug of coffee from his filter machine, he shook off the fug of slumber and allowed his brain to transit into the cold light of day. At ten o'clock, he joined a Zoom call with a man called Professor Michael Simmons. Simmons worked for the MHRA – the Medicines and Healthcare products Regulatory Agency. From Nick's research, he'd discovered it was the main body in the United Kingdom that had to sign off on new medicines before they could be approved. These were the same people who had okayed the Covid vaccines and Nick hoped that the pasty, balding man who appeared on-screen would have the information he was after. Once both sound and video were mutually confirmed, Nick thanked Simmons for agreeing to be interviewed.

'So if you don't mind, I'll be recording our call,' Nick said. 'It's just for my notes.'

'No problem,' the professor said. 'Fire away.'

'Thanks,' Nick said. 'I'd like to understand the kind of scrutiny new medicines are put through before they're considered fit for human consumption. I mean, I know there are clinical trials.'

'Trials are one part, sure,' Simmons said. 'But long before that, there's a rigorous process of research and development. In fact, it usually takes around twelve years before an experimental drug makes it to the shelf.'

Nick was surprised at this. 'Seriously?'

'Oh yes. And for every drug a pharmaceutical company will test, tens of thousands will fail along the way. Hundreds of thousands of experiments are discarded at fairly early stages because of the sheer volume and the costs associated with it all. If the risk-to-reward ratio isn't stacked in their favour, they'll kill a project dead long before it's had the chance to show real promise.'

'If all pharma companies only care about is profit, it's a wonder they succeed at all,' Nick said.

'Yes, except the rewards for when a drug does pay off can be huge. Especially if you've got the only patent. But there are more steps yet. Once scientists have figured out a certain compound has a certain effect on, say, a diseased cell, they have to prove that the effect is safe for humans. That means extensive computer modelling, followed by animal trials. Less than half of those trials make it through to the next stage.'

The more Nick processed this, the more twelve years sounded like no time at all. 'What's the next stage, then?'

'Applying for a CTA, or clinical trial application, with us. And after that, all trials must also be approved by an independent research ethics committee before they can go ahead.'

Nick bit the inside of his cheek as he considered how to

phrase his next question. 'Is there any way drug companies could lie to you guys? Maybe falsify the safety data?'

'I can't see how,' Simmons said. 'We have protocols and checks in place to ensure that never happens. And we inspect the trials personally.'

This sounded reassuring to Nick, though he was also aware that he was only dealing with the UK situation. He asked about the standards elsewhere.

'All international regulatory bodies come with equivalent safeguards,' Simmons explained. 'Whether it's the FDA in America or the European Medicines Agency. Standards and levels of safeguarding, especially in the West, are high.'

Nick nodded. He checked his notes. There was a question he was hoping to challenge Simmons with. 'What about Thalidomide?' he asked. 'Didn't that pass all these trials originally? And presumably all these safety checks?'

Simmons had a downcast look about him as he answered. 'A tragic but very rare case,' he said. 'At the time, scientists didn't believe any drug pregnant women took could pass through the placental barrier. But that was over sixty-five years ago. Our understanding, our clinical protocols, have come on in leaps and bounds since then.'

Something seemed to change in Simmons's expression. Nick thought it might be a look of suspicion.

'Is there a particular drug you were curious about?' the professor asked.

Nick stared him straight in the eye. 'What do you know about Nostal?'

Simmons raised an eyebrow. 'Novel as that drug might seem to many, it's gone through exactly the same process as any other medicine. I presume you're referring to the recent murder case?'

'Mark Doyle,' Nick confirmed. 'You know about that?'

'Word gets around,' Simmons said. 'Look, I don't pretend to know what happened exactly. But I'm happy to go on the record right now and tell you that tens of thousands of people were given it in controlled conditions, and not one of them murdered anyone. The consensus of the medical community is that it's as safe as any other approved drug.'

Nick frowned. 'I get that, Professor,' he said. 'But, in all fairness, isn't that what they said about Thalidomide?'

After he'd thanked Simmons and signed off the call, Nick made another coffee. He drank it slowly, listening to the sounds of occasional traffic passing by outside his window as he recapped the interview in his mind. Another dead end. He wondered if he was ever going to find any empirical evidence that Nostal was dangerous. His phone beeped. It was a notification from InMeet, the prison chat app, telling him he had a new message. He opened the app and his messages, and retrieved a longer voicemail.

'Hello, is this Mr Winters? This is Mark Doyle. I'm so glad you got in touch. I've talked to my barrister and he's keen for us to all meet. I want to tell you my side of the story. I feel so bad about what happened, Mr Winters, I can barely eat or sleep. I wake every night seeing that man's face. You have no idea. Can you come here on Monday afternoon? Visiting hours are between two and five. My phone privileges are only an hour a day, so if you could get back to me soon, I'll put you down on my list. Thank you again.'

Nick was elated. He hit reply and left his own message, telling Doyle he would be more than happy to visit on Monday. Getting Doyle on the record was going to be a real coup. He could now go into his weekend knowing he was making significant progress. But then he remembered his plans for the evening and his high instantly vanished. It was replaced, instead, by a heaviness he'd rather not carry. But he also knew he must.

TWENTY-TWO

(0)

He sat opposite Heather in Little India. The curry house had been a favourite of theirs whenever they had travelled into London as students. Cheap, cheerful and mercifully still in business after all these years, it sat under a railway arch in King's Cross. As pleasantly reminiscent as this was, however, Nick was struggling to bring up the conversation he needed to have. For the last twenty minutes, there had been nothing but small talk.

'Isn't this wonderful?' Heather said, looking around. 'Remember when we used to get pre-loaded on cheap vodka on the train up here?'

He smiled weakly. 'I remember.'

She reached into her handbag under the table and placed her bottle of Nostal on the table. 'Come on, get yours!' she said with a grin.

'Heather . . .'

She must have seen something in his expression, because her smile dropped. 'What is it?'

He looked into her eyes. Again, they were familiar, but distant, lacking the radiance they had when she was last dosed. He searched his feelings but found only the faintest passion there, barely a trace of what he'd experienced when he was doped. His heart sank. And then he told her. About Sam, about the gagged story. About Doyle and the trial. Everything. He was talking so fast he barely noticed her reactions to it. But when he was done, she looked confused.

'I don't understand,' she said. 'This means what? That Nostal is dangerous?'

'It could be,' he said. 'That's what I intend to find out.'

They sat silent for a while, while Heather appeared to process it all, the lines on her forehead furrowing deeper into her brow.

'But this Mark Doyle guy. He could have just been acting crazy, though, right? It might have had nothing to do with the drug.'

'I don't know,' he admitted.

'So what does this mean?' she said. 'For us?'

'It doesn't have to mean anything,' Nick said. 'If we don't want it to. But I don't think we should take it anymore.'

Heather pulled herself back, crossing her arms and shaking her head. 'But this won't work unless we do.'

'It won't?'

'I don't feel the same feelings,' she said. 'I mean, don't get me wrong. I like you. I think you're a nice person. But I don't love you. Not when I'm not . . .'

She stared ruefully at the Nostal, then back at him. Their eyes locked on to each other, and Nick wondered if she was trying to see if she could jolt her old emotions by looking into his soul.

'It just . . . it just won't work without it,' she said, at last. 'Those feelings. They've been gone thirty years.'

He opened his mouth, wanting to protest, but he couldn't

argue. What she was saying was true. But that didn't mean there wasn't another way.

'Do you think . . . ?' he began.

But she cut him off at the pass. 'You mean without it? No, Nick. There's just no way.' She paused, re-crossed her arms the other way. 'Why?' she said. 'You think you could?'

He opened his mouth once again, only to shut it once again.

'That's what I thought,' she said.

She closed her eyes, her fingers gripping her elbows hard. When she opened them again, she had a determined look about her that made him uneasy.

'Nick, could you be mistaken? What are the odds there's something wrong with the drug, really? Think about it. You said you spoke to a regulator, right?'

'Someone from the MHRA,' he confirmed.

'So what did he say?'

'He was pretty certain it was safe.'

'Right,' she said. 'That makes sense. I mean, if Nostal was actually bad, we'd know about it by now, right? Millions of people are taking this all over the world. How many murders have you heard about?'

He bit his lip. 'I guess so.'

'So isn't it more likely that there's another explanation for what happened to that banker?'

The waiter appeared, ready to take their order. Nick politely waved him away, asking for a few more minutes. When he was gone, he took a sip of water and met Heather's gaze again.

'What about all these other people?' he said. 'They're all claiming Nostal did things to them too.'

'Maybe it did,' Heather said. 'But some people just have bad reactions to medicines. It's not uncommon. Have you spoken to any of them? Verified their claims?'

He thought about the two people on the list he'd already reached out to. 'Some,' he said.

'Any proof?'

The words were like a hammer of reality knocking at him. She was right to ask. He admitted he had nothing conclusive.

'Fine,' Heather said. 'Then I'd say you don't have any facts. Just speculation. I may not be a journalist anymore, but I can still tell the difference.'

'Heather, I—'

She held up a hand to shut him off. 'Nick, this whole thing was your idea. You were the one who got in touch, saying we should try it. I was hesitant. But you persisted. And now here we are.'

'I know,' he said, softly. 'Look, I wish I hadn't found this out, but—'

'That's bullshit,' she said.

He was taken aback at her tone. He hadn't seen her angry for a long time. Not since they first dated, in fact.

'You love it when you've got a good story to chase,' she said. 'It's always been that way with you. Do you even remember why we split up?'

He did but thought better of speaking.

'You were obsessed,' she continued. 'As soon as you got your first job at your first serious grown-up paper, you never quit. Always chasing one lead after another. Trying to prove yourself. You worked nights, weekends. I never saw you.'

'I know,' he said, daring to interject. 'It's my biggest regret. Losing you. It took me thirty years to realise it, but I eventually did. Being with you has been . . . incredible.'

Heather uncrossed her arms and tapped a finger on the green bottle.

'I agree. But this is what made it possible. *This*. You know how it feels when it wears off. The magic goes. It's horrible, I know. But true.'

'Heather—'

'You know, my life's been pretty empty,' she said. 'I'm nearly fifty. Divorced. My only son has left home. I thought my chance to be happy again was gone. Then you showed up. I was telling my friend last night what a crazy roller coaster this week has been. But I've been happy, Nick. More than happy. Like anything is possible. Just like those cheesy ads say. And now, we're here all over again.'

'But this drug could be hurting us,' he said.

'But you don't know that,' she insisted.

It was his turn to shake his head. 'I know what you're saying, Heather. But something in my gut says Lakefront Sciences are covering something up.'

'Your gut. Yes, of course. Got to follow your gut.'

For the first time in their conversation, he felt a flash of irritation towards her. 'What's your point?'

'Don't you see?' she said. 'You're repeating history all over again. Prioritising chasing a story over us being together.'

'But it's a story that could affect us,' he protested.

'Every one of your stories affected us,' she said. 'In the end.' She huffed. 'Nick, I don't want to give this up. Can't we just take a pill, enjoy ourselves? What if we agree to keep using it until we know the facts? You find actual evidence that Nostal is dangerous, and I'll be the first to stop.'

He said nothing, looking down at the tablecloth.

'Of course you can't,' she said.

She snatched up the bottle, shoved it back into her bag, and stood up, pushing her chair back.

'Heather!'

He rose too, but she was already walking away too fast, shouting back at him not to follow her. Stunned, he watched her go. Potentially slipping away and out of his life again, as she had thirty years before.

TWENTY-THREE

(0)

He barely slept again that night. Just when he thought he was about to drop off, another snippet from their fight played out in his mind. He'd tried calling her several times before he went to bed, but she hadn't responded. It was hard not to feel sympathy. He had just sprung the news on her out of the blue. At least he'd had a couple of days to get used to it. The worst part was she had also been right. Nick didn't have any conclusive proof. And it wasn't like he didn't sympathise. Every minute he'd spent under the spell of the wonder drug had made him feel alive in a way he hadn't in decades. He didn't want to stop any more than she did. But what choice was there? Heather would see that, given time. Surely she would. When morning finally came, he made himself get out of bed and showered, trying to shake off the feeling that he had blown things again, this time permanently. The decision was made. He was going after the story. What mattered now was finding the vindication he needed that he'd been right to do so. And that meant focusing on the task at hand. His phone rang just as he was eating breakfast. The screen lit up with an unknown number. Nick hesitated, then answered.

'Is this Nick Winters?' said a woman's voice.

'Who's this?'

'My name's Rebecca Hughes,' the voice said. 'I'm the Global Head of Public Relations at Lakefront Sciences.'

Nick held his next breath. Though morning sunshine filled the kitchen, he felt as though there was a sudden chill in the air. 'What, um, can I do for you, Ms Hughes?'

'Actually, it's what I can do for you, Mr Winters.'

Rebecca Hughes had a well-spoken, home counties accent. Her voice also had the edge of authority, hinting at someone who was used to being in charge. He was thinking about what to say next when she spoke again.

'I know you're looking into the trial of Mark Doyle,' she said. 'I thought perhaps we could talk. Off the record.'

He frowned. How did she know about him? How did she even get his number? 'I, uh . . . what is it you want to talk about?'

'I'd rather discuss that in person, if it's all the same to you,' she said.

Nick hesitated. He wasn't sure what could possibly be so important that it couldn't be discussed over the phone. But he was a journalist. And he was curious. 'Okay. When and where?'

'How's Monday morning? In my office.'

Nick had his interview with Mark Doyle on Monday, but that wasn't until the afternoon. 'I can make that,' he said.

'Fabulous. My driver can pick you up.'

'Driver? That won't be necessary,' he said.

'I insist,' Rebecca Hughes said in that authoritative tone. 'Nine o'clock work for you?'

He confirmed that it did. As soon as the call ended, Nick texted Julia, asking her to get in touch when she could. She rang him back immediately. He told her about his mysterious phone call. 'Anyone talk to you at work?' he asked. 'Or did you speak to anyone?'

The long silence on the other end was tangible.

'I haven't told a soul,' she said, at last. 'Do you think they know about me? Oh my God, what am I going to do?'

'Don't panic,' Nick said. 'I'm sure if they knew, someone would have spoken to you by now.'

'But then how did they know to call you?' she asked.

Nick could sense she was trembling on the phone. He wished he had an answer for her. 'Look, I'm meeting them on Monday. Let me see what's what. In the meantime, just go into work as normal. I'll call you when my meeting's done. Try not to freak out.'

'Easy for you to say,' she said.

He acknowledged that indeed it was, but tried to reassure her that whatever he discussed with them, he wouldn't give her up. 'Never revealed a source, never will,' he reminded her.

He ended the call, his mind buzzing. How else might this Rebecca Hughes know about him? Maybe Charles Mills's or Lenora Cox's lawyers had passed his name on to her. But then what reason would they have had to do that? For an awful moment, Nick worried that maybe they *did* know about Julia. Perhaps someone in the company's IT division had been monitoring staff emails. Could they have found an email Julia might have sent to Sam? But Julia wouldn't have used her work email to get in touch, surely? She was young, sure, but she was smarter than that. He had too many questions, and his brain kept flipping over possibilities. Monday felt like an eternity away.

TWENTY-FOUR

(0)

It *was* an eternity. As he expected, the time dragged. Nick spent most of the weekend indoors, tidying the flat and typing up the notes he had on the story so far. Occasionally, he texted Heather with yet another apology. By the time Sunday evening came around, he knew she wasn't going to reply. Perhaps ever. He endured an uneasy sleep on Sunday evening, but eventually Monday morning arrived. And when the doorbell rang at nine sharp, he answered. The stranger he found standing on his doorstep looked less like a driver and more like a debt collector. Beneath a sharp, tailored suit, Nick noticed bulges of muscles he didn't even know could exist on a human body. The look was completed by a stocky face, buzz cut and a pair of black sunglasses perched on a misshapen nose that might have been broken more than once.

'Good morning, sir,' the man said with surprising cheer. 'The name's Ben Cooper. I work for Rebecca Hughes.' He had a cockney accent but spoke with affectations that suggested he was trying to suppress it. 'If you'd like to come with me, sir,' Ben prompted gently.

Nick stared at the black stretch limo parked on the road. It didn't seem like a dangerous thing to do, did it? It was a limo, for God's sakes. Not some dodgy transit van.

'Sir?'

Nick looked at the driver, then back at the limo. 'Sure,' he said. 'Let's go.'

'Was that your bike I saw parked outside?' Ben asked congenially. He was speaking through the limo's internal comms system. They were driving down Hampstead Road.

Nick was in the back, sitting on one of two rows of leather seats. 'What's that?'

'The bike, sir,' Ben said. 'The Honda. Is it yours?'

He turned left onto the Euston Road, while Nick peered through the tinted glass at the buildings they passed. 'You, uh, into bikes?' Nick asked.

'Bit of a weekend passion,' Ben said. 'I like to take mine out when I'm off duty.'

'What's your ride?'

'I'm a Ducati man, through and through,' Ben told him. 'Can't go electric though. It's just not the same.'

'Couldn't agree more.'

Nick had never even considered anything but petrol, but he knew the way all bikes were going, it was soon going to be inevitable. He sank further back into his seat. It was strange being alone in such an expansive vehicle. Given the slightly cloak-and-dagger invitation, he had half expected to find the mysterious Rebecca Hughes inside the limo when he'd first got in, talking in metaphors that were thinly veiled threats. But he knew that was just his overactive imagination. Their conversation apparently over, Ben the driver went back to ignoring him on the other side of the divider glass. The limo snail-crawled through Monday morning traffic. They arrived in Moorgate just after ten. Ben turned off the street and down a ramp that took them under a new glass building, one of so many that had shot up in London in recent years. Rows of vans and trucks filled its subterranean car park. Blazoned across each of them was a graphic that cleverly combined ripples in water with a double helix. The official Lakefront Sciences logo. The limo pulled up sharply into one of a series of bays marked 'VIP'. Feeling awkward, Nick fumbled to open the door before the chauffeur could do it for him.

'This way, sir,' Ben said.

Nick followed him past several BMWs and Mercedes-Benzes towards a lift at the far side. Ben swiped an employee ID card and they stepped inside. They rode up in silence, Nick counting off thirty-five floors before the doors opened. As soon as he exited, he had to draw in a breath. The entire floor was open plan, with floor-to-ceiling glass all the way around, offering a stunning panoramic of the city. He moved instinctively towards the glass wall nearest him, hypnotised by the hundreds of intricate rooftops of period buildings and, beyond them, the sparkling Thames.

'Quite something, isn't it, sir?' said Ben, in that constrained cockney accent of his. 'Now, if you'll follow me . . .'

Nick allowed himself to be taken past a maze of meeting rooms that culminated in a corner office that was clearly the domain of someone with seniority in the company. A sheer glass wall on one side offered a god's eye view of the City of London. Through the door, he saw a woman in a dark grey suit sitting at an oak desk. Behind her was the room's only solid wall, painted eggshell white. The woman was shuffling papers, looking serious. Ben knocked gently. She glanced up and hastily waved them in.

'Mr Winters,' she said, rising from her chair. 'I appreciate you coming.'

Nick studied her as she approached them. Shoulder-length, raven hair. Minimal make-up. Early forties maybe. She was wearing a long necklace with what looked like a pendant dangling from it.

'You're Rebecca, I'm guessing,' he said.

He took the hand she had already extended, her firm grip matching the voice on the phone. She flashed him another smile that made Nick feel strangely disarmed.

'I'm grateful for your time, Mr Winters. Benjamin, would you mind . . . ?'

'Of course,' the driver said, excusing himself from the room.

He closed the glass door behind him, leaving Nick alone with Rebecca Hughes. And an ominous feeling in his gut.

TWENTY-FIVE

(O)

Rebecca asked if he'd like something to drink. When Nick declined, she invited him to sit in one of the red Chesterfield chairs that faced her desk. She, meanwhile, perched herself on the corner so that she had an elevated view of him. Establishing her dominance. It occurred to Nick that she hardly needed to do that. The entire office was intimidating enough. A framed picture loomed large on the wall behind the desk. It was a painting of an old kitchen table replete with fruit and surrounded by vases. It looked like an original Cézanne, but Nick was no expert. Black marble stands, in the shape of giant hands, were dotted around the room, some carrying large bouquets. On the south end of the office, several luxurious-looking chairs surrounded a low-level glass table. This meeting area also featured an oak bar, its open shelves stocked with a variety of bottles, some of them wine that probably belonged in a collector's cellar. Nick leaned back in his chair, trying to appear relaxed as if he took meetings in offices like this all the time.

'So,' he said. 'How did you get my number?'

'From your website,' Rebecca said.

'I mean, how did you know . . . about me?'

'Would it surprise you to know that we pharmaceutical companies work in close conjunction with the regulatory bodies?'

Nick frowned.

'We know you contacted the MHRA,' she explained.

Nick experienced two emotions simultaneously. The first was relief that they hadn't found him through Julia. The second was annoyance that his name had been passed on so readily. 'Professor Simmons?' he guessed.

'He's due to retire next year,' Rebecca said. 'We've offered him a consulting role here. Quite a generous salary, a couple of days a month. I suppose he considered it a courtesy to let us know you'd been in touch.'

'Well, wasn't that nice of him?' Nick said.

Apart from his disappointment in the apparent incestuous nature of the medicines industry, he also wondered how much of Simmons's interview he could now trust. Was the professor covering up something for his future employers? Something that had gone wrong in the trials? But he had more immediate questions too.

'What did Simmons say about me?'

'Only that you were asking about drug safety. I'm guessing you know about Mark Doyle's trial. Mind if I ask how?'

Nick answered her carefully. 'Word gets around,' he said, borrowing the phrase Simmons had used during his interview.

'You do know we have a super-injunction out on this, right?' she said.

He felt anger rise up in him. 'Yeah, congratulations on that, by the way. Great way to gag the free press. You guys must be proud of yourselves.'

Rebecca shrugged. 'We're just trying to do our best to ensure a fair trial.'

Nick almost laughed but managed to stop himself. 'Selfless,' he said. 'Never mind that your drug might be harming people.'

She gave him a look that was borderline pity. 'I didn't realise you were so against fairness and objectivity, Mr Winters,' she said quietly. 'I would have thought you of all people would appreciate the importance of facts.'

'Well, I know for a *fact* that you're scared of people finding out what happened.'

'That's true,' she admitted. 'I'm not a big fan of the court of public opinion. It's bad for business. And our share price.'

'Yeah, funny that,' he said.

She shook her head. 'You think we're the bad guys here just because we don't want the jury tainted? Would you deny us a chance to prove there's nothing dangerous about our product in a court of law?'

Nick's irritation remained. 'If you're so confident about being vindicated, why not let the media report on the trial?'

'Maybe we will,' Rebecca said. 'Once the verdict goes our way.'

He shook his head in disbelief. There was no excuse for curtailing the freedom of the press. And he told her so.

She gave him a half smile. 'You know, I asked around about you.'

'I'm flattered.' Except he wasn't. He didn't like the level of intrusiveness. It felt almost threatening.

'It seems when you think you're onto something, you want to get the bit between your teeth,' Rebecca said. 'I found your article about the Saudi Embassy.'

Nick's first thought was she must have spent a fair amount of time on his website. The article was five years old.

'It was a good piece,' she said. 'The Home Secretary doing dodgy deals with the head of a Saudi arms company that also happened to give munitions to fundamentalist Wahhabi groups in Nigeria and the Philippines.'

'It was a big story at the time,' he admitted.

'I remember it. Stephen Harvey had previously denied ever having any connection with Mohammad Badawi, even before becoming Home Secretary. Yet you exposed Harvey was a major shareholder in Badawi's firm.'

'I remember,' he said.

'Only that's not what got you fired, is it?' she said. 'You published the story against the express wishes of your then employer, who was very good friends with the Home Secretary.'

'You really have done your research,' he said.

'I still have friends in the media. Some of them speak very highly of you. And with good reason.'

He breathed in deeply through his nostrils, trying to clear the annoyance he felt at this entire conversation.

'I know you're aware of the potential consequences for defying a super-injunction,' Rebecca said. 'But I also know that won't stop you. Which is why I asked to speak with you.'

He faked a smile, producing his phone from inside his leather jacket. 'Great!' he said. 'Care to comment on the record, then?'

Rebecca moved off the desk and over to the glass window, where she looked out across the London vista. 'Look, Mr Winters, I asked you here because I have a proposition for you.'

He wondered when she was going to get around that. 'Okay, so what is it?'

'I'd like you to work for us,' she said.

TWENTY-SIX

(O)

For a moment, he was too stunned to speak.

'You obviously care about the truth,' Rebecca said. 'What if I offered you an opportunity to seek the truth, right here? Working from the inside?'

'I . . . I don't understand,' he said.

'Doyle isn't the only issue for us,' she said. 'We have an unprecedented number of people trying to take us to court. Insisting that Nostal compromised them in some way. It could be very damaging for us.'

Nick realised he was gripping the arms of his chair. Was she testing him? Did she know about Julia and the leaked names he had on his USB? He told himself to relax and met her eyes, looking for signs of duplicity. They sparkled back at him with what he read as earnestness, though it was hard to be sure. He decided the only safe choice was to play dumb.

'What people?' he asked, frowning. 'Compromised how?'

'It varies,' she said. 'Look, we don't need to get into the

weeds here. Long story short, the Doyle trial, combined with enough of these other claims, could be disastrous for us.'

He still wasn't following. 'What do you need me for?'

Rebecca shrugged. 'We've made a perfectly safe drug that brings happiness to millions,' she said. 'Doyle's lawyer is clearly lying. These other people. They're lying too. We just need someone to prove it.'

Nick whistled softly. 'You want me to write the opposite story to the one you don't want out there?' he asked, incredulous. 'Are you kidding me?'

'Not a story, no. An internal report. Just for Jeremy Gladstone and the board.'

Nick recognised the name. Gladstone was the global CEO of Lakefront Sciences.

'It's Jeremy who suggested we hire you,' Rebecca said. 'He's been most distressed. He believes, as do I, that the science is definitely on our side. And that means anyone claiming Nostal is dangerous has ulterior motives.'

'Motives?'

'In Doyle's case, he obviously had a grudge against Richard Wendell. And these other people. Well. Chances are, they probably just want money. And I suppose they assume we have more than enough to throw around. But we still need proof. Of their ill-intentions.'

He laughed. 'What?'

'We'll pay you very well.'

'I don't doubt it,' he said, looking around at the room's decor.

'I mean, really well,' she said. 'Sixty thousand pounds.'

Had he accepted the drink Rebecca had offered him earlier, he would likely have spat it out. 'Sixty *thousand*?'

'If you deliver it in four weeks. The trial's in six weeks, so you'll have to work fast. Tell you what. We'll make it seventy if you accept today. What do you say, Mr Winters?'

Nick could barely believe what he was hearing. Seventy

thousand pounds was a lot of money, just for one report. But there was also a reason the offer was so generous.

'You're trying to stop my article,' he said.

'Yes,' Rebecca said. 'That would certainly be a beneficial by-product. But that doesn't mean I would expect you to compromise the truth. To be clear, I'm, we're, offering to pay you for some genuine investigative work. Into Doyle and into these other people. See if you can find anything that reveals they're lying. That's all.'

Nick thought about his interviews with Charles Mills and Lenora Cox. He was pretty sure they weren't making things up.

'What?' she asked. 'Why do you look so sceptical?'

Nick tried hard to put his poker face back on. Rebecca Hughes obviously had no idea he'd spoken to two of these so-called liars already. For Julia's sake, he couldn't let on that he knew more than he did.

'I don't believe in getting something for nothing,' he said. 'If I was to do this . . . *investigative* work, I don't buy that you'd really want me to be objective. I think you'd want me to write the conclusions you'd already decided you want me to come to.'

'That's a very cynical attitude,' Rebecca said.

'How else could I see it?' he asked.

She fiddled with the pendant on her necklace as if contemplating how to respond. 'You know, you shouldn't just assume that we're the villains here. Big pharma does a lot of good in the world. Our products help people. Forgive my bluntness, but we spend a lot of time and money making damn sure they're safe. I'm convinced there isn't a scrap of evidence that will say otherwise. And if we hire someone with your reputation to confirm that, no one can say we were afraid of scrutiny.'

Nick shifted uncomfortably in his chair. 'Look,' he said. 'I'd like to believe that. But applying for a super-injunction doesn't exactly sound like you have nothing to hide. And I can't, I *won't*, take anyone's hush money. However it's dressed up. I'm afraid I'm going to decline your generous offer. I write the stories I want to write.'

She prickled at this. 'And how is that approach working out for you financially?'

The comment landed with Nick, but he tried not to show it. The truth was his website had few subscribers and it had been hard to make ends meet the last few years.

'This could help you,' Rebecca said. 'Fund you to do more of the journalism you love.'

Nick bit the inside of his cheek. His bread and butter, including countless consumer tech reviews he wrote, didn't pay anywhere near seventy grand. Not even close. But he wasn't about to get his hands grubby.

'Thank you for the offer,' he said. 'Genuinely. But I'm really not interested.'

He got up to leave and Rebecca handed him a business card. 'Please,' she said. 'Just think about it?'

He repeated his answer but took the card anyway. After all, it had her direct contact details on it. And when the story he wanted to write was ready, he could always use it to reach out to her for comment.

TWENTY-SEVEN

(O)

The hulk of a chauffeur was waiting dutifully outside Rebecca Hughes's office. He offered Nick a ride home, but he declined politely, saying he'd prefer to use public transport. He didn't want to spend another second with these people. The moment he stepped outside the imposing lobby, he felt a weight lift off. He texted Julia Conway as he walked down the street. She called him a minute later.

'It's okay,' he told her. 'They don't know anything.'

He sensed the immediate relief on the other end of the phone. But it was soon replaced by confusion.

'What did they want with you then?' Julia asked.

He told her about Professor Simmons and the internal report Rebecca Hughes had asked him to write.

'I think they're just looking for a way to own me,' Nick said. 'If I accept, they'd probably make me sign a non-disclosure agreement. Stop me from publishing my original, intended story.'

'Will you do it?' she asked.

Nick didn't need to think about his answer. 'Not a chance.'

Julia was quiet for a moment. 'So they don't know about me,' she said at last. 'That's good.'

Nick agreed that it was. 'Ears open, but head down,' he reminded her. 'I'll be in touch.'

He hung up, realising he'd already walked all the way to Bank station. But instead of hopping on the Tube, he looked at his watch. His interview with Doyle was in three and a half hours. He could skip going home, just start walking north, slowly. He could do with clearing his head anyway.

The streets were summer-hot and busy. In Islington, Nick stopped for lunch in a sandwich chain, where he munched on a cheese and salad roll while he searched online for Jeremy Gladstone on his phone. He found the CEO's Wikipedia page first. The photo was current, depicting Gladstone in his seventies, with his silver hair and styled beard. He had been working for Lakefront Sciences for the better part of twenty years, but had only been in charge of the global business since 2018. There was very little about his background, apart from a business book he had written in his forties that still sold well. Nick would have loved to interview Gladstone at some point, perhaps further down the line, but he was pretty sure he'd be denied, especially now he'd told the company's head of PR where to go. He threw his wrapping away as easily as he'd discarded Rebecca's assignment and strolled on through King's Cross and along the Caledonian Road towards Pentonville prison. He felt nervous at the prospect of meeting Doyle and his barrister. Hopefully the meeting would go well. At the prison gates, he pressed the buzzer and stated his name clearly and who he was visiting. A garbled voice mumbled something incoherent through the speaker. For a moment, Nick thought he was being ignored, but then he heard a bolt sliding across the wooden door. An overweight man in a guard's uniform stepped out through it.

'Mr Winters?'

'That's right.'

'My name is Jason Grant. I'm one of the guards on duty here.'

'Okay,' Nick said.

He was starting to feel something wasn't right.

'I'm afraid that your visit will not be able to go ahead today,' the guard said.

'Oh. I see. Mr Doyle was supposed to put me down on the visitor's register,' he blurted. 'He's granted me permission on the app thing, you know the—'

'I'm sure he did. But I'm afraid that it will still not be possible.'

Jason Grant lowered his voice as he looked around him, even though they were the only two people standing at the entrance.

'Mr Doyle was murdered in his cell this morning,' he said.

TWENTY-EIGHT

(0)

Forty minutes later, Nick was sinking his second pint in a nearby pub. He sat at a table by the window, watching the passing traffic, his brain still trying to absorb the news. He called Julia Conway and told her what had happened.

'Killed? Oh my God. When?'

'They found him this morning,' Nick said. 'Throat slit. The police are there now, interviewing the inmates.'

'Oh dear,' Julia said. 'That's just so awful. The poor man!'

Nick held the phone to his ear, neither of them speaking.

'Is there any . . . I mean, are they saying why . . . ?'

'From what I understand, he got into an argument with someone inside. These things can happen in prison. The guard said they'll know more once the investigation is complete.'

Silenced followed before Julia said, 'What do you mean *know more*? What do you think happened?'

Nick considered his answer carefully. Doyle's unexpected death felt wrong. Something felt off. His gut reaction was this was foul play. *Is that crazy?* he wondered. A hit job from the outside? It was, after all, a mighty coincidence that the one man who could single-handedly decimate Lakefront's share value just happened to be shivved before his trial. Handy for those shareholders, anyway.

'Nick?'

'The timing's a little strange,' he admitted.

'Oh my God,' Julia said. 'You're not saying the company might have had something to do with it?'

'I suspect *something*,' Nick said. 'I need to look into it.'

'Oh. My God. What sh-should I do?'

He felt bad for calling her now. All he'd done was make her scared again. But something in him said she was better off knowing. Just in case.

'Carry on as normal,' he said. 'Same as before, ears open, but head down. But if you hear anyone talking about this, let me know.'

'I . . . ok-okay.'

'Don't worry,' he said. 'You're safe.'

He wasn't sure why he said it so emphatically. But Julia sounded grateful for the reassurance. It was only after he'd hung up that he realised he had no right to tell her any such thing. He was in the dark now, he knew that. This story hadn't just changed gears, it had changed direction. Mark Doyle had been killed. And Nick needed to find out who was responsible.

PART TWO

TWENTY-NINE

(0)

A few days later, Nick returned to Pentonville prison. This time, he was greeted by a female guard, who checked him in on an iPad. He was led through the gate and taken straight to the visitor centre. There, he was made to empty his pockets before being frisked by a second male guard. After his passport was examined, he was escorted through a series of clanking jail doors and unceremoniously dropped off in a central room that resembled a 1970s school cafeteria. From the rows of Formica tables and chairs, it was clear this was the main visiting hall. The room was only half full, containing a handful of convicts in blue overalls and their visitors. There were, however, plenty of guards. Nick picked one of the empty tables at random and sat down. He tried to steady his nerves as he waited. Finally, he heard the heavy clunk of keys turning. A new prisoner was escorted into the space. The guard pointed at Nick. The prisoner nodded and plodded towards him, his eyes zeroing in.

'You Winters?'

Nick nodded, looking his interviewee up and down. Carl Ellis. Currently serving eight years for GBH and burglary. The first thing that struck him was how skinny he was. Like someone had started with pipe cleaners and tried to pack human flesh around it as an afterthought. He looked like he would be easy pickings for any other inmates who fancied a go. But looks could also be deceiving. Nick rose to his feet. Handshakes were not permitted, so he simply invited Carl to sit down. When they were both settled, the convict clasped his tattooed arms behind his head and grinned.

'So,' he began, 'when do I get the money?'

Nick stared at the missing tooth, briefly wondering if one of Carl's previous convictions had been for the possession of crystal meth.

'I think there's been a misunderstanding, Mr Ellis,' he said.

'Bollocks,' Carl replied, dropping both his arms and his smile. 'Five grand if I tell you what I know. Or you can stick your fucking interview.'

Nick shook his head. 'You didn't mention that you were hoping to gain financially from this.'

Carl snorted. 'What are you, fucking stupid? You can read between the lines, can't you?'

Nick winced. It made sense now. On Tuesday morning, he had called the press office for the Ministry of Justice to ask who Mark Doyle had shared his cell with. Once he had Carl's name, he emailed the governor's office. Before he knew it, Carl had reached out to him on the InMeet app. The convict had agreed to be interviewed but had also mentioned something about hoping it would be worth his time. Stupidly, Nick hadn't picked up on the extra meaning.

'Look, Mr Ellis,' he said. 'I'm not sure I have any budget to pay you for any—'

'That's bollocks! I know the newspapers pay thousands of pounds for stories.'

'Maybe the tabloids do, for certain types of stories, but I don't actually work for—'

'Listen here, pal. You want to know what happened, don't you? I was there, mate. I can tell you.'

Nick leaned back in his chair. This was getting nowhere. He needed to know what this man knew, but it was clear he wasn't shifting.

'Look,' he said. 'I can't promise you anything without knowing what you're holding.'

Carl's brow knitted. He seemed to be contemplating whether to be offended.

'Tell me what you know, and then we can discuss whether it's worth something,' Nick offered.

'Fuck that,' Carl said.

Nick sighed. Maybe it was time to call the man's bluff. 'Okay, fine. Have it your way,' he said.

He pushed the chair back and stood up. 'One question though. How many other journalists do you see here?'

Carl ground his teeth, looking down at the floor. He remained that way for a long time. 'All right,' he said at last. 'But you better pay me what I deserve.'

Nick sat down again. 'Why don't we start at the beginning?' he said.

He placed his phone on the table and asked if Carl objected to being recorded. 'I promise to keep your name out of it,' he added.

The convict shrugged, which Nick took to be consent.

'So how well do you know Len?' Nick asked.

Carl's furrowed brow tightened further. The prison's official statement about the incident had reported that forty-two-year-old inmate Leonard Griffin had been the one caught with a bloody shiv next to the freshly stabbed corpse of Mark Doyle. Griffin was no stranger to violence and was already serving a life sentence for murder.

'I don't know Len personally,' Carl said. 'But I know who

he is. And I know the type of people he hangs around with.'
Carl glanced over his shoulder before continuing. 'The way it
works in here, you have a hierarchy,' he said. 'Some are at the
top, some at the bottom. The ones at the top, well, they get
first pickings . . . cigarettes, booze, drugs . . . anything really.
You get me?'

'I think so,' Nick said.

'So sometimes someone new comes in, you know.
Someone who some of the fellas might take a liking to.'

'You're saying that's what happened to Mark?'

'I'm saying it happens a lot.'

'And did Mark know about this . . . rule?'

'He suspected it, yeah. He overheard some of the blokes in
the caff talking one day. He was terrified. He'd never been in
prison in his life, you know. Fucking white-collar boy. He
absolutely shat himself. So he starts confiding in me because
we're banged up in the same cell. Asking me how it works. Is
there any way he can avoid getting picked? He wants to
know if he has to join a gang. Him? In a gang? I proper pissed
myself, I can tell you.'

'So what advice did you give him?'

'I told him he needed to keep his head down. Not like
that. I meant, keep a low profile. Maybe he'd be left alone.'

'Is that what happened?'

'At first. He was here, untouched, for weeks. Then Len
made a claim on him.'

'A claim?'

'First pickings, like I said. Len's top of the tree. But I was
so fucking surprised, I couldn't believe it.'

'Why was that?'

'Well, I know for a fact Len ain't queer. Back in the day, he
used to run a bunch of knocking shops in Soho. Strip clubs
with a little extra service. Had a reputation for taking his
payments in kind.'

'So he only likes women?'

'Exactly. Not even jail queer, if you know what I mean.'

'Right. And what did you do when you learned about this ... claim?'

'I told Mark straight away. Told him to just let Len do whatever he wanted. Pressed upon him that, horrible as it was, it was best not to resist.'

'Because ... ?'

'Because Len is right at the top of the hierarchy. Right. At. The. Top. It don't get any higher.'

'So I'm confused. You're saying Len wanted Mark for sex after all?'

'No,' Carl said. 'It was a trick. So he could be completely alone with Mark in the cell. There's a certain understanding, see. If someone's high up the tree and claims dibs on a new mark, we give them the privacy they need. Out of respect.'

'Why lie though? If this Len guy has the rep you say he has, and he wanted to kill Doyle, why not just demand his time alone? Why pretend it's a sex thing?'

Carl looked around and dropped his voice to a whisper. 'Because not everyone is okay with covering for murder,' he said. 'You want to do for a fella in here, that's your business. But you involve other inmates, you make them accessories. It's not part of the code here, no matter how high up you are. So you won't get co-operation.'

'Co-operation? From who? The other inmates?'

'Exactly. Some cons look the other way. Others watch out for screws. That sort of thing.'

'You mean you all help facilitate a rape,' Nick said.

He realised he was developing a visceral disgust for Carl Ellis. But the man simply shrugged. 'Look, you don't have a choice in these things, mate. You either respect the hierarchy or get what's coming to you. Everybody understands the rules.'

Nick ran his fingers through his hair. 'Okay,' he said. 'So talk me through how it happened.'

'In the mornings, they open up our cell doors and we all step out for the count. Then we all march down for breakfast.'

'Okay . . .'

'So while this is happening, Len's already put the order out. So Mark's been grabbed and held back inside his cell.'

'Who grabbed him?'

Carl didn't respond.

'You?' Nick said.

The other man looked away. 'Like I said, it was all a trick. I didn't know what Len was planning to do. Nobody did.'

'All right. So then what happened?'

'Then Len arrives. He tells me to fuck off. So I stepped out.'

'Where the hell are the guards?'

'They're all being distracted. The line down to breakfast, it keeps moving, but slowly. But there are lots of little, ordinary delays. Fellas stopping to chat shit with the screws, slowing the line down. Others bending down, pretending to tie their shoelaces. That sort of thing. Making it look like nothing else is happening, but really providing cover for Len.'

'It doesn't sound like the sort of distraction that would work for very long.'

'It doesn't have to. It ain't a romantic weekend away. The idea is a fella goes in and out, if you'll pardon the language. No flowers, no dinner. A few stand outside the cell door with their backs to them, again for privacy.'

'You included?'

He couldn't be certain, but Nick thought he caught a flicker of shame flash across Carl's face. But it vanished almost as instantly. 'I told you, I didn't know what Len was planning. First I hear is Mark screaming loudly, saying no, no, no. All the usual shit when some poor sod's marked. Normally you'd expect to hear their voice get muffled very quickly, hand over the mouth, you know. But not this time.

There was a choking sound, like someone spitting up water. That's when I knew his throat had been cut.'

'You witness the actual murder?'

'Not the moment it happened, no. But I didn't need to. I turned round, saw Len standing there. Calm as fuck. Holding his broken bit of mirror. He's smiling, blood all over him. Screws rush in, take him down, that's that. You know?'

Nick exhaled, blinking hard in an effort to rub out the image of Mark Doyle, his neck slit, eyes wide as he bled out across the cell floor. It didn't work.

'The news is saying Len is protesting his innocence,' he said. 'How can he, given what you've just told me?'

'That's just his pride,' Carl said. 'Len's never fessed up to anything in his life. Not to Old Bill. But it pissed the rest of us off no end, I can tell you. We had no idea what he was going to do. He made us a fucking part of it.'

'I see. Why do you think he did it?'

'He never knew Mark. Never even met him. There was no way this was a beef. The only thing I can think is he was ordered to.'

'By someone on the outside?'

Carl nodded.

'Any idea who?'

The convict hesitated, his eyes wandering, refusing to meet Nick's own.

'There's only one geezer Len would willingly risk losing any chance of parole for. Scarier than fucking Len even.'

'And who's that?' Nick pressed.

Carl chewed his lip and finally met his gaze. Then he gave him a name. 'That's all I'm saying,' he said, crossing his arms. 'The rest you'll have to figure out. Now, how much are you going to give me?'

Nick stopped the recording and stared directly into Carl's eyes. He spoke calmly, keeping his voice even. 'I appreciate you talking to me, Mr Ellis. But now let me tell you what I think is fair. I think the right amount to pay someone willing to be complicit in a sexual assault that then becomes a murder is absolutely nothing. I'm sorry.'

Carl's face contorted as he processed the words. Then he snarled and flung himself over the table at Nick. Fortunately, the guards reacted quickly, rushing forwards to restrain him. As they led him away, and back to his cell, the convict cursed him in every conceivable way. Nick watched him go, feeling disgusted. But not in the least bit bad about not giving him a penny.

THIRTY

(0)

Back at the flat, he made himself a sandwich and searched online for the name Carl Ellis had given him. He started with Facebook. There weren't many Adam McCreadies who fitted the age and demographic. And while Nick didn't like to stereotype, when he came across the only one with a skinhead and a square jaw, he was pretty sure he'd found his man. Both McCreadie's Facebook and Instagram accounts were locked, with only a thumbnail-sized profile picture still visible, so Nick switched to a general search. He found more results than he was expecting, and not in a good way. Adam McCreadie was connected to a series of court cases involving everything from sex trafficking to drug running. In every case, he seemed to get off due to lack of evidence, but it was pretty clear even to the casual researcher that he was a very bad man indeed. Nick was still wading through various news articles when his phone rang.

'Christ,' Sam said. 'I've only just heard about Doyle.'

The story of a prisoner being murdered at Pentonville had

been circulating for a number of days, but with no one allowed to mention what Doyle was on trial for, it was a short piece with scant details that was easily buried under newer breaking stories. Nick was surprised Sam had spotted it at all.

'Why didn't you mention anything?' his old editor asked.

'I've been busy trying to find out what happened,' Nick said. 'I talked to his cell mate this morning.'

'So what *did* happen?' Sam asked. 'He piss off the wrong gang in there or something?'

'I think something worse.'

Nick brought Sam up to speed, including the interesting conversation he'd had with Carl Ellis. 'So the man who might have arranged it is called Adam McCreadie. He's the head of one of London's largest criminal gangs, apparently.'

He told him all the bad things he had discovered from the web so far.

'Jesus, Nick. What the hell are you getting yourself into?'

'That I don't know yet,' he admitted.

'Well, hold fire,' Sam said. 'You may not want the story if it isn't your exclusive any more. I've left a message with our legal guys to see where the press stands with regard to the super-injunction, now the trial isn't going forward.'

'I'm way ahead of you, Sam,' Nick said.

Nick had already spoken to Julia Conway, who had updated him on the discussions her department was having in the wake of Mark Doyle's death. What she had to report had taken Nick by surprise.

'The injunction still holds, regardless,' Nick said. 'The wording explicitly forbids any reporting on the existence of the trial, past or present.'

'For a trial that never happened? Are you fucking serious?'

'This is what Lakefront's own lawyers are saying,' Nick said. 'And they should know. As long as it could be argued that word of its existence could damage their reputation, the gag stays in place.'

Sam was silent.

'Well, then it's still down to you,' he said at last. 'But I really don't like where this is going. Criminal fucking gangs? You need to be careful, okay?'

'I will be,' Nick promised. 'It'll be worth it if it leads back to Lakefront Sciences.'

'You honestly think there's a link?'

Nick had been chewing over the question all week. He'd considered the possibility that Doyle might have owed McCreadie money or something, but not for very long. Mark Doyle was a chartered surveyor. That didn't preclude him from becoming involved with the wrong people, but Nick still couldn't see Doyle's world ever mingling with theirs.

'I think it's a possibility,' he told Sam.

'Just watch your back,' Sam said. 'This is all sounding a little dangerous.'

Nick promised him he would.

For the rest of that afternoon, Nick delved deeper into his quest. He'd hit a wall, having been denied access to McCreadie's public social media. But then he had an idea. He decided to search for Len Griffin instead. See what he could find out about the killer himself. Len's social presence was displayed for all to see. His accounts hadn't been active for a while, likely because of his limited access from prison. Nick scrolled down and discovered Len had been a regular poster on Facebook before his incarceration. He was a keen Chelsea supporter and most of his updates were at football matches. Nick found picture after picture of pre- and post-match drinks. Len, with his mates, all cheersing and boozing. He stopped at a random group photo of the lads all sitting around a table inside a pub. Some wore the tribal colours of their team, others were in civilian clothes. But it was the gentleman at the end of the table that caught Nick's eye. Bald, mean-looking and dressed in a charcoal grey suit. He recognised Adam McCreadie's face from his profile picture. He went back into Len's posts, scrolling through the photos with more scrutiny. No pub names in the posts, but many were location-tagged in Soho. In four separate pictures posted on different dates, Nick spotted the same craft beer pumps on the bar. The upholstery was the same deep ruby red too. There was no doubt all these socials took place in the same pub. And although Nick found no more photos of McCreadie, he could tell from how he looked so at home in the group that he belonged to it. Nick visited the website of one of the craft beer brands. There he found a list of pubs that sold their trademark ales. The embedded locations map showed him an expansive cluster of red dots scattered across London. He zoomed in on Soho. Fifteen venues to choose from. Frustrating. Another idea. He searched for Chelsea fan forums, combining the names of two of the brewery's ales. The fifth result down, he found an unofficial fan site for the club. One Chelsea4eva34 had started a thread about trying to get a few of the site's visitors together after a match. It had been posted two years ago but that didn't matter. A comment on the bottom of the first page mentioned a pub that served one of the craft beers. The Barrel Inn, off Berwick Street. Nick checked the pub's own website pictures and confirmed it was one and the same place. Switching websites, he checked the football listings for the following day. And whistled. He felt a small pinprick of adrenaline. He instantly knew what his next step should be. But he also recalled Sam's warning. He would need to tread very cautiously.

THIRTY-ONE

(0)

On Saturday morning, Nick rode to Soho. It was a part of London that had changed a lot over the years. Almost all the seedy clubs and bars he remembered had been replaced by new-build flats or homogenous coffee chains. Nick's current coffee, however, was being consumed in the back room at the Barrel Inn. The pub was empty, and the cappuccino he'd ordered disappointingly bland. But he had deliberately chosen location over taste buds, specifically, the long table that, according to Len's photos, McCreadie and his associates liked to gather at. Nick was assuming a number of variables here, but one of them was his belief that humans were creatures of habit and especially so on match day. He took another reluctant sip of his drink and went over his plan. His phone buzzed loudly on the table.

'Heather,' he answered softly, having seen her name flash up on the screen.

'Am I disturbing you?' she asked.

'No, of course not. You okay?'

He hadn't heard from her since the previous Friday when she had stormed out of the restaurant. And he'd stopped sending her any more texts.

'I'm sorry I didn't respond to you,' she said. 'I've just been doing a lot of thinking, you know.'

He nodded. 'Sure, of course.' He sensed she was trying to find the right words.

'I thought about everything you said,' she said. 'And I was wrong to get angry. I just felt disappointed. But I get why you wouldn't want to take any more of that stuff. It's just that without it—'

'I know,' he said. 'I get it.'

She asked him how his investigation was going. Nick debated about what to share with her. She hadn't mentioned anything about Mark Doyle, which meant she probably hadn't read that he'd been murdered. It was probably best to avoid mentioning that. Or indeed criminal gangs. There was no point in worrying her needlessly.

'I'm making good progress,' he said, choosing his words carefully.

'Oh, good,' she said.

She sounded sincere, he thought.

He weighed up his next question and decided he had nothing to lose. 'Will I see you again?'

He could feel her struggle to answer.

'I don't know,' she said.

His heart sank. He wanted to tell her the real reason he'd suggested the Nostal. About how his health scare had made him realise just how much he had regretted losing her. But then she surprised him.

'I've been doing some research of my own,' she said. 'Did you know that back in the seventies and eighties, therapists would prescribe ecstasy to couples having relationship problems?'

Nick told her he had not.

'They figured it would help,' she said. 'Maybe bring back the old feelings the couples used to have for each other. They kept trying it until it was banned. It's a crazy story that not many people know about. You should look it up.'

'I will,' he said. 'It sounds pretty crazy. Did it work?'

'For a few people,' Heather said. 'Some of the couples apparently started feeling residual effects after a while. As in, their old emotions started to slowly come back again. Even once the doses wore off, they would still feel a kind of lingering fondness for the other person. And things got better from there.'

He felt hopeful, suddenly. 'You think that would work with us?'

'Honestly? I don't know,' she said. 'I don't think we took enough Nostal to make that happen anyway. Unless you've changed your mind about taking it again?'

His heart seemed to be getting heavier now, sinking past his stomach. 'I don't think it's wise to,' he said.

'I get it,' she said. 'And maybe you're right. It probably wouldn't have worked in the long term. The truth is, at our age, we're very different people now anyway.' She breathed out slowly. 'Go do your story, Nick. Find out what the hell is up with this drug. Maybe, if you come up empty, we can talk again.'

'Maybe,' he said. He liked the idea of that, even if he wasn't sure how realistic an outcome it would be.

'I . . . I just really wanted to let you know I haven't deliberately been ignoring you,' she said.

'It's okay,' he said, gently.

He sensed they were about to say goodbye, and so blurted out one more thing. 'I'm here,' he said. 'If you change your mind. If you want to give this another go. Without the Nostal, I mean.'

'I know,' she said. 'Take care, Nick.'

She hung up. The heaviness continued to press down as he removed a reel of duct tape from his jacket pocket. He ran his fingers over it, wondering whether it would do its job. Would any of this lead him closer to what he was looking for? If nothing else, he owed it to himself and Heather to find out.

THIRTY-TWO

(O)

Nick returned to the Barrel Inn several hours later to find Saturday night officially underway. The pub was heaving. There was the usual assortment of tourists – women who wore too much make-up, men who likewise had overdosed on cologne, wearing shirts that were ironed too pristinely and shoes that were over-buffed. These were mostly Brits, treating themselves to a West End weekend. But there were a few foreign tourists too, marked by all the usual bags, from Hamleys to the M&M store. Nick weaved through the mixed crowd and ordered half a cider at the bar. The match had finished hours ago and the pub's two large-screen televisions had been muted. Instead, awful pop music filled the front of the venue.

Taking his drink, he made his way towards the back room and took a casual look around. The tables were all full, and the room buzzed with raucous conversations. He leaned against a pillar and studied the scene. There was a gathering at the long table of men dressed in Chelsea colours. Even from this distance, the conversation was noticeably bawdy. After a few minutes, Nick concluded that Adam McCreadie wasn't among the group. But he did notice a straggly man with spiky ginger hair. It was a distinctive feature that Nick recognised from the Facebook photos, which he was certain the man had been tagged in. His name was Paul something, Nick was sure of it. Paul was clearly drunk, roaring with laughter as he clinked pints with others around the table, more of whom Nick was also slowly recognising from the pictures. This was the same lot all right.

He sat down when a table nearby became free. Plenty of people drank alone in busy pubs like this, so he felt relatively blended in. Popping in his wireless ear pods, he reminded himself to mumble occasionally so that people would assume he was on his phone. This assumption would be more correct than they realised because his phone was currently directly under the long table, strapped to the underside with duct tape. It had taken him a while to configure the settings, turning off all notifications and putting it on silent. But he had finally done it. For the last few hours, his mobile had been acting as a listening device, recording the voices around the long table through a special app. Or so he hoped. Nick pressed a small button on the left ear pod, connecting it remotely, and turned up the volume. He was relieved to hear that the phone's mike was more than powerful enough to pick up the group's conversation. He struggled to make out some individual words, but that was down to all the ambient noise around him. Hopefully, the playback would be much clearer when he listened to it later, at home. What he could detect, however, was the obvious tribalism within the group. These guys were all on intimate terms with each other. Nick risked a glance across the room. Ginger Paul was standing up, gesticulating with his hands to indicate he was intending to buy a round. Nick saw an opportunity. He packed away his ear pods and stood up, following Paul casually to the bar.

There, jostling amongst thirsty customers, they ended up shoulder to shoulder. Nick leaned in and shouted into the man's ear.

'Hey, aren't you a friend of Adam's?'

The other man sprang back from him as if he'd been punched in the face. 'Who wants to know?'

'Oh,' Nick said. 'I've met him once or twice down here. You know, after watching the Pensioners. I assumed he'd be here, being match day and everything. Nice bloke. He coming tonight?'

Ginger eyebrows raised. 'Do I fucking know you, mate?'

'Oh. No. Sorry. Look, don't worry about it. Was just curious.'

'Wait, who are you? What the fuck do you want?'

'Easy, fella. I didn't mean any harm. Sorry.'

Paul puffed his chest out towards Nick like a territorial peacock. 'Why don't you just fuck off, mate?'

Nick held up a hand. 'Sorry, didn't mean any offence.'

Paul's eyes said everything else that needed to be said. They blazed with such coldness that Nick felt a shiver trickle down him. Enough so that he backed well away from the queue and turned around. He'd made a silly mistake, he realised. Drawn attention to himself. It was time to go. He made his way slowly towards the exit, hoping he was already being lost in the crowd. But with every step he took, he swore he could feel those eyes burning into the back of his head.

He found refuge in a restaurant around the corner that served excellent Malaysian food. Sitting in a red booth, he dipped Roti bread into a curry and occasionally checked his watch. Through the window, he watched the street outside, feeling uneasy about his encounter with Paul. He had the feeling the man wouldn't have thought twice about attacking him. Nick had hoped it would come across as a casual enquiry from a fellow fan in the pub, but it had clearly made Paul suspicious. All he could do now was stay the hell away from the place and wait. Eleven o'clock took an age to come around, but when it did, Nick was grateful that the Barrel Inn didn't have a late licence. He paid his bill, much to the relief of the waiting staff, who had been too polite to comment on the fact he'd drawn his after-dinner espresso out by an hour and a half. Nick thanked them, then hurried out onto Berwick Street, where he hid behind a tree as the punters dispersed, stumbling into the night. He stayed out of sight, waiting until the noises died down. When it sounded like everyone had left, Nick hurried to the pub door, which was locked. He banged on it repeatedly until a junior member of staff appeared in the window.

'I'm really sorry, I left my phone in there,' he said.

Luckily, the kid took pity on him and opened up. Nick ran to the back room, which was empty, with the lights off. He found the long table and reached under it. He was pleased to discover his phone was still there. Ripping the duct tape, he stashed the device in his pocket. Had it captured anything useful? He'd know soon enough once he got it home.

THIRTY-THREE

(0)

From the Barrel Inn, he headed towards the NCP car park a couple of streets away. His bike was parked where he'd left it. Nick freed his helmet from the cargo netting and started the Honda up. After he punched his ticket and exited the car park, he made his way onto Lexington Street, heading north towards Oxford Street. The traffic was heavy, typical on a Saturday night. The phone in his pocket felt like precious cargo. He tried not to get his hopes up too much. There was no guarantee it would lead him any closer to knowing whether Lakefront Sciences had anything to do with Doyle's murder. But at least it was a start. As he snail-crawled behind two black cabs, he wondered if his suspicions were right. Perhaps Doyle did have some other, unrelated beef with McCreadie after all. But it still seemed unlikely. It was surely too much of a coincidence that the man had managed to piss off a notorious criminal *and* Lakefront Sciences for entirely different reasons. And why would McCreadie want to have

Doyle killed anyway? He would need a pretty good reason. At least Lakefront had one.

If that theory was right, he wondered whether Rebecca Hughes had any knowledge of what had happened to Doyle. Global Head of Public Relations might sound like an impressive title, but it didn't necessarily make her part of the company's inner sanctum. Maybe Jeremy Gladstone had a close personal cabal around him prepared to execute the unscrupulous stuff. If Nick wanted more answers, he would probably need to dig deeper into Gladstone. He was just trying to figure out how to do that when he heard a powerful rumble behind him. He glanced in the side mirror and discovered the source. A biker, dressed in black leathers, weaving their way up Lexington Street, swerving aggressively around other vehicles, surging forward with single-minded intent. Nick realised two things at that point. First, the mysterious rider, a man, was headed straight towards him. Second, he was pointing a gleaming cylindrical object directly at him. Nick was no expert, but he was pretty sure that it was a pistol with a silencer fitted to it.

THIRTY-FOUR

(0)

Within seconds, it became a frenzied game of cat and mouse. Nick scrambled around cars, trying to put distance between himself and the gunman. At a zebra crossing, he almost knocked over a group of tourists, but they leapt out of the way just in time. The thunderous rumble grew louder as the biker closed in behind. Nick figured his best hope was to try to lose his pursuer in traffic. He took a sharp left onto Oxford Street, mounted the pavement, then swerved back onto the road. He undertook two buses and hit the accelerator. After a few seconds, he risked another quick glance in the mirror. The gunman was still coming, turning the same corner. He rode with skill and precision, sweeping around the buses until he was in front of them too. *Shit.* Where had he come from? How did he even know how to find him? Nick felt his throat clam up as the mirror revealed a gun barrel aimed in his direction. He heard a muted *cheep* noise as a chunk of lamp post to his left exploded. Definitely a silencer.

Nick jerked his head back, barely registering the damage

the bullet had caused, before revving his bike and surging forward. His heart was pumping fast. Maybe too fast. But conversely, he also felt like his brain had frozen. All the autonomy of his decision-making centre was stuck in some sort of mental mud. The Honda shot towards the junction of Oxford Street and Regent Street, but Nick could not decide whether to turn left or right. He started to panic. Something skimmed the side of his head. It happened again, this time hard enough to feel like someone had punched him on the side of his helmet. He wobbled, careering clumsily onto the pavement again. A crack appeared in a clothes shop window next to him. Another bullet. *Fuck.* He was gaining on Oxford Circus station, his momentum still propelling him forwards. Think, *think.* He swallowed, risking another look in the side mirror. His would-be killer had mounted the pavement thirty feet or so behind him. The long pistol flashed yellow. *Ping, ping.* Nick thought he might have felt a bullet hit the wheel spokes. But the bike was still moving, and so was he.

He rumbled back onto the street, leaning as far to the right as he could until his knee almost scraped the tarmac. He was sure he heard shots fly overhead, where his back had been just a second before. Still staying low, he looped around a Toyota Prius and finally reached the station. Now there would be even more cars and people to negotiate. He righted himself as he made a left turn. Time was running out. He couldn't stop to call the police, but what if he stopped a police car? They were everywhere in London, weren't they? He just had to keep riding until he found one and called for help. He accelerated again, boosting the bike along the bus lane and undertaking another black cab. The now familiar rumbling grew louder behind him. He sped up, overtaking the next bus on the right. And there it was. A white car with all the right livery and a blue siren. It was going at a snail's pace among the other traffic. He could pull up, knock on the window. Hope faded as quickly as it had sprung, however. To alert the officers inside the car, he'd need to slow down, even if to just rap on the window. And he'd be shot before he could get the first word out. Another loud whizzing noise next to his left ear confirmed his theory. He couldn't risk slowing down, not even with the police car here. As long as he remained a fast-moving target, he still had a chance.

Towards the end of Regent Street, he had another idea. Nick choked the throttle and the Honda surged forward, narrowly avoiding two more bullets that crunched into the back of a red bus. By now, the police car was no longer around to witness it, having already turned left onto Beak Street. Nick drove over the island, dodging oncoming traffic, and mounted the pavement on the opposite side of the road. People screamed as he rode through their midst, but he had no intention of slowing down. Part of him was worried the gunman might accidentally shoot an innocent pedestrian, but he had already committed to the plan.

To his right lay the narrow covered passageway that was Burlington Arcade. The shopping arcade was a handy shortcut to Piccadilly if you were on foot. Nick turned sharply and careered straight down the passageway. He flicked his head back just in time to confirm his assassin had overshot it. Whether the gunman rode on or doubled back, he figured he had bought himself around thirty seconds, which he intended to make the most of. At the exit, he killed the engine and leapt off the Honda, throwing the bike down on its side. *Five seconds.* He tore his helmet and gloves off, dropping them quickly down on the ground and ran across the street. *Ten seconds.* A red double-decker bus moved slowly along the lane towards his position. It was the kind inspired by the old Routemaster, with open rear doors that allowed passengers to hop on and off. Nick sprinted towards it, grabbing the pole on the low platform and pulling himself on. *Twenty seconds.* He ignored the stern look the conductor gave him, squeezing himself into the throng of passengers, which provided his camouflage. *Thirty seconds.* The bus continued its snail crawl along Green Lane. Though pressed between bodies, Nick still had a view through the side windows. Through the glass, he saw his pursuer cruise slowly past in the opposite direction. The stranger had pocketed his weapon and was intensely scanning the environment around him. Nick was struck by his helmet. It was black with silver streaks on top, resembling a crown of thorns – it made him look like a weird Norse deity.

The assassin looked sharply right, straight at the bus. Though Nick was confident he was well hidden among the other passengers, part of him couldn't help feeling like the gunman was staring right at him through that tinted black visor. He looked away again, and Nick let out a breath. A moment later, the gunman rode away. Nick remained on the bus. His breathing slowly returned to normal, the sweat cooling on his body. It might have been his imagination, but he could have sworn he'd sensed hatred behind that dark faceplate. He felt his adrenaline begin to drain now, and almost collapsed in the wake of it. He crossed his arms, determined to wait out the shaking in his body. Nick hoped it would pass soon. Just as he hoped his assassin didn't know who he really was. Or be waiting for him when he got home.

THIRTY-FIVE

(O)

Fortunately, no one was waiting for him. When he opened his front door, all that greeted him was his empty lounge. He didn't think he had ever been more grateful to be back in his flat. He poured himself a whisky and flopped his bone-tired body onto the sofa, sipping steadily until he felt numb. Just to be safe, he'd stayed on the bus, riding it all the way to Tottenham Court Road before he felt brave enough to hop off. Then he had made his way back to Burlington Arcade in search of his bike. Remarkably, it had been propped against a lamp post by some good Samaritan and was otherwise untouched. His helmet and gloves, too, had been thoughtfully hung on the right handlebar. How he had ridden all the way home he had no idea.

He downed the rest of his single malt, his thoughts circulating like noisy wasps with nowhere to land. There were many questions, but most of them would be for the police. He probably should have gone straight to the nearest station, but all he wanted to do was get home safe. His phone was still in his trembling hand, but Nick had never felt so drained. Maybe the cops could wait until the morning. As soon as he allowed himself that thought, he gave himself permission to shut his eyes. He discovered it was such a blissful feeling. He put down his drink and savoured the experience of just being still and alive. It soothed him to hear the sound of his own chest rising and falling, a steady, affirming rhythm repeating itself over and over. Exhaustion pulled him under and he succumbed, falling briefly into a deep but welcome darkness. It felt like only minutes had passed before the doorbell buzzer sounded, waking him back up with a start.

THIRTY-SIX

(0)

He blinked in confusion at the bright sunlight that streamed into his living room. *Shit.* What time was it? How long had he actually been asleep? The buzzer was still going. Someone had their finger pressed down on it. He felt his heart skip. What if it was the gunman who'd chased him? But that was ridiculous. Even if he had tracked him here, which was highly doubtful, he was hardly going to be as courteous as to knock on his door. He looked at his watch. It was just after 7 a.m. His visitor was probably just a Jehovah's Witness doing their Sunday rounds. He staggered over to the front door and peered cautiously through the peephole. In the oval lens, he saw a blonde woman. Her smart casual dress, which included a white blouse, navy blue jacket and trousers, made him suspect she was indeed from the local Kingdom Hall. But when he glanced back through the window, he saw a police car parked outside the gate, and two uniformed officers making their way down the path. Hesitantly, he opened the door.

'Are you Nicholas Winters?' the woman asked.

'Ah, yes.'

'Detective Inspector Flynn.'

She produced a wallet from inside her jacket and held it open. He stared at her ID badge in confusion.

'I-is there something I can help you with, Inspector?' he asked.

'May we come in?' Flynn asked.

He nodded, stepping aside so the trio could enter. In the kitchen, he invited them all to sit. His brain was doing cartwheels. What were they doing here?

'Get you anything? Cup of tea?' he said, just blurting out words.

'Actually, that would be lovely,' Flynn said with a warm smile. She turned to the officers. 'Boys?'

'No thank you, ma'am,' said the one on her left as his counterpart shook his head.

Both looked about twelve to Nick, though their beards said otherwise. They seemed to pale in Flynn's presence. She was a large-framed woman, with hefty limbs and a strong, oval face. But it was her disarmingly pleasant manner that Nick found most intimidating. He shifted nervously over to the kettle and filled it with water.

'I was going to call you guys, actually,' he said hurriedly. 'A weird thing happened to me last night. I was—'

'—chased along Oxford Street by a man with a gun. Yes, we know. I'm very happy to see that you're okay.'

'Wait a minute,' Nick said. 'How do you know about that?'

'We'll get to that in a bit,' Flynn said. 'Tell you what. Let's have that tea first, shall we?'

He brought over her mug, and sat with one himself, opposite her.

'This is a nice flat,' Flynn said cheerily as she looked around. She took a sip of her English Breakfast and sighed happily. 'You live alone?' she asked. 'No wife or kids?'

He was still wondering what she was doing here, but he answered her question. 'Ah, no,' he said. 'And no kids. You?'

He wasn't sure why he had returned the question. A mixture of politeness and nerves probably.

'Married with two,' Flynn said. 'Kimberly's three and Tommy's just turned five.'

'How nice,' he said. 'They must be proud having a policewoman for a mum.'

Policewoman for a mum? Why on earth did he say that? He could have sworn he felt his cheeks redden.

But Flynn only chuckled. 'They're proud as punch,' she said, beaming. 'My husband worries they're a bit young to know their mummy deals with criminals. But they're perfectly okay with it. Funny thing about kids. They can be a lot more grown up than we give them credit for. A lot more.'

Nick didn't know what to say to that. The last thing he wanted to do was continue having a cosy chat. But Flynn seemed determined to get to things in her own time. He sipped his tea and gave her an earnest look.

'Want to tell me why you're really here, Inspector?'

Flynn calmly put down her mug. 'We're aware that you contacted Mark Doyle in prison,' she said. 'You were down to visit him on the day of his death.'

She said it like it was a statement of fact that she wasn't expecting him to confirm or deny. Nick let out a small breath. He had no idea the police would be looking into Doyle's visitors so thoroughly. But he supposed it made sense, given what had happened.

'I was pursuing a story,' he said.

'Is it by chance one you're not legally supposed to report on?' Flynn asked.

Nick noticed the same breezy tone she'd used when chatting about her children. It put him on his guard.

'Actually, I'm not allowed to publish it,' he clarified. 'But there's nothing stopping me digging into what happened.'

He tapped his right knee under the table like he was sending an urgent, secret telegram as he waited for the DI to respond.

'Yes, you're absolutely right,' she said. 'And I assume you were looking into Richard Wendell's death at first? But then you found yourself with another murder story on your hands. Was that what led you to visit the Barrel Inn pub last night?'

'How did you—?' Nick began.

'We're the police, Mr Winters. It's our job to know things. For example, we also know you interviewed Mark Doyle's cellmate. I'm guessing he was the one who told you about Len Griffin's connection to Adam McCreadie and his lot? Truth is, we've had McCreadie's gang under observation for a few days now.'

Nick's heart froze. McCreadie's gang. *Of course they're a gang.*

'One of our undercovers spotted you in the pub last night,' Flynn said. 'You might not have known it, but you walked into a surveillance operation. One we put a lot of effort into.'

Nick squeezed the handle of his mug. He'd been a fool. So busy chasing after his story that he forgot the police would be investigating the murder too.

'Why *were* you there last night?' Flynn asked. 'You weren't expecting any of those men to agree to an interview, were you?'

'Not exactly,' he said. 'I was looking for a link . . . back to Lakefront Sciences.'

Flynn raised an eyebrow.

'Something doesn't add up,' he said. 'I think they might have had something to do with Doyle getting stabbed.'

'I see,' Flynn said.

He blurted on, still driven by nerves, telling her all about his secret recording on his mobile.

Flynn shook her head, a wry smile on her lips. 'Very clever,' she said. 'Did you capture anything incriminating?'

'I don't know yet,' he admitted.

'We'd love to take a listen,' she said.

'Of course,' Nick said.

Flynn looked at the two junior officers, then back at Nick, who stared back at her, puzzled.

'You see, Mr Winters, your suspicions are correct. We have good reason to believe that Lakefront Sciences may well be involved in criminal acts. And we intend to prove it.'

THIRTY-SEVEN

(O)

Nick put down his mug. Now Flynn had his full attention.

'Is it to do with Nostal?' he asked her. 'Are they covering something up?'

'Honestly? We don't know,' she said. 'But they might well be, yes.'

His interest was even more piqued. 'So is it actually dangerous? Did it make Doyle kill that guy?'

Flynn waved a hand. 'Let's just say we don't have sufficient evidence of that. *Yet*. But we do have good reason to believe that Jeremy Gladstone employed McCreadie's services.'

'Gladstone? The CEO?'

Flynn nodded. 'We believe the orders to kill Mark Doyle came from the top. That Gladstone, or maybe someone he knows, has a contact in the criminal underworld. One of our snitches, see, a man who does occasional work for Adam McCreadie, told us that Gladstone and McCreadie had a meeting together . . . and that during this meeting they discussed a fee for the hit.'

Nick sat back, absorbing what she was telling him.

'But now you may have set our investigation back. A lot back, actually.'

He shut his eyes.

'You got yourself spotted,' Flynn said. 'You spoke to a man called Paul Forrester, who probably marked you as undercover. I don't know what you said to him, but he had you pegged as soon as you opened your mouth.'

Nick bit his lip. He knew he'd made a mistake talking to Forrester. It was a stupid move.

'You ruined our whole operation,' Flynn continued. 'Now Adam McCreadie and his gang will assume we're watching them. They'll stop drinking at the Barrel Inn and lie low for a while. And, wherever they go, they'll all be looking over their shoulders . . . for us.'

'I'm sorry,' Nick said. 'I didn't know.' He buried his face in his palms and ran his fingers through his hair.

Then he snapped his head back up. 'What about the guy who chased me? You saw that too?'

'Not at the time,' Flynn said. 'Our undercover spotted Forrester make a short phone call after you left. Then, a few minutes later, we got a report of two bikes racing down Oxford Street, with a possible firearm involved. I checked the CCTV footage and figured it was you.'

No one said anything. Flynn reached across and gently touched his wrist. 'You were very lucky you escaped with your life. Very lucky.'

'I know. It all happened so fast,' he said.

Now that Flynn was here, he actually felt relieved to be able to talk about it. 'So the man who chased me? He didn't follow me from the pub?'

'We think he's an associate,' Flynn said. 'Maybe someone they had on speed dial. A fixer, they call it. Somebody nearby, ready and available at short notice. It's the kind of service you need from time to time if you're in their line of work.'

'Can't you arrest them, then?' Nick asked. 'You saw what they almost did to me.'

'We can't, not yet,' Flynn said.

'Why not?'

'Not enough proof,' Flynn said. 'Same reason we can't arrest Gladstone. At the moment, all we have is hearsay and conjecture. And now you've interfered with any evidence we could have got from our surveillance operation.'

Chastened, he stared at his tea. He breathed in deeply. 'Shit,' he said. 'I'm really sorry.'

Flynn nodded. 'What's done is done. It just means our investigation will probably take longer now. Unless you have something you can share with us? Anything you've discovered so far?'

He nodded. 'Well, I do have an inside source,' he said.

Flynn's eyes widened in surprise.

'A whistle-blower,' he clarified. 'Lakefront employee. Someone who wasn't happy about the super-injunction. And some of the other things Lakefront is hoping to hide from the public.' He told Flynn about the USB stick, with the list of claimants on it.

The DI listened in astonishment. 'Very interesting,' she said. 'So, who is this whistle-blower?'

Nick's heart quickened. He had promised not to reveal Julia's name, even if it was to the police. Fortunately, Flynn seemed to pick up on his concerns.

'It's all right, Nick,' she said, holding up another hand. 'I understand if you can't tell me. I don't have to know his name. But I am concerned for his safety. If Jeremy Gladstone finds out he has a leak inside his own company, I worry about what he'll do.'

Nick took a second to register Flynn's accidental misgendering. He had not specified whether the source was male or female. Now he realised he could take advantage of that, further preserving Julia's anonymity.

'Don't worry, Inspector,' he said. 'He's been very discreet. He knows to keep his head down.'

Flynn's expression became serious. 'Have you ever gone into the Lakefront Sciences building to meet him?'

No,' Nick confirmed.

Flynn stared at him as though weighing up this answer. 'Because if you have, that might have put him in danger.'

'I haven't,' Nick said.

Flynn took another sip of tea, looking pensive. Her eyes moved hawk-like across the kitchen table, locking on to an object resting on top of a pile of mail. Nick followed her gaze to a white card with a double helix logo embossed on it. Rebecca Hughes's business card. He'd forgotten he'd left it there.

'Mind if I . . . ?' Flynn said, snatching the card up before he could respond. She examined it, raising a quizzical eyebrow. 'You've spoken to Rebecca Hughes?' She flipped the card round to show him, even though he knew whose name was on it.

'Yes,' Nick said, 'but I never told her about my source.'

'Of course not. But Ms Hughes did give you an interview?'

'Actually, she interviewed me,' Nick said.

Flynn gave him a quizzical stare. He swallowed and told her about the job offer Rebecca Hughes had made. And about his refusal to take it. Flynn took this in, nodding.

'Good for you,' she said. 'These are bad people. You don't want to be getting into bed with them.'

She placed the card back down, finished the last of her tea. 'And are you sure they don't know about your source?'

'Pretty sure,' Nick said.

'That's good to hear,' she said. 'We need to keep him safe.

Tell me, do you think he might have been privy to anything else that could help us build our case?'

Nick thought it over and shook his head. 'I don't think so. But if that changes, I'll let you know.'

'Thank you,' Flynn said. 'I need you to share anything else he tells you that connects Lakefront to any criminality, okay? Can you do that?'

Nick told her he would.

'And please tell your source to be careful with what he says around his colleagues, okay?'

'I already have,' Nick assured her.

She stood up. 'Thank you for your time, Mr Winters.'

She handed him a card as the trio made their way slowly towards the door. 'I'm based at Holborn station,' she said. 'If you need to get hold of me, just ask for DI Flynn and they'll put you straight through. There's an email address on there too. Send us that recording, okay?'

'I will,' he said.

Before leaving, Flynn turned back one last time, a look of worry clouding her face. 'Promise me you won't do anything risky without telling us what you're planning first, all right? You need to keep us in the loop from now on. At all times.'

He promised. Then the front door was shut, and Nick was left alone in his flat with his thoughts. What a morning. It was all so overwhelming, and the lack of sleep wasn't helping. He retrieved his phone and opened the recording app. At least three hours of pub conversation had been captured on there. Nick attached the audio file and emailed it over, marking it for Flynn's attention and adding his contact details. He planned on listening to the recording himself too. But not right now. Now all he wanted to do was climb into his bed and shut off the world.

THIRTY-EIGHT

(0)

He slept for two hours, a broken sleep but his body still felt better for it. He realised he was starving and raided the fridge, never happier to discover a leftover bowl of three-day-old noodles he was confident were still in play. He'd barely finished before his phone went off.

'Mr Winters? Sorry, me again.'

He recognised DI Flynn's voice.

'Listen, I've been mulling things over, and I think I've had an idea.'

Nick frowned. 'An idea?'

'How would you like to make amends for botching our surveillance op?'

Nick listened to Flynn's proposal.

'You want me to tell them I've changed my mind?' He could barely believe what he was hearing.

'This could really help us,' Flynn said. 'You could play your part in assisting us in taking Lakefront Sciences down.'

He wasn't following. 'How?'

'You could use this job offer to get close to Rebecca Hughes. Work her, maybe.'

'Work her?'

'Yeah. We're not sure how much she knows,' Flynn said. 'It's one of the missing pieces of the puzzle for us. But you could be our man on the inside. Get her to trust you. See what you can find out.'

Nick blew out a long plume of air. Continue working with Lakefront even though he now knew they were behind Doyle's murder? That was a tall order. But the sincerity in Flynn's voice told him she was deadly serious.

'Look,' she said gently. 'You take the job, you'll be well placed to get us the evidence we need. And we do need more evidence.'

He gripped his phone tighter. 'What if everything's changed now? If she knows, if they know, it was me snooping around—'

'How could they?' Flynn said. 'None of McCreadie's men know who you are, right? There's no way Gladstone or anyone he's working with could know it was you in that pub. True?'

Nick frowned, thinking her argument over. She was technically right. But still. It felt a little like she was asking him to go back into a lion's den.

'This could be good for both of us,' Flynn said. 'You're investigating this story, aren't you? This is your chance to go deep undercover, find out the truth. And at the same time, help us.'

He chewed it over some more. But Flynn wasn't done yet.

'Right now, you're the only way we can get to Rebecca Hughes without alerting her. And our best shot at putting Jeremy Gladstone behind bars.'

He hesitated, unsure what to say.

'Look,' Flynn said, softening her tone. 'Lakefront Sciences thinks it's above the law, but I will make damn sure they face justice. I'll do it with or without your help. But I would much rather you wanted to be part of that.'

Her words lingered in the silence. It was hard for Nick to assess the swarm of emotions he felt. He wasn't keen to put himself in any danger, but at the same time, he had to contend with a horrible truth. Lakefront's hands were dirty. Like it or not, his suspicions had been confirmed. And Flynn was right about him investigating his story too. His gaze wandered over to the medicine cupboard. Wasn't he desperate to find out the big secret Jeremy Gladstone was prepared to kill for? To know what he had given up his second chance with Heather for? He drummed his fingers slowly on the table.

'All right,' he said. 'Tell me what you need me to do.'

She talked it through with him, giving him specific questions she wanted him to find answers to. Things Flynn's team needed to know, if possible. How close was Rebecca to Gladstone? Did she have access to his diary? Did she know where Gladstone was the day when he reportedly met Flynn's source? Flynn's words blurred in Nick's mind, even while he nodded along silently. What he was really wondering was whether this had any chance of working. But he supposed they would find out soon enough.

THIRTY-NINE

(O)

At noon on Monday, Nick returned to the Lakefront Sciences building. On his first visit, he'd arrived through the trade entrance, so had missed the impressive spectacle that was the vast and cavernous lobby. He felt dwarfed by the towering columns that ferried glass lifts up and down with dizzying speed. His footsteps echoed across the white marble floor as he approached the reception desk to announce his visit. He took a seat, and a moment to calm himself. The truth was, he wasn't sure Rebecca Hughes was going to believe his sudden change of heart. He'd called Flynn earlier in the morning to relay his concerns, but she had dismissed his insecurities, emphasising that she had full faith in him. Wasn't he an investigative journalist? Surely he could easily pull something like this off. Nick had told her he'd do his best, but now that he was here, his nerves were stubbornly returning.

A familiar, well-spoken voice interrupted his thoughts.

'Nick?' Rebecca Hughes said. 'Good to see you again. Please come with me.'

He followed her to the lifts where she swiped her ID card across the reader. They rode up to the forty-first floor and the doors opened onto an impressive restaurant. A host standing behind a podium ticked off Rebecca's name, then led them past a series of glass tables until they reached one by the floor-to-ceiling window. Jeremy Gladstone was sitting with his back to the London skyline, sunlight glinting off his thin-framed round glasses.

He rose and shook Nick's hand. 'Mr Winters. Please, sit.'

Nick swallowed. He hadn't expected this meeting. He thought he was just in to see Rebecca Hughes. But then he remembered Rebecca telling him it was Gladstone who had been keen to recruit him. It made sense that he would want to meet in person. Nick took the seat to Gladstone's left, while Rebecca placed herself opposite the two men. Nick couldn't help staring at Lakefront's CEO, with his pristine suit and overly styled silver hair. Adrenaline pumped through him as he tried not to think about the fact that this was the same man who arranged for Doyle's murder. As for Gladstone, he seemed placidly unaware that Nick was scrutinising him. Or else he was just hiding it very well. The CEO smiled, handed them both menus and beckoned a uniformed waiter over. He ordered a bottle of mineral water and invited Nick to pick whatever he wanted. 'On us,' he added.

When Rebecca had first mentioned lunch, Nick had wondered if a drink might be on the cards. He figured it wouldn't hurt to appear affable, so had left his bike at home just in case. Now he was glad he had. He ordered a much-needed beer. After Rebecca asked for a large chardonnay, he made himself meet Gladstone's eyes until the waiter returned.

'Rebecca tells me you had a change of heart,' Gladstone said. 'That you've agreed to help us, after all.'

Nick felt certain muscles in his body tense, and for a moment was worried that Gladstone would see through his pretence. He needed to tread a fine line here. The CEO would never believe he had suddenly become their ally, but he needed to make his reasons sound convincing. It was time to channel the confidence DI Flynn had put in him.

'Well, to be honest, it wasn't my first choice,' he said. 'But things have been slow, financially.'

'Happy to help in that department,' Gladstone said. 'Anything to expose these awful people. They really have created a headache for us.'

Nick ignored the last comment and instead gave the CEO an earnest look. 'But more important to me is that Ms Hughes here told me there wouldn't be any interference. That I'd be free to write whatever I find. I hope you meant that.'

'Of course,' Gladstone said. 'We wouldn't expect anything else.'

Nick nodded, hoping he looked like a man who was being convinced.

'Rebecca says you're an excellent journalist,' the CEO said. 'That you used to work for the *Sunday Record* once upon a time?'

'Once upon a time,' Nick agreed.

The drinks arrived and he took a sip of his beer, keeping his hand steady. So far, so good. Gladstone seemed to take Nick's insistence on objectivity as further proof of his new-found willingness to take the job. Of course, he had no idea whether Gladstone really would be happy to let him write whatever he wanted. But hopefully his mission here would be over long before he had to type a single word.

'You know, this is fabulous news,' Gladstone said. 'We need these chancers to be scrutinised by someone of your calibre.'

Rebecca glanced at Nick. 'I'm sure you'll do a fine job. I'll put money on them all hiding something. Or else being out for a quick payday.'

'Sad,' Gladstone agreed, with a glum expression.

Nick stared in disbelief at the pair, who gave every indication that they believed this to be the case. Gladstone, especially, had the look of a sullen child who'd been wronged somehow. And there was one bit of news neither seemed keen on discussing.

It would be strange not to bring it up, he thought, so he did. 'I guess there's one name you guys can scratch off the list of opportunists,' he said.

The reaction was instant. It was like he'd slapped both of them across the face. Gladstone turned pale and Rebecca stiffened.

'You're referring to Mark Doyle,' Gladstone said quietly.

'Yes,' Nick said. 'Pretty tragic, what happened, wouldn't you agree?'

He watched them closely.

'Awful, awful thing,' Rebecca said. 'We wouldn't wish that on anyone.'

Nick studied both their expressions. Rebecca did look genuinely pained, while Gladstone's expression appeared neutral. He was careful not to stare too long. He didn't want to arouse suspicion. The CEO poured some more water into his glass before looking off into the distance.

'Doyle's death was . . . unfortunate,' he said solemnly. 'My heart goes out to his family.'

Yeah, Nick thought. *I bet it does.*

But the CEO hadn't finished. 'And, sadly, it also robbed us of the chance to prove the safety of Nostal in a court of law, which we would have relished doing.'

Of course you would have, Nick thought.

'But these other claimants,' Gladstone continued. 'They're still very much alive. And they could do serious damage to our good reputation.'

Nick nodded. 'I guess your injunction doesn't cover them any more now there's no trial?'

'It does not,' Gladstone said. 'But that's irrelevant. None of these people have any proof our product's defective. But it's not just negative press we're worried about.'

'No?'

'These are not isolated incidents. We've had other claims of a similar nature. In other countries and markets.'

Nick raised an eyebrow. This was news to him.

'There are opportunists to be found everywhere,' Rebecca said dismissively. 'Fortunately, the numbers are still low enough not to attract widespread attention.'

'The reason they're low numbers is because our drug is perfectly safe,' Gladstone said with gritted teeth.

Nick bit his tongue, but his mind was still processing. Of course, it made sense that the UK wouldn't be the only country where some people would experience adverse side effects. But was it all connected?

'The sooner we can expose the ones here at home, the better,' Gladstone said. 'Before word spreads too far.'

'Too far?' Nick asked. He was feeling a little lost.

'There are other ways that news can spread besides the news,' said Gladstone.

'Loose lips,' Rebecca Hughes explained. 'Particularly among our employees. It's only a matter of time.'

Nick did his best to maintain his poker face. He hoped they had no idea about Julia.

'We like to think our people are loyal,' Gladstone said. 'But despite whatever confidentiality clauses people have in their contracts, it's human nature to spread gossip.'

'And gossip can spread to our shareholders,' Rebecca said.

Now it was starting to click into place.

'So that's why you need me,' Nick said. 'You're hoping my report will reassure them.'

'I'm confident it will,' Gladstone said. 'Especially coming from you.'

Although he knew he'd made the point already, Nick felt the need to emphasise it again. 'Look, I'll investigate these guys. But you need to know that I will only report what's true.'

Rebecca turned to Nick. 'Honestly, I don't think you need have any concerns. These claims are unsubstantiated bullshit, if you'll excuse my French. I have no doubt you'll discover that.'

Nick thought back to Charles Mills and Lenora Cox. Neither of them struck him as bullshitters, but he kept his mouth shut.

'Well . . . to an honest report, then,' he said, raising his bottle.

Jeremy Gladstone and Rebecca Hughes looked at each other, then raised their own drinks to him.

'To an honest report,' Gladstone said.

He turned to Rebecca. 'Let's get the paperwork drawn up straight away.'

FORTY

(O)

Rebecca escorted him back to the elevator and rode down with him to the lobby. They were alone in the lift. Nick was quiet, observing her body language carefully. He'd wanted to ask some of the questions Flynn had suggested. But it would be too suspicious to start launching into them all straight away. Today's task had been to convince Rebecca and her boss that he was genuinely interested in working for them. But looking at her stance, cross-armed, slightly turned away, made him wonder if he hadn't been as convincing as he'd hoped.

'Everything okay?' he asked.

She turned to meet his eyes. 'Fine,' she said coolly.

He raised an eyebrow.

'Okay, okay. I'm glad you changed your mind, but if I'm honest, I wish you were a little more on our side.'

'How do you mean?' he asked.

'It would be nice if you didn't just assume big pharma are automatically the bad guys,' she said.

He bit the inside of his cheek, considering his response. 'I don't,' he said. 'I'm only interested in the truth.'

'And you'll find it,' Rebecca said. 'You do your job right, your investigation will show that we've done nothing wrong. But my point is it would just be nice if people like you could appreciate all the good we do in the world.'

He was about to offer a cautious reply when the lift doors pinged open. They were back in the lobby. Waiting for them was driver-slash-debt collector Ben Cooper. He was dressed as sharp as ever, the collar of his shirt threatening to rip under the pressure of his tree trunk of a neck.

'You've got that meeting in Richmond, ma'am,' he said. 'I tried to message you.'

'Oh yes,' Rebecca cried. 'Sorry, I had my phone on silent. It's my fault.'

'Please don't apologise,' Ben said in his cheery voice. 'Shall I fetch the limo?'

'Thank you, Benjamin. If you wouldn't mind.'

Ben smiled and disappeared. Rebecca invited Nick to wait with her outside the building's revolving doors.

'Where'd you find that guy, anyway?' he asked. 'He reminds me of a doorman in a posh Mayfair club.'

She smiled. 'Yes, he does, doesn't he? Benjamin is my minder and driver. And my personal assistant for a lot of the time, as you can see. He's ex-military. Served in Afghanistan.'

'I can believe it,' Nick said.

'Jeremy hired him. I don't know how they know each other, but I think there might be an army connection. Jeremy was in the service too once. I remember he said I should have someone who could not only drive me about, but be useful if I ever got myself into a fix.'

'Fix?' he asked, puzzled.

'I suspect he meant that I could be a target for someone with a grudge, perhaps. Big pharma might not be big tobacco, but we're still the villains in some people's eyes.' She gave him a fixed look.

'Point taken, Rebecca,' he said. 'And I promise I'll write my report with an open mind.'

Her cobalt eyes softened. 'That's all we ask. I'll get the contract over to you in a few hours.'

A black limousine pulled slowly up by the pavement.

'Ah, here's Benjamin now. Can we drop you anywhere?'

'No, I'm good,' he said. 'I think I'll walk. Speak later.'

'Good luck with your investigation,' she said. 'Remember, we're counting on you.'

When the limo had disappeared in the distance, Nick called Holborn police station and asked to speak to Flynn.

'Nick! How did it go?'

'I met Jeremy Gladstone,' he said.

He told Flynn about the lunch and that he believed he had convinced them overall.

'Well done,' she said. 'This is good!'

'Yes,' Nick said. 'Although I didn't get much of a chance to talk to Rebecca.'

'That's fine,' Flynn said. 'You've done the important bit. How's your source? Have you checked in with him today?'

'I have,' Nick said.

He had texted Julia that morning to say he would be in the building later and not to be surprised if she spotted him. Moreover, he had called her late last night and told her about his visit from the Met police and Jeremy Gladstone's suspected involvement with Doyle's stabbing. Naturally, Julia had panicked. Nick reminded her no one knew of her existence within Lakefront and assured her that not even the police knew her identity. Eventually, she had calmed.

'You know, I'm happy to talk to him personally,' Flynn

said. 'If you think it'll help reassure him he's doing the right thing.'

Nick didn't hesitate in politely refusing. 'Sorry,' he said. 'I promised to keep him anonymous.'

'Of course,' Flynn said. 'I get it. But you should tell him he might be called as a witness if we get our day in court.'

'I will,' Nick said. 'We'll cross that bridge when we come to it.'

'Okay, then,' Flynn said. 'Listen, you let me know if either Hughes or Gladstone contacts you, okay? I need to be in the loop at all times.'

He promised her he would and cut the call. He was outside Moorgate Tube station now, ready to take a train back home. As he trotted down the steps, he thought about what Flynn had said about how this was his chance to investigate the truth. He knew she was right. He would go wherever the story took him. His thoughts turned to Heather, and he wondered briefly if he'd made the right choice. He'd be sad to lose her, if that was what it cost. But there was no way he could let this story go. Especially now that he had almost been killed for pursuing it. His train wasn't coming for five minutes, so he waited patiently on the platform, looking at the ads to pass the time. The six-sheet opposite was advertising a Honda dealership nearby. As he stared at it, he remembered something Ben Cooper had said the first time Nick had ridden with him in the limo.

I'm a Ducati man, through and through.

And then what Rebecca had said about him.

Someone who could be useful if I ever got myself into a fix.

He recalled Flynn's words about the man who had tried to kill him on Saturday night.

A fixer, maybe. Somebody ready and available at short notice.

It was then that he realised that the man who drove Rebecca Hughes around all day was trained by the military. And that he also rode a motorbike.

FORTY-ONE

(O)

He rang Flynn back as soon as he arrived home and shared his suspicions that Ben Cooper had most likely been his would-be assassin.

'That does make a lot of sense,' she agreed. 'Do you think he knows it was you he was chasing?'

'I don't know,' Nick said. 'It's certainly possible I guess.'

'All right, let's not take any chances. I'll assign a detail to keep an eye on him, okay?'

'Detail?' he asked, confused.

'Someone will follow him twenty-four-seven,' Flynn said. 'Make sure he doesn't go anywhere near you.'

'You can do that?'

'We have the resources, don't worry,' Flynn said. 'We'll keep a close eye on him.'

He heard steel in Flynn's voice and felt reassured.

'We'll check the CCTV again too,' she said. 'The footage was blurry, so I know we didn't get plates. But maybe one of my team clocked the model. If it's a Ducati, we know we've got our man.'

'Sounds good,' he said. 'Thank you, Inspector.'

'Tracy,' she said. 'Please.'

'Okay. Thank you, Tracy. And please, call me Nick. Appreciate you looking out for me.'

'Don't mention it. That's my job . . . Nick.'

After he hung up, he was alone in the flat, his thoughts buzzing around like flies again. He felt safe knowing Flynn's team was on the case, but unanswered questions still vexed him.

Assuming Ben Cooper was his pursuer, how had he located him so easily? Had he just scouted the area looking for a man who happened to match the description Forrester had given over the phone? Nick figured Ben must have spotted him before he reached the NCP car park. Because after that point, he'd been wearing his helmet, which would have obscured his features. But if that was the case, wouldn't Ben have got a good look at his face? And there remained another possibility. Cooper could have also noticed his Honda and put two and two together that way. The man knew what Nick rode. The two of them had been moving at such high speeds, however, that it was far from certain. At the end of the day, if Ben had identified him that night, he would surely have told Gladstone, his old army buddy. So had Gladstone been leading him on earlier? Pretending not to know what had happened? Or was Nick missing something else? Some other clue. Including, perhaps, where Rebecca Hughes fitted into the picture exactly. One thing he knew for sure. He would need to be super careful if he ever saw Ben Cooper again.

. . .

Things took an unexpected turn shortly after 3 p.m. when Julia called him and asked if he was able to talk. Even from the select few words she had spoken, Nick could tell she was spooked.

'What's happened?' he asked, concerned.

'W-we had a visit from IT,' Julia said. 'We've been told to hand over our computers. They're doing some kind of sweep. They're taking company phones too.'

Nick exhaled softly.

Julia explained that an IT task force was literally going floor to floor. An email had also gone out from Jeremy Gladstone himself, saying there was a potential breach of security. No more details were given, but the CEO had been firm in stating that every Lakefront employee needed to co-operate fully with the tech team.

'Where are you now?' Nick asked.

'Outside the building. It's all right, no one can hear. But I'm scared. You still sure they don't know about me?'

'I doubt it, Julia,' he said. 'If they did, they'd have come straight for you. But it sounds like they might suspect a leak. You haven't got anything incriminating on your computer, have you?'

'Definitely not,' she said. 'I've only ever used my personal mobile. I think they'd have happily taken those too if they'd been allowed to.'

Nick believed her. He wondered what might have prompted the CEO to issue such a sudden edict. Was it mere coincidence that he had only just met Nick for lunch? Was it possible Gladstone suspected something was up? That maybe Nick's sudden willingness to write their report seemed a little too suspicious? But why would Gladstone suspect an inside leak just because Nick had experienced a change of heart? What did one have to do with the other? He remembered how Gladstone and Rebecca Hughes had talked about the dangers of loose-lipped employees. Maybe they simply suspected everyone or anyone. The timing could just be a coincidence.

'Look, Julia, this is probably nothing more than a fishing exercise,' he said. 'There's no way they've rumbled you.'

'So you think I'm still safe?' she asked. 'There's no way they can know?'

He didn't. But in his mind's eye, he pictured Julia being hauled into a meeting room and interrogated about her emails. Not because of anything she'd let slip, but perhaps as a routine exercise where she would simply be one of hundreds of other employees being routinely quizzed. He couldn't see her remaining calm and stoic. In fact, he was pretty sure she would give herself away within seconds.

You have any annual leave left?' he asked.

'Yes, loads. Three weeks at least.'

'Can you take a few days with zero notice without raising suspicions?'

'I-I think so,' she said.

'Okay, is there anyone you trust you can stay with? Maybe a friend or family member? Anywhere where you can lie low for a couple of weeks?'

'Um . . . my aunt's, I guess,' Julia said.

'Great. Act normal but book the time off, starting tomorrow. And don't tell anyone where you're going. You're going to hide out at your aunt's until you hear from me. Okay?'

'What about keeping my ears open?' she asked.

'You've already done that, and brilliantly. Besides, I can be the inside man now. You can just remove yourself from the equation. All right?'

'O-okay,' she agreed to Nick's relief.

'Text me tonight,' he said. 'Let me know you're there.'

She promised she would.

FORTY-TWO

(0)

Nick was too preoccupied to cook that evening, so he ordered a takeaway. Two empty foil cartons later, he sat replete at the kitchen table, his mind still churning. A contract also lay on the table. Lakefront Sciences had wasted no time, dispatching a non-disclosure agreement to his flat that afternoon. Nick had only skimmed over the document, but he knew the gist of it was him promising not to publish any articles while he was in the company's employ. He had protested this possibility at the very start with Tracy Flynn, but she had tried to assure him the NDA made no difference. After all, if he was prepared to risk breaking a super-injunction, what did it matter if he signed another piece of paper? 'Besides,' Flynn had said, 'if we slap a pair of handcuffs on Jeremy Gladstone for murder, how likely is it the courts will care about any paperwork, including the super-injunction?' Flynn might have had a point, but Nick still intended to leave the contract exactly where it was for as long as he could get away with it.

His phone pinged. A message from Julia, to tell him she

had arrived at her aunt's house in Hampshire. *Good news*, he thought. Now she was safely ensconced, he could put her out of his headspace and get on with his investigation. He was half tempted to open a bottle of wine, but he needed his wits about him. He moved next door, settled into the sofa and placed his ear pods in. When he was ready, he retrieved the recording from Saturday night. He knew he didn't have to bother. Flynn and her team would likely go through it in detail. But he wanted to know whatever they did, for the sake of the story. He pressed play and listened closely. It took a while to focus on the voices around the table, which competed not only against each other but with other conversations in the background. Nevertheless, Nick was pleased with the overall audio quality. In fact, if he turned on the volume all the way, he could hear the men talking as clearly as if they were sitting next to him. At first, all he heard was random banter, some of it apparently about the day's match and how Chelsea had foolishly missed a number of opportunities. This, of course, was only natural because Nick had set the app to start thirty or so minutes after the match was due to end, factoring in the possibility of extra time. As he continued to listen, the conversation broke into smaller clusters among the group. Where he could make out individual chats, they seemed to be on such a personal level they would only make sense inside their respective cliques. One was about a woman one of the men had apparently started dating. Another a series of in-jokes about a past night out that only those who had been there would understand. After about forty minutes in, Nick began to doubt there would be anything of value. He'd been hoping for something, anything, that might link the McCreadie gang to Gladstone or Lakefront Sciences. Especially a mention of Mark Doyle, or the stabbing. He went into his second hour, still with nothing. But then, twenty minutes later, he caught an interesting snippet. He rewound the recording so he could replay it slowly. It was an exchange between two voices, one of which Nick thought might be Forrester. He listened closely.

This session on expenses then or what?

<laughter>

Maybe. I heard the coin came in okay.

Surprised he even knows how to use ToroPay. He don't look the type.

ToroPay. Nick fetched his laptop and returned to the sofa. He dropped the name into search. It turned out to be an encryption-based payment platform that utilised several different crypto-currencies. It was a fairly new service by the looks of it too. He frowned. It was a clue for sure. But what he was to make of it, he couldn't tell. He returned to the audio. For the next couple of hours, the conversation fell back into banal chatter, with voices increasingly talking over each other, making each thread difficult to follow. At one point, it became clear that they were all intent on moving from the pub. No one explicitly said why, though it would have been around the time Nick had been spotted, so perhaps Forrester had already raised concerns that they were being watched. Nick would have liked to have heard Forrester's warning, not to mention the mobile call he'd placed to the gang's mystery fixer. But both were impossible to pin down among all the noise. Just like many of the answers Nick sought.

He went to bed around midnight. A deep sleep pulled him quickly under, a sign of his mental exhaustion perhaps. His slumber was a welcome balm, a blissful nothingness that lasted until around one thirty, when his eyes snapped open as an idea struck him. He rolled out of bed and almost ran to the kitchen, switching on the light and blinking against its glare. When his eyes had adjusted, he sat in front of the laptop at the table. The conversation that had caught his attention earlier clearly referenced a financial transaction. And Nick was pretty sure it would be one they wouldn't want traced. Opening a new browser window, he downloaded the latest version of Tor and installed it on his machine. It wasn't the first time he had accessed the dark web. In his time, he'd written articles on criminality spanning drug smuggling, weapon sales, illegal pornography and much more. As a result, he had done a fair amount of research on this grubby belly of the internet. On the Tor homepage, he clicked on a link called 'hidden Wiki', which he remembered led to an index of sites of exactly the ilk he was looking for. He picked the top one under the category of 'shops and services' and was soon on a site calling itself the Black Road. There, he searched for 'ToroPay'. A long list of forum-style posts appeared, classified ads of various sorts. He quickly scrolled through them, skimming the first line or two of results. Knowing he had a limited window of dates to work with, Nick confined his search to posts made after Doyle had been arrested, but before the day of his murder. He found a series of posts, a back-and-forth trail of a conversation between a user named TrueBlue651 and someone who called themselves MeaNonCulpa. It was a guess, but he figured the first username might well be a reference to Chelsea FC. He started the thread in the middle, where the word ToroPay had been highlighted from his search.

TrueBlue651: *use ToroPay again, ok? cant be traced*

MeaNonCulpa: *Yes yes I know. Have you got the link?*

TrueBlue651: *here www.blackroad.onion and you just put in my username like last time*

MeaNonCulpa: *Right-o.*

There was a time interlude before the posts and replies started again.

MeaNonCulpa: *Right-o, I've really got the hang of all the crypto pay do-dah.*

TrueBlue651: *I see the payment cheers*

MeaNonCulpa: *When will it be done?*

TrueBlue651: *tomorrow, mate, leave it with me.*

MeaNonCulpa: *I look forward to hearing from you*

Nick scrolled up and started from the beginning. The initial post was by MeaNonCulpa. The content was deleted but they had added a second message.

MeaNonCulpa: *Where are you? Did you read this?*

TrueBlue651: *m8 please delete your request.*

MeaNonCulpa: *Done!*

TrueBlue651: *thanks. can't be too careful, sometimes you get old bill sniffin round. just don't mention the geezer's name any more okay? or what prison. got to be smart and that*

MeaNonCulpa: *Always.*

The conversation went on to the discussion about payment. Nick tapped the sides of the laptop. Was it possible that TrueBlue651 was Adam McCreadie? Or maybe one of his underlings? There was no way to say for certain. He clicked on the user's profile, but none of the bio fields had been filled in. What was he expecting on the dark web? TrueBlue651 could be anyone. The football connection couldn't be a coincidence though. According to the thread, TrueBlue651 had asked MeaNonCulpa to delete their initial message, apparently a *request*, because it had revealed too many details. Nick suspected Mark Doyle might have been mentioned by name in said request. Neither party seemed to have noticed they had still referenced a prison in what was still left in the exchange though. Realising he had no idea how long the thread would stay live, Nick took screen grabs of the entire chat. Once that was done, he returned to the browser, chewing his lip. He stayed fixed on TrueBlue651's profile. He tried copy and pasting the username into the search bar in the top corner. The results revealed a series of conversations between TrueBlue651 and MeaNonCulpa. Not surprisingly, many of the posts had blank fields that carried the message 'This user has deleted this content.' The posts that survived lacked any meaningful details. He sighed. Some clues, for sure, but no hard proof that he could see.

He cleared the search and returned to the home page.

Hmm. One more thing he could try. He typed 'MeaNonCulpa' into the search bar and hit return. As he suspected, MeaNonCulpa also only had conversations with TrueBlue651, including the one he'd just read. Nothing to discover there. Except . . . he blinked at the screen to make sure he wasn't mistaken. But, no, there it was. A fresh post from MeaNonCulpa, time-stamped just ten minutes ago.

MeaNonCulpa: *It's time for another package. Can you pick up tonight?*

Nick looked at TrueBlue651's profile again. According to the site, he or she was still logged on. Sure enough, a minute later, they answered back.

TrueBlue651: *you dont give much notis do ya?*

MeaNonCulpa: *Can you or can't you?*

A pause before the next reply came.

TrueBlue651: *i can do it mate. just tell me where the package is*

Then the same person who might have ordered Mark Doyle killed typed out the word *'warehouse'*, followed by a postcode. Nick took a screenshot before it could disappear.

TrueBlue651: *okay mate i'll be there around 2 a.m.*

Nick let out a whoop. Now he had a time and a place. Now he fucking *had* them.

FORTY-THREE

(O)

Nick frantically dialled Holborn station and asked for Flynn.

'I'm afraid DI Flynn is off duty,' the call handler on the switchboard said. 'Would you like to leave her a message? I can make sure she gets it.'

'Uh . . . no thanks,' he said.

Nick mentally flipped over his options. He could hang up and call 999. But this wasn't strictly an emergency. And what if the sight of flashing blue lights scared the two mysterious parties off? Alternatively, he could try and explain why he was calling. But by the time he unpacked it all and was transferred to the right person it would be too late. He'd have lost his only lead. The transaction, the exchange, whatever the hell this was, was going down in less than twenty minutes. If he didn't get moving, he would lose the trail.

He closed the front door behind him. The hot day had morphed into a cold starry sky, but his full leathers more than compensated. Zipping up his jacket, he mounted the Honda and slipped on his helmet. Minutes later, he was riding through Camden Market where, fortunately, the roads were clear. His mind raced ahead, thinking about what on earth he was going to do when he got to the rendezvous point. Nothing maverick, that was for sure. If TrueBlue651 really was McCreadie or one of his associates, Nick needed to make sure he wasn't seen. But first, he needed to get there in time. Taking the Hampstead Road down to Tottenham Court Road, he tried to figure out the fastest route. The meeting point was something of a puzzle. The map app on his phone showed a warehouse all right. Yet the site didn't have a business name linked to it like all the other commercial units that surrounded it. Why they had arranged to meet there was a mystery, as was the nature of the package that TrueBlue651 had agreed to collect. Nick's best guess was drugs. Perhaps MeaNonCulpa was a cocaine fiend and simply liked to conduct all their shady activities through one channel. It was strange to think that the same criminals who literally offered hit jobs would also have a sideline in drug dealing, but what did he know about their operation, really?

His brain was still turning over possibilities when he crossed over into Hackney. He found the warehouse easily enough. As the map graphic had suggested, it was unoccupied. The windows were boarded up and the only entrance points were a steel-slatted garage door, padlocked, and a single black door. Nick couldn't believe his luck. Somehow, he'd managed to get here before either party had arrived. He slowed the bike and pulled into an alleyway on the other side of the road. He looked at his watch. The drop-off was meant to be in three minutes. If only he'd been able to reach DI Flynn. But perhaps it wouldn't matter if he could provide her with everything she needed. He crouched behind the corner of a brick wall in the alley, hoping he would be inconspicuous. Unzipping the jacket, he pulled out his phone.

He opened the camera and put it on night mode, then pointed the lens towards the front of the warehouse. He checked the screen. Despite low-level street lighting, he had a crisp image of the entrance to the building. *Good.* He lay prone, the phone camera peering around the corner. Just waiting.

Two o'clock came and went. Nick wondered whether he had made a mistake, or whether the transaction might have been cancelled. But then the black door opened and a man and woman emerged. Nick touched the screen, zooming in closer. The man had a beard and was wearing a red suit. Nick guessed he was in his forties. The woman was younger and dressed in a yellow T-shirt and denim dungarees. Her hair was in two neat pigtails, and she was wearing pink wellington boots. She was giggling, perhaps laughing at something the man had said to her. Or maybe she was just high. They were an odd couple, for sure. He began taking pictures, zooming in and capturing their individual faces before getting some shots of them together. The man was helping her carry a black holdall, which presumably contained the package. The couple stood out in the night air for a while longer and then bright headlights washed over them, forcing them to shield their eyes. Nick adjusted the camera's filters accordingly as a white van pulled up outside the warehouse. Two silhouettes were in the front cabin, too dark to make out. The transit blocked Nick's view of the couple, stopping him from getting any sense of what was taking place. He strained his ears, trying to catch snippets of their conversation. A man's voice just about carried over the van's engine. More laughter from the girl, though he couldn't make out what anybody was saying. The far passenger door opened, and Nick saw a shadowy shape clamber out. Then came the sound of the sliding cargo door, out of sight, followed by more laughter. This time, everybody was chuckling away like they were all old friends. He heard the door slam shut and the black shape returned to the passenger side. The van's driver grunted and the transit pulled away slowly. Only the man in the red suit was left behind, watching the vehicle disappear. The holdall was gone. After a minute, the man re-entered the warehouse. Nick pulled up the gallery view on his screen. He'd taken several shots before the vehicle rolled up, but the last few showed nothing but the side of a white van. No clear shots of driver or passenger. Or even a number plate. He really had no choice. He would have to follow the van.

FORTY-FOUR

(O)

Nick tried to keep far enough back so as not to be conspicuous. His bike probably stood out a mile, especially on empty roads in the early hours of the morning. His strategy was to keep at least a street's distance away. Luckily, the lack of traffic meant he had a clear view of which way the van turned, so he could take his time following on. This subtle cat and mouse took him all the way past Enfield along the Great Cambridge Road – and then out of London altogether. The van joined the M25, heading northbound and east. There was more traffic between them now, so Nick had to close up the gap, but he made sure he still kept at least two vehicles behind. His paranoid brain imagined they'd already spotted him. But if they had, they gave no indication of it. The van didn't speed up or change lanes erratically. His brain was more likely a liar. And that gave him his next idea. If he could get a decent look at the driver and passenger, he could pass on a physical description that might be useful to Flynn and her team.

He sped up, swiftly changing lanes and accelerating as fast as he dared. As he passed the driver's window, he got his glimpse. The first man behind the wheel was unknown, but he had been at the Barrel Inn. The second sported spiky ginger hair that Nick recognised immediately. Paul Forrester. He felt a chill that had nothing to do with the night wind, and changed quickly back to the slow lane, grateful for the visor that obscured his face. The van overtook him on his right. With a bit of luck, they wouldn't have given him a second's thought. He watched the vehicle's tail lights disappear into the distance and allowed himself to process what he had now established. First, that TrueBlue651 was definitely one of McCreadie's boys, likely Forrester or the driver of the van. Second, that they had picked up a package for whoever MeaNonCulpa was and were dropping it somewhere out of London. But who were the other couriers, the woman in the van and the man in the red suit who had stayed behind? More importantly, who was MeaNonCulpa? Gladstone? Rebecca Hughes? Perhaps even Ben Cooper, the hired-thug-assassin working on their behalf? There were vital pieces of this puzzle that just weren't in the box.

Nick followed the van off the exit towards Cambridge, where it travelled along a series of A-roads until they were deep in the countryside. He turned off a roundabout and onto a narrow country lane with nothing but moonlight and hedges to guide the way. Eventually, the van made an abrupt left onto private property. An iron gate rolled open to grant access to a long and snaking driveway. Nick sped past the gate, glancing over just in time to see the van pull up to a stately home at the end of the drive. When it was safe, he made a U-turn back to the closing iron barrier. The distant mansion looked eery under the moon, like an old Bedlam hospital. Nick spotted a rotating CCTV camera above the gate's main pillar and quickly pulled out of sight before it caught him. A quarter of a mile down the road, he left the kickstand down and examined the hedgerow that grew along the perimeter of the property. Behind the foliage was a high brick wall. Crossing over to the other side of the lane, he took more pictures on his phone. Beginning with the hedgerow, he panned the camera lens across. More CCTV cameras were mounted all along the wall, perhaps half a metre apart. Some faced the grounds, while others were pointed at the road. Fortunately, the latter were angled down towards the hedge perimeter and not at his position. He kept panning until the gate came back into view, then zoomed in. He made out dark shapes on the driveway and heard a faint murmur of men's voices. Although he was sure he hadn't been detected, he didn't want to linger for too long. Returning to his bike, he debated what to do next. It was almost 3 a.m. now. He was hungry and fatigued from the drive. All he wanted was to head home, crawl back into bed. But he had come this far, hadn't he? He couldn't turn back yet.

FORTY-FIVE

(0)

He picked a spot half a mile south, resting the bike on its side on a grassy knoll. Nick lay beside it, trying to stay low and hidden in the moon and starlight. Camping here was a gamble. It assumed that once the package had been delivered, the van would return to London. There was no guarantee of that, of course, but it made logical sense. As it turned out, he didn't have to wait long. He saw the van approaching and pressed himself further into the grass. Though protected by his full leathers, he still felt the damp dewiness brush against his cheeks. Twin beams of LED headlights swept the tarmac, but the dispersal wasn't wide enough to reach the bank. The van passed. Nick raised his head, waited a few seconds and got to his feet. He flipped up his bike, kick-starting it back into action. The chase was back on.

The van stopped at services on the M25 and Nick followed it down the slip road. He parked on the edge of the petrol forecourt adjacent to the restaurant, which was closed for the night. Though it was an ungodly hour, there was a smattering of cars and two other motorbikes waiting at the pumps. Nick killed his engine and stayed where he was, retrieving his phone while the van pulled up at the next free pump. A moment later, Forrester clambered out from the passenger side and headed straight for the pump nozzle. Nick clicked the camera button repeatedly as he filled the tank, making sure to capture the registration number of the van. No one else got out of the vehicle. After he was done, Forrester crossed the forecourt and entered the shop to pay. It was only then that Nick noticed his own fuel gauge was bordering on empty. He'd need to fill up if he hoped to get back to London. This ran the risk of losing his quarry, but petrol wasn't a luxury. He glanced across at the van and saw Forrester had returned with an armful of snacks. The vehicle set off again. Cursing inwardly, Nick watched them go.

He was back on the motorway again within fifteen minutes, but the lanes were even busier now, bolstered by early shift work traffic and holidaymakers catching early flights at the airports. As he suspected, it had been more than enough time for the van to gain a significant lead. He looked down at the speedo. Even if he went full throttle, he had little hope of finding them. He had his photos. It would have to be enough.

FORTY-SIX

(0)

It was 4 a.m. when he got back home. Nick collapsed on the bed and passed out. It felt like two minutes later when he was woken by the sun streaming on him through the bedroom window, which explained why he was also sweating. He stripped off and made a beeline for the shower. After breakfast, he emailed a selection of the photos he had taken with a message for DI Flynn, requesting she call him as soon as she could. With that out of the way, he made coffee.

Once he had a hot mug in his hand, he opened Google Maps and tracked his previous night's journey, tracing the route out from the M25 halo and along the country lane, which he now learned was the A1386. He switched over to street view, leapfrogging in quarter-of-a-mile gaps until he recognised the familiar stretch of hedgerow. He stopped when he saw the gate. The sight of the house appeared very different in the cold light of day. Less Bedlam hospital and more National Trust estate. The property looked like it was built around the nineteenth century. It also had a name. A sign at the gate, which he hadn't spotted in the dark last night. *Dove's House*. He copied the postcode, went to the Land Registry website, and did a search. It matched a property registered to DPR Holdings. From there, he visited the Companies House website, where he discovered DPR Holdings had reported a turnover of over fifty million pounds, though it didn't say what products or services the company traded in. He switched back to his browser and typed 'Jeremy Gladstone Director'. Plenty of results about the man himself, but no link to DPR Holdings. He tried another string, this time 'Lakefront Sciences DPR Holdings.' No web pages linked the two terms together.

He stared at the cursor, then returned to Companies House. On closer inspection, there was a tab called 'People'. He clicked on it and discovered the name of the single director and CEO. It wasn't Jeremy Gladstone, but a Lord Davenport-Ross. Nick switched to Wikipedia, where he found his bio. Tristan Davenport-Ross. Born in Sussex, Eton educated, a distant relation to the Royal Family. His family invested in mines in Namibia way back in the nineteenth century, which was where most of their modern wealth had come from. Tristan Davenport-Ross had been elected to sit in the House of Lords. A hereditary peer, and technically a baron. Pretty silver spoon stuff.

In the late nineties, Davenport-Ross had founded DPR Holdings, described as an international commercial property investment company, registered in the United Kingdom. So. The mansion house belonged to a lord. Or a lord's limited company at any rate. Nick wondered what sort of role the mansion could possibly play. The Wikipedia article said that Davenport-Ross resided in the family home in Sussex. As nice as Dove's House was, it wasn't the lord's primary residence. So who was in there? Who was at home to receive the drugs package last night? He tried an image-only search using Davenport-Ross's name. The chubby face that came up was a much older version of the one on the Wiki page, with added white, thinning hair and ruddy cheeks. Locations showed the lord at a variety of society and gala events. Nick scrolled down the photos, scrutinising the meta-data and trying to decide what was worth clicking on. And then he saw something at the bottom of the first page. Nick clicked. The image was hosted on a popular celebrity gossip site, part of a feature about a charity event. Some benefit for cancer at the Royal Albert Hall. The photograph had been taken in one of the bars inside the famous dome-shaped venue. In it, Davenport-Ross was dressed in a black tuxedo. His head was thrown back in mid-laughter as one arm held up a flute of champagne. The other arm was firmly around the shoulders of Jeremy Gladstone.

FORTY-SEVEN

(O)

Nick was mulling over this particular new twist when his phone rang.

'Nick!' DI Flynn said. 'What on earth have you sent me?'

'Just a few souvenirs from last night,' he said. 'I thought you might be interested in seeing them. Hang on, I've got something else I need to ping over too.'

'Okay, send it to my direct email. It'll be quicker.'

She read it out and Nick typed it into his phone. He attached the screen grabs of the forum chat and sent them across.

'Got it,' Flynn said a moment later. 'What is it?'

'A snippet of conversation that I caught on the dark web.'

'You went on the dark web?' she asked, her tone laced with suspicion.

'It's okay,' he said, 'it was just research. I've been on it before. For work.' Nick told her what he had discovered the previous evening, starting with an apology. 'I couldn't reach you and I didn't have time to wait.'

He explained how he'd camped outside the warehouse in Hackney and followed the white van all the way out of London.

'There were two guys from the Barrel Inn,' he said. 'Part of McCreadie's gang. The woman in the photo went with them. I don't know who the guy in the red suit is, but I think she was the one who had the drugs on her.'

'Drugs?'

'Sorry, I'm going too fast.'

Nick laid it all out again from the top. He finished by telling Flynn who the mansion belonged to and the picture he'd just found that showed Lord Davenport-Ross and Jeremy Gladstone together.

'They clearly know each other,' he said. 'But I don't know what other services McCreadie's boys are doing for them. Last night was a package. I'm guessing drugs, but I don't know for sure.'

He could almost hear Flynn's astonishment at the other end of the phone.

'Wow,' she said. 'I don't know what this all means, but you might have found us another connection back to Jeremy Gladstone.'

'I hope so,' he said.

'Though it was a bit reckless of you. What if you'd been spotted?'

'I wasn't,' he said. 'I was really careful to stay out of sight.' But he knew she had a point. 'I'm sorry,' he said. 'I just didn't want to lose the lead. It all happened so fast. And I was worried if I waited for you, it'd be too late.'

She sighed. 'All right, Nick. I can't say I approve, but I also can't argue that this isn't useful evidence. I just don't want anything bad to happen to you.'

'I know,' Nick said. 'And I appreciate that. I was extremely careful, I promise. There's nothing like having an attempt made on your life to keep you on your toes.'

'I bet,' Flynn said.

'Speaking of which, are you still watching Ben Cooper?'

'Like a hawk,' Flynn assured him. 'So far he's just been going to work and straight home. Nothing out of the ordinary.'

'Any news on the CCTV footage?' he asked.

'It's not good I'm afraid. The bike was going too damn fast. It could well be a Ducati but there's no way to be sure. I'm sorry. But, like I said, we've got eyes on Cooper day and night, so don't worry.'

Nick was disappointed, but not surprised. 'So what now?'

'We'll take a look at the photos you've got here. See what we can learn from them. In the meantime, carry on as normal with your official assignment. Try to get friendlier with Rebecca Hughes like we talked about.'

'On it,' he said.

'I'll let you know what else we find,' she promised.

True to her word, his phone buzzed just after lunch.

'Thought you'd appreciate a quick update,' she said. 'We ran the plates on the van, but the vehicle's not registered with the DVLA. Or, rather, we suspect they've been counterfeited to make the van untraceable.'

Nick whistled. McCreadie's boys were undisputedly up to no good.

'We're still trying to get an ID on the unknown man and woman, but nothing so far. We'll let you know if we get a match.'

'What about the warehouse?' Nick asked.

'The building is listed as commercial,' Flynn said. 'But no one's currently on the lease. I sent one of my officers over to take a look, but he said it was abandoned and locked up. Are you certain you saw people come from inside?'

'One hundred per cent,' Nick said.

'Strange,' Flynn said. 'My officer swears the building is vacant.'

'Maybe they were squatting there,' he suggested.

Flynn didn't seem convinced. 'I don't know how they'd have added the locks. Perhaps you imagined them exiting the warehouse. It would be an easy mistake to make.'

Nick bit his lip and thought back to the pictures he'd taken. None of them actually showed the couriers passing through the black door. Could he have imagined it? Now he wasn't sure.

'Look, it's not important,' Flynn said. 'The warehouse looks like a dead end anyway. I just wanted to double-check.'

She promised to keep him looped in on any further updates, and the call ended. Confused, Nick opened his camera roll and scrolled through the photos carefully. Had he made a mistake? Did it really matter? There was definitely no open black door in the shots. Never mind, he'd come back to it later. There was an important call he needed to make first.

FORTY-EIGHT

(O)

Rebecca Hughes's mobile was engaged, but she rang him straight back a minute later.

'Sorry to have missed you,' she said. 'How goes your investigation? Any progress?'

Nick had an answer prepared for that very question. 'Yeah, I've interviewed a guy called Charles Mills,' he said. 'He's the eighty-year-old who went bungee jumping. I haven't found anything yet but it's early days.'

'Well, please press on,' Rebecca said. 'There are lots more people on that list.'

'Understood,' he said. 'Look, Rebecca. The reason for my call. I wondered if I could ask you something.'

'What is it?' she asked.

Nick hesitated. This was a gamble on his part. He wasn't sure how well Rebecca knew Jeremy, but he figured she was the best person to ask. And he wasn't going to risk quizzing Gladstone directly.

'It's just something I was curious about,' he said. 'You

knew when you offered me this work that I had certain ethical boxes I needed to be able to tick, right?'

'Yes,' she said with a sigh. 'What's bothering you now? Is this about the NDA we sent you?'

Nick looked at the contract still on the kitchen table, where it remained unsigned. 'I . . . er, no. This is more about political connections.'

'Political?'

Nick shut his eyes and hoped he could navigate this delicately without appearing to be too curious. 'It concerns Jeremy,' he said.

'What about him?'

The tightness in her voice told him he would need to tread delicately. 'Meeting him in person, he seems like a decent enough man. But I was just remembering some background research I did a while back when I was starting my article.'

'All right. And?'

'You know of a guy called Lord Davenport-Ross?' Nick asked.

She paused. 'A little. What's this about, Mr Winters?'

'Please, call me Nick. And it's probably nothing. But just out of interest, you ever see him at any Lakefront events?'

'Events?'

'You know. The type of soirees you PR types probably attend.'

'Why is this important?' she asked with what Nick took to be mild irritation.

'He appears to know Jeremy very well,' he said. 'I noticed they seem to operate in the same circles. I've seen them at a few charity gigs, that type of thing. Mostly medicine related. Any idea why?'

'Why do you want to know?'

He paused, forming his answer before speaking. 'I was just curious how close they are,' he said. 'If Jeremy is the kind of guy to use a relationship like that to curry political favour. I don't know. Maybe I'm being oversensitive. I guess I don't much like the idea that Lakefront might have undue influence in parliament. I'm hoping you can put my mind at ease.' He waited, hoping he sounded convincing.

All right,' Rebecca said, eventually. 'Lord Davenport-Ross is a major shareholder in Lakefront Sciences.'

Interesting, Nick thought.

'But I don't know what you're implying,' Rebecca said. 'Jeremy has never, would never, exploit Davenport-Ross's position. It's true that as a company we do our fair share of lobbying the government, like any other industry. But nothing underhand and nothing illegal. Does that satisfy you?'

Nick felt her exasperation. It was time to dial it down a little. 'Sure,' he said. 'Sorry. It was just bugging me.'

'It's fine,' she said tightly. 'Davenport-Ross has the biggest stake in the company. I'm surprised you didn't know that.'

Nick hadn't. So far, he'd had no cause to investigate any of Lakefront's shareholders. But he would make it a priority now.

'So are he and Jeremy close?' he said, trying to sound casual.

'Honestly? I don't know,' Rebecca said. 'They don't act especially friendly when they're in shareholder meetings. And Jeremy's never talked much about him to me. I'd say they were acquaintances at best.'

'And you don't know him that well either?'

'I've never really spoken to him at length. He's the sort of man who likes to speak *at* people. He does in our meetings anyway. I can tell you he's really not happy about our share price at the moment.'

'Yeah, I bet,' Nick said. 'You know much about his other businesses?'

'What businesses?'

'He owns a mansion in Cambridge. It's listed as business premises. Nothing to do with Lakefront Sciences?'

'Not as far as I'm aware,' Rebecca said.

Okay, Nick thought. *That's enough. You need to drop it now.*

'Listen, Rebecca. I appreciate you indulging me. Like I said, it comes with the job. I've written so many stories about politics and corruption and I guess my radar is probably over-tuned. Just forget I mentioned anything.'

'Gladly,' she said.

'I just want to know I'm working for a decent, above-board company.'

'For the thousandth time, Nick, you are. You really want a scandal? Go and find out what those claimants are lying about.'

And with that, she hung up on him.

FORTY-NINE

(O)

For the rest of the afternoon, he debated whether he should have quizzed Rebecca about Davenport-Ross. He still had no idea how much she knew or what she was involved in. His hope was that asking about Gladstone's connections would have seemed natural enough, something she would almost expect from him. But now that the deed was done, he couldn't help wondering if he'd taken an unnecessary risk. He considered updating Flynn, but it was getting late. And, besides, it wasn't like he had learned anything key from his conversation.

He wondered how her side of the investigation was going. Whether her team was any closer to identifying the mystery man and woman he'd photographed. He picked up his phone from the arm of his sofa and pulled up the pictures he had taken to examine them once again. Was there anything else he had missed? The photo on the top left of his camera roll was of the courier and the man in the red suit, standing outside the entrance to the warehouse. He expanded it, zooming in on the woman first, scrolling up and down her body, examining her clothes. Apart from the bizarre dress sense and clashing pink wellingtons, there was nothing else in her apparel that gave any more clues as to her identity. Same went for her scarlet-clad companion. He pulled back to the wide shot again. Another mystery. What was the deal with the building behind them? Had he imagined them coming out of that door? If they had been inside, what business did they have in there? For a few moments, he imagined a coke lab inside the warehouse, full of naked people wearing face masks and measuring ground product on scales. He pictured the mystery couple, fully dressed, supervising the operation. In his mind's eye, the man was holding a pick 'n' mix shovel, serving himself a dollop of white powder from a large pile sitting on a metal lab counter. He handed it to the woman, who poured the powder into an opaque freezer bag. When she was done, she unzipped her holdall and placed the bag inside, where it sat with several others just like it. Cut to the sound of last night's van pulling up outside. The two of them run for the door, armed guards with sub-machine guns nodding at them respectfully as they let them pass. *No, no, no.* That was Hollywood nonsense. The warehouse would not be some clandestine crack factory. Not least because it looked like his memory had been wrong. Flynn's own officer had checked it out and declared the building empty. Not just empty, abandoned and locked up. The description continued to bug him like an increasingly persistent itch. It made no sense. He might not have the photo to prove it, but he was convinced his recollection was correct. He could have sworn the two of them *had* been inside the warehouse. Was he imagining things? Was the building truly empty? The itch became stronger and stronger until Nick knew he needed to double-check his sanity. He decided he would ride over there tonight. Take a look for himself.

FIFTY

(O)

Hours later, Nick stood in the same alleyway as before, his bike parked in the same spot. But compared to his previous visit, everything else was different. Whatever Flynn's man had seen, it was the complete opposite of what he was looking at right now. There was plenty of activity going on in front of the warehouse building tonight. In fact, people had been coming and going with some regularity since he arrived. There had been a constant stream of visitors for the last hour. Every so often, someone would approach the single black door and give it a special knock. The door would open, and they would be hastily ushered inside. It was strange. Almost as strange as the anomalous outfits people were wearing. Everyone was dressed in bright, garish clothes. It reminded Nick of the rave scene of the early nineties, where ravers would gather illegally inside disused buildings. As he continued to observe them, the similarities only grew stronger. Whenever the door opened to let people in or out, there was a hint of flashing lights. And, though he couldn't be sure, he thought he heard faint bass coming from inside the building. His burning curiosity now blazed white-hot. So much for empty and abandoned. But Nick also knew that if he really wanted to know what this was, he would have to take a closer look. Much closer, in fact.

He had been debating it for a while, given that Flynn was concerned about his safety. But the reality was, he didn't sense any danger. All these visitors looked like ordinary members of the public which, in his opinion, made it far less likely his drug den slash cookhouse fantasy really did exist behind that black door. No, all the evidence pointed to some sort of rave. And how dangerous would a rave be? Before he could talk himself out of it, he crossed the street as calmly as he could, trying his best to ignore the voice inside his head that was asking him whether this was a good idea.

He heard subdued music pumping from the warehouse as he drew closer. Though he couldn't tell the genre from here, it didn't sound like electronica. But he couldn't be certain. At the black door, he stopped and listened carefully. No sound came from inside, except the soft thudding of whatever tunes were playing. He knocked hard. Two times, then three. The secret rhythm he'd watched the others do. He didn't have to wait long. The door swung open and a chunky man appeared, wearing a red suit. He stared at Nick through beady eyes.

'Password, mate.'

'I'm sorry?'

'Password,' the man repeated.

A large woman stood behind him. She was also dressed in a red suit. Nick blinked at the two of them, and then at the room. A number of observations hit him, one after another. First, this was a reception area. There was padding on the walls, soundproof cushioning composed of PVC in a shade of olive green. Two black leather sofas sat empty in the centre. The lighting inside the room was low and ambient. Seedy almost. There was another door on the far side too, covered in the same green cushioning. It was where the music was emanating from.

'Password,' the man repeated, this time more insistently.

'I . . .' Nick was momentarily speechless. What was this place? Some kind of speakeasy? He tried again. 'I'm not sure I know—'

'What is it with you, Greg?' the woman said. 'Can't you see it's his first time? He's just nervous.'

The man gritted his teeth and snapped his head back at her. 'But what if he's Old Bill?' Greg turned back to give Nick a hard stare. 'He *looks* Old Bill,' he added. 'Look at how he's dressed for a start.'

'I'm not with the police,' Nick said, realising how weak that sounded.

'Ask if he's got cash.'

'Do you?' Greg said.

'Cash?'

'Fifty quid.'

Nick frowned. The woman smiled at him from behind the sofas. He reached for his jacket pocket and removed his wallet. Lucky for him, he had the money. Greg held out his palm and Nick counted the notes. Admittedly, this wasn't at all how he had envisaged this going, but he played along.

'Okay,' Greg said. He seemed happier now that he had pocketed the money. 'Let's test you out.'

'Test me?'

'Come sit down, love,' the woman said warmly. She swept a chunky hand across one of the sofas. 'Don't be nervous,' she said. 'It *is* your first time at Play Ground, ain't it, darling?'

Nick hesitated. 'Yes,' he said. What the fuck was going on here? He moved across to the sofa and took a seat.

'My name's Brenda,' the woman said. 'Greg Grumpypants you've already met. Please don't be nervous. I promise we'll look after you.'

Brenda took a seat on the opposite sofa while Greg closed the door and moved across to stand over Nick. Nobody said anything for a moment.

Greg took out his phone. 'It's nine fifteen now,' he said. 'We're going to wait twenty minutes, just to make sure you haven't just swallowed a pill.'

'Pill?'

'You're not supposed to bring your own,' Brenda said. 'It'll have said so on the WhatsApp we sent. You'll have seen that.'

Nick ran his palms slowly up and down his thighs, caressing the denim. It was a poor attempt at trying not to fidget. He tried to work out what was happening. Music continued to bang lightly from the inner door.

'We'll pass the time with a questionnaire,' Greg announced. He opened his phone screen and started to read something out loud. 'Now, the important thing to remember is the test is not about knowing the right answers,' he said. 'Rather, it's your comprehension of the questions themselves. They are designed to engage the brain's higher cognitive levels, namely those present in an adult human.'

Nick swallowed.

'Question one,' Greg said.

Brenda gave Nick a big beaming smile.

'What is your understanding of the concept of God?'

FIFTY-ONE

(O)

The questions continued in a similar vein, either philosophical or logical. Some invoked lateral thinking. Nick relaxed his shoulders, trying to look as though he knew exactly what was happening. It appeared to be working on Brenda. She nodded encouragingly as he told them how he would leave a fictitious fox with a sack of grain on one side of a river and return one final time for the hen.

'You know, I always get confused by that one,' she said, winking at him.

Greg cleared his throat in protest at her interruption. 'Question eighteen,' he said. 'If you hosted a dinner party, who are the five people you would invite?'

'I wouldn't,' Nick said. Though he was still mystified, he was growing more confident as he watched them buy his act. 'Host, I mean. I'd book us a restaurant and let someone else do the cooking.' He flashed them what he hoped was a sincere smile.

'Good enough for me, Greg,' Brenda said. 'Come on, that must be it.'

Greg looked at his phone screen. 'It's nine twenty-seven. We're a bit under. But I'm satisfied. He's clean.'

'Thanks, love,' Brenda said, turning to Nick. 'I'm sure you understand we can't have people dose up beforehand. That'd send you right far back.'

'Crib oblivion they call it.' Greg chuckled. 'Fucking impossible to take care of you then. Plus, you'll probably shit yourself.'

This prompted Brenda to guffaw too.

The two of them snorted for several seconds while Nick looked from one to the other. He pushed out another smile, hoping to convince them he shared the joke, whatever it meant.

'Ah, well,' Greg said. He was still crying, wiping his eye with his sleeve. 'Okay, mate, I'm satisfied you're your own age. Which I'm guessing is . . . late forties?'

Nick looked at Brenda, then back at him. *Play along*, he thought. 'Forty-nine,' he admitted.

'Ha. Close enough! Here you go.'

Brenda moved across to his sofa and opened a metal tin. The tin was divided into separate compartments. Nick stared at the green pills they contained, all too familiar, despite their lack of packaging. Brenda picked three tablets from three different sections.

'Take these,' she said, depositing them in his hand.

Nick brought his palm up, examining the inscriptions. A minus thirty, minus fifteen and minus three. Combined, they would give him the mental age of a toddler. He could be jailed for up to five years for taking these.

'Hurry up, love,' Brenda said. 'Don't forget, you'll have to wait for it to come on. You don't want to miss any more of the fun.'

He felt the throbbing of the music from the door again. *Fun*. Nick closed his fist on the pills. What was this? Maybe he should get the hell out of here, right now. But the two faces looking at him expectantly frowned, their expressions slowly turning suspicious. Whatever else they were, they were bouncers. Their job was to keep out troublemakers. The longer he hesitated, the more likely their puzzlement would turn into aggression. He looked again at the door. He'd come all this way, hadn't he? Wouldn't it make more sense to go down the rabbit hole? Find out what the hell was going on? Sensing their impatience, he met their eyes. 'How, er, long does it last?' he asked.

'No more than the usual,' Brenda said softly. 'A couple of hours.'

'Have you got any water?' he asked.

They looked at each other, and he saw their faces relax.

'Oh shit, of course,' Brenda said.

She went to the corner of the room to a mini fridge that Nick hadn't spotted before. When she returned, she handed him a carton.

'Juice?' he said, taking it with his free hand.

'The punters love 'em,' Greg said. 'It's a little touch, but you'll appreciate it on the other side.'

Nick examined the carton. It was strawberry flavoured and featured cartoon characters on the front.

'We've orange if you want,' said Brenda.

Something about her voice changed too. Became more sing-songy. Tender. He smiled at her, pierced the straw through the foil and took a sip. Rabbit hole it was. He placed the pills on his tongue one at a time, and gently swallowed.

'What's your name, love?' Brenda asked.

'Huh?'

'So we can tell them on the inside. So they can look after you.'

'Nick,' he said.

'Nick. Okay then. All sorted.'

Nick nodded, though at what he couldn't say. *You'll appreciate it on the other side,* Greg had said.

What other side? he wondered.

PART THREE

FIFTY-TWO

(-48)

Everything was so bright, and so full of colours. His arms were moving, his fingers waving almost spastically. The song was loud; it was inside his head. He remembered a word. *Fun.* Yes, this was fun. Who had said that word? He frowned. It was hard to do thinkies. His head became sore and he didn't like it. He looked down. There was a juice in his hand, but it was empty. It had tasted yummy, he remembered. He threw the packet onto the floor in protest. Where was he? Inside a room. A big, big room. This was where the song was playing. There were a lot of people playing too. Some running around. Giggling. Boys chasing girls. Girls chasing boys. All bigger than what they should be. Like giants, he thought. There was a slide up ahead. It was so tall and so big. *Wow.* His jaw dropped. How he got into this big room was a mystery. Vaguely, dimly, he was aware that he had been somewhere else before, but it felt like sleep. Besides, he no longer cared. The only thing that mattered was the slide now. It looked so much . . . *fun.* The music went *boom-boom-boom.*

He recognised the words. It was about a postman who had a cat. A black and white cat. *Postman Pat, Postman Pat!* His lips moved giddily as he sang along, joining in the chorus with all the others, bellowing out words at the top of his lungs. Skipping now, bounding across a yellow play mat that he noticed for the first time. It covered the whole of the big space, and it meant when boys and girls fell down they wouldn't get hurted. He reached the slide. There was a queue already, everyone waiting by the ladder at the end.

'I want to!' screamed a boy, pulling a girl and throwing her onto the floor.

Concerned, he ran to her. But she wasn't hurted. She had fallen onto the play mat and had already sprung back on her feet.

'Philip!'

Everyone in the queue looked around. A person stood in front of them all, dressed in red clothes. It was funny. They were not much bigger than any of them, but something about the way they moved and the voice they used was different.

'Philip!' the person shouted.

They had a scary voice, he thought. It made him want to hide.

'Philip, no more pushing the others or you will get a smack. Do you hear me?'

Philip grinned cheekily but nodded.

'All right then. Now listen, all of you. You need to learn how to be patient. And to share. There's time for everyone to have a go on the slide. I don't want to see anyone pushing or shoving, all right? Or there'll be trouble.'

Then the person left and went to stand by the far wall, where they continued to watch everyone running and playing.

'Wow,' he said aloud. 'Who was that?'

'He's one of the Bigs,' a voice explained.

When he turned around, he saw another boy dressed in

shorts and a T-shirt with superheroes on it. The boy was carrying a stuffed bear.

'What's a *Big*?' he asked the boy.

'They're the ones in charge. We're just Littles. We need them to look after us.'

This was new information and it required new thinkies. He scratched his head, deliberately slowly so he looked like a monkey. It made the other boy laugh. When he was finished, he pointed at the bear.

'Is that yours?' he asked.

'Bearbah,' the other boy confirmed.

'Bear . . . *bah*?'

'*Mistuh* Bearbah.'

He looked at the bear and nodded. 'Okay,' he declared.

He studied the boy again, suddenly feeling shy and awkward. He tried to think of something to say. 'Why do the Bigs shout?' he finally asked.

'Cos we can be silly,' the other boy said and giggled.

He giggled too, then pointed at the boy's skin. 'Why are you brown?'

'I don't know. Why aren't you? What's your name?'

'My name is . . . um . . .' He frowned. What *was* it?

'I'm Anuj,' said the boy.

'I'm . . .'

'Don't worry,' Anuj said. 'It's hard at first but you will member it.'

He beamed. It felt nice to have a friend. It was hard to remember how he had got here, but it didn't really matter. It was nice here. And there were Bigs looking after them. Most important of all, there was a *slide*.

FIFTY-THREE

(-48)

'Weeeeeeeeee!'

He slid off the edge and his bum hit the yellow play mat. Anuj tumbled past, just seconds behind him.

'Wooooooooooo!'

'Again!' he yelped, excitedly.

'Okay!' his new friend said.

'This time let's go upside down,' he begged as they slowly made their way to the back of the queue again.

'Head first!' Anuj agreed.

'You've done it before?'

'Yes! It's good. Very good!'

So they slid down again, this time head first. After, Anuj told him he needed a wee. Now that he thought about it, he needed the toilet too. And so he followed his friend across the . . . what was this? A big playroom. Lots of fun! Spotlights and brightly coloured lights swept the walls and floor, covering all the other Littles in a kaleidoscope of colours. He recognised the new song that was playing now. It was about all the fat round ones. *Tinky Winky! Dipsy! Laa-Laa! Po!* All the Littles were singing it at the top of their lungs. He giggled. Mr Bearbah bashed against the backs of Anuj's legs as he dragged him behind. Anuj was humming; *he* was humming as he tried to keep up. Where were they going next? He'd already forgotten. It was so hard to do *thinkies*.

FIFTY-FOUR

(-48)

He was aware of being inside his head again. When he tried to remember where he had just been, the thinkies hurting came again. But one thing he did know. He wanted an ice cream. The van was parked in one of the corners of the big play area. It was painted with bright colours and played happy, tinkly music. Anuj appeared, holding two ice creams with flakes. He licked his lips greedily while his friend explained how you could just walk up to the van as many times as you wanted and ask for your favourite. You didn't even need to give them any monies. The only trick was not getting caught by the Bigs. They would often tell you off for making yourself too sick and some Littles had been known to have eaten so much they *made* a sick on the floor. They laughed when they imagined the Littles rolling around holding their sore tummies. It was funny. Funny tummy funny. When he'd finished, he saw Anuj had stopped laughing and now looked sad, like his eyes were made of water. He was looking over at a Wendy house in the other corner of the playroom. It looked nice. Lots of Littles were busy running in and out of it and there was even a table outside where some others were pretending to have tea. But while it looked *fun*, Anuj was staring at it like it had hurt him.

'Did you fall?' he asked, wiping the remains of his ice cream across his chin with his wrist.

Anuj sniffed and stared at him like he was having a hard thinkie.

'I mean in the house. Did you fall and hurt you?'

'No,' Anuj said. 'I miss my friends.'

'What friends?' he asked.

'Tom,' Anuj said. 'And Will. And Sophia. We used to play in the Wendy house here. But then they went to Fun Land. But I miss them. I want to play with them.'

He felt sad now too. 'Don't you want to play with me?' he asked.

'Yes,' Anuj said. 'But you're not them.'

He took a bold step closer and put his arm around Anuj. 'I can be your friend,' he said. 'I can be your friend now. Okay?'

Anuj still didn't look sure.

'Hey,' he said, an idea forming in his mind. 'Why don't we go draw?'

He pointed to another table that had been set up in the big playroom, this one surrounded by Littles scribbling on lots of paper with crayons. Anuj stared at the activities as if doing hard thinkies.

'Can I draw my friends?'

'Only if I can draw Superman!'

'Okay! Then we swap!'

Anuj swallowed, then put his own arm around him. A trace of a smile appeared on his face. The prospect of playing with crayons seemed to cheer him up.

'Okay,' Anuj said. 'Let's draw.'

He grabbed Anuj's hand and led him off to another part of the play area. He did not know who all these other friends were, but he knew *his* friend was feeling sad. And so he would do his best to make him happy.

FIFTY-FIVE

(-48/0)

Nick opened his eyes to find Greg and Brenda were looming over him with grinning faces, like the world's creepiest aunt and uncle.

'Wakey-wakey!' Brenda cried.

He was lying on one of the black sofas in the reception room. Nick groaned and gently touched his head. He felt disorientated, like he was waking up from a strange but deeply immersive dream. Fragments of memories spiked inside his brain. Bits of a playground. Music. Ice cream. Most of all, the unsettling sense of being much smaller than he was, as though he had swallowed the 'Drink Me' potion from *Alice in Wonderland*. What the hell was this?

'Whoa there, fella,' Greg said as Nick sat bolt upright. 'This is your first regression. You have to take it easy.'

Nick buried his face in his palms. His mind felt like it was swirling around as if someone had shoved it into a food mixer. Slowly, however, reality reasserted itself. The room around him felt gradually more present and real.

'How did I get here?' he asked.

'Everyone has a Big timing them,' Brenda said cheerily. 'When the Nostal wears off, they come and take you out. The transition is always a bit weird. It's because you're sort of waking up, you see? 'Cos if you think about it, a toddler's brain isn't the same as ours, is it? It's probably a bit like a dog suddenly becoming human!' She laughed.

'Don't worry if you feel all out of sorts, Nick,' Greg added. 'Your whole world has been topsy-turvy for a while. And now it's back the right way up again.'

He nodded slowly.

'How'd it feel?' Brenda said.

'I don't have any words for it,' Nick said.

'Ha ha, you'll soon get used to it.'

Greg patted him on the back. 'Well, in your own time,' he said. 'There's the door. It's been a pleasure having you. Come back soon.'

Nick looked at him, and then back at Brenda.

'Er . . . thanks,' he mumbled.

Outside, the sky was onyx black and peppered with brilliant stars. He couldn't have been under the spell of the overdose for more than a couple of hours at the most. But it felt a lot, lot longer. It felt like days. As he crossed the street, he spotted a mixed group of friends walking away from the warehouse. They were all wearing bright clothes that stood out a mile, the secret dress code of the initiated. Nick could only assume they had exited just before him. As he caught up with them, he thought he recognised one of the group – an Asian man, dressed in a superheroes T-shirt and shorts. He felt . . . familiar somehow. Nick was drawn towards him. Before he knew it, he had wandered into their midst. One of the girls in front stopped talking. The Asian man stared at him.

'Excuse me. Do I . . . do I know you?' Nick asked thickly.

It felt heavy and emotional to see the stranger, and he wasn't sure why. The man looked into his eyes. 'First time regressing?' he said.

Nick nodded.

The man turned back to the group. 'Guys, give me a moment?'

They murmured and agreed, and the man fell behind to keep in step with Nick. To his surprise, he placed a gentle hand on his shoulder.

'Don't worry, it's going to feel weird for a while. Your first time always does.'

'I feel like . . . I know you, somehow,' Nick said. 'Did we talk to each other . . . ?'

He pointed back towards the warehouse. 'In there?'

They passed under a yellow streetlight, where Nick saw the other man's eyes were full of kindness and compassion. 'Yes,' he said. 'I remember you. We went on the slide.'

'Slide?' Nick frowned. He searched desperately for the memory. It wasn't that it was not there, it was just foggy and elusive. 'I . . .'

'It's okay,' the man repeated. 'It takes a long time to adjust. I'm a regular, so it's all pretty normal to me now.'

Nick hesitated. 'I . . . I feel confused.'

The man smiled. 'You got somewhere to be?' he asked.

'Me? No.'

'Let's grab a quick coffee,' the man said. 'I know a place.'

FIFTY-SIX

(0)

The man took him to a greasy spoon café a few streets away, tucked deeper into the industrial estate. It was one of those twenty-four-hour places that served black-cab drivers, as evidenced by all the hackney carriages parked outside. They sat opposite each other in Formica chairs at one of twenty-odd tables. The man poured sugar into his mug of tea, while Nick sipped an instant coffee. The place was busy, at least half full. From a hidden kitchen behind a long order counter came a plethora of frying sounds and the clanking of pots and pans. The smell of bacon and sausages made Nick's stomach grumble.

'So how often do you do this?' he asked.

His table companion shrugged. 'Whenever I can. It's hard to get away sometimes. I work pretty long hours.'

'Really? What do you do?'

'I'm an IT director for a global investment bank,' he said. Nick nodded.

'How much do you remember?' the man asked.

'Just fragments, really,' Nick said. 'Music. Balloons. A Wendy house.'

'I remember,' the man said, smiling. 'It's always so different, each time,' he added. 'Sometimes you think you remember parts of it but then you'll talk to a mate who was there and they'll say "No, we didn't do that, we did this" and you'll question yourself. But if you think about it, not knowing what's real and what's your imagination . . . that's kind of how our minds worked when we were little kids.'

Nick stared into his coffee mug, contemplating this. 'I think we had fun playing together,' he said after a while.

The man smiled again. 'Anuj,' he said, shooting his hand out.

He took it. 'Nick.'

Anuj grinned wider. 'Pleased to meet you, Nick.'

Nick relaxed his shoulders. 'So, how did you first get into this? If you don't mind me asking?'

'Not at all,' Anuj said. 'A friend of mine told me about it. A girl I used to work with. She asked me what I'm about to ask you.'

Nick raised an eyebrow. 'Ask me what?'

'Do you believe in fairies?'

'I don't follow.'

'It's from *Peter Pan*,' Anuj said. 'It's a great story, *Peter Pan*. A warning about the dangers of growing up.'

Nick remembered the story. Peter had never wanted to be an adult, with all its scary responsibilities. It made him think about a slogan he'd seen on a T-shirt once that read: *DON'T GROW UP. IT'S A TRAP.*

'So it's about feeling like a kid again?'

'Yes, but also more than that,' Anuj said. 'It's about wonder. Magic.'

'Magic?'

'Fairies. Dragons. Flying carpets. There was a time when these things were as real to you and me as breathing.' Anuj looked wistful as he continued. 'But we forget. As we get older, we start putting limits on our imagination. In time, we forget how incredible it actually felt to believe in a truly magical universe, where anything is possible. That vanishes forever. Only now we get to go back.'

Nick reflected on the experience in all its surreality. 'It was kind of magical,' he agreed.

'I remember my friend asking me if I remembered believing in Father Christmas,' Anuj said. 'How fucking exciting it felt. And how would I like to feel that kind of thrill again, without my stupid adult brain getting in the way?'

Nick nodded. He had carried his own belief in the man with the white beard until he was eight. He remembered looking at the stars with his mother one Christmas Eve, convinced he could hear the jingle of sleigh bells from the sky.

'Some people take MDNA or LSD to get some high, out-of-body experience. But there's no greater high like living inside a child's mind, with all its fun possibilities.'

'I don't remember any fairies, though,' Nick said. 'Or dragons for that matter.'

Although he also knew that if anyone had suggested he had wings and could fly while he was in there, he would have readily accepted it as fact.

'Every session is different,' Anuj said. 'One time, you might be an astronaut, another time a fireman or a princess. What matters is how limitless the possibilities are. Even something as simple as going on a swing is just the most amazing thing *ever*. You ever see a toddler turn a banana into a phone?'

Nick smiled.

'Everything is an adventure,' Anuj said.

Nick studied this stranger. They had been laughing and joking together before. He remembered a teddy bear. For a brief moment, he had a giddy sensation in his stomach. A slide. Yes, he remembered more now. And Anuj was one hundred per cent right. It *had* been an adventure.

'Listen, you'll feel strange for a while,' Anuj said. 'The Nostal's probably out of your system, but it takes a while for your brain to normalise. Don't sweat it.'

'I do feel strange,' he admitted. 'Guess that's why it's illegal, right?'

'It's perfectly safe,' Anuj assured him.

'The clubs ever get raided?' he asked.

'Sometimes. I was in one that did once. It was horrible. We all woke up in a police station jail. There were about fifty of us. No one knew what had happened. A few people could remember the raid, the cops putting some of us in cuffs.' He gripped his tea mug harder. 'The law's so fucking stupid,' he said. 'We should be able to do what we want with our own bodies.'

Nick wasn't entirely sure what he thought about that – or any of it at the moment.

'Plus, it's legal,' Anuj continued. 'It's a legal substance. Why should it be any different from alcohol? You don't see the police arresting people for having one too many. The clubs are run responsibly. You can see that, right?'

'Actually, I think I can,' Nick said.

He had a fuzzy memory of an army of people in red suits who he remembered looking out for him while he was under.

'If there's one thing I've learned about the scene is that it's all done responsibly,' Anuj said. 'A monitored environment, people who supervise us. Just like you would have at any nursery or creche.'

Anuj went on to explain to Nick that the people who were part of the Little scene, even the promoters who took on the risk of illegally booking, hosting and planning each night, were all about safety first. The punters wanted to explore their infantile minds without having to worry about doing something stupid. That's why there were always Bigs around to supervise.

'The organisers can keep taking my money,' he said. 'Experiencing being Little, how liberating it feels. I'm happy to keep coming.'

'Who *are* the organisers?' Nick asked.

'Who cares? Just a bunch of people out to make a buck, probably. But good on them. They do a fantastic job. Tell me you didn't have one of the best times you've had in years.'

'It was very weird,' Nick said. 'But yes. Also kind of wonderful.'

'And that's why you'll be back,' declared Anuj confidently. He stood up, scraping his chair, and leaned forward to pat Nick on the shoulder. 'I'll see you next time, my friend.'

He left, banging the glass door of the café behind him. And leaving Nick to finish his coffee while still feeling mesmerised. And, if he was honest, overwhelmed.

Nick returned to his bike and leaned on the seat. He still felt a little unsteady on his feet. There wasn't anything wrong physically. He was just having more flashbacks. He could remember more scenes, like getting back bits of a dream that had faded when you woke up. But the memories seemed to belong to someone else. He removed the helmet from the netting and placed it over his head.

He was glad he had met Anuj. The entire experience had felt so alien. Regressing that far back shouldn't be something you did alone. Not only that, Anuj had given him some good insights into this whole scene. The way it was organised really did remind him of the old rave scene from the early nineties. Taking pills and getting on it. An undisclosed location, known only to those in the loop. Prone to cancellations and last-minute venue changes if the police caught a whiff of what was going on. He wondered why he'd never even heard of this. Was he really that out of touch? He'd read about people experimenting with overdosing. But this was something different. This was a real subculture. For the curious, it provided a safe space for people to go much further back than the law currently allowed. As he pulled out of the alleyway and back onto the road, he passed another group, a mixture of thirty- and forty-somethings. They were headed towards the black door. A girl led the way, laughing as she did the knock for all of them. They were just about to start their unearthly trip to a world of infinite fun, where fairies and magic could still exist.

Strange as it was to admit, Nick envied them.

FIFTY-SEVEN

(O)

Back at home, he drew a glass of water from the kitchen tap. As he gulped it down, he closed his eyes and tried to recapture the lucidity of the emotions he had experienced during his regression. But all he felt were the barest tinges, like flickers from a fire that was fading fast. He slept badly until sunlight eventually roused him again at 5 a.m. His dreams had been of amorphous shapes, full of bright and luminous colours. Psychedelic swirls that reminded him of the old children's show *The Magic Roundabout*. His subconscious, he supposed, replaying his time in the enchanting Play Ground. He sat up in bed and wiped his brow. He felt it again, that nebulous sense of longing. The more he thought about it, the more he wondered if those few hours might literally have been the happiest of his life. There was something so pure, so innocent about it all. It was hardly surprising people were prepared to break the law just to get back to that state of being.

He showered and dressed quickly, then emailed Flynn

asking her to call him. He wondered what she'd make of last night's strange adventure. He spent the next couple of hours googling regression clubs and finding out what he could about this bizarre subculture. His phone rang while he was in the thick of it, a name flashing on the screen that wasn't Flynn's.

'Rebecca.'

'Hello, Nick. I don't suppose you're at home, are you?'

He confirmed he was.

'I know it's short notice but I'm in the neighbourhood. Are you free at the moment? There's something I'd like to show you.'

'I . . .'

'Great!' she said before he could object. 'I'll be there in ten minutes.'

He waited outside the flat. True to her word, the limousine soon appeared. As it pulled up at the front gate, he couldn't help but feel a degree of trepidation at the first glimpse of Ben Cooper's stony face behind the windscreen. He swallowed. No. Whatever this was, it was going to be fine. Yet his anxiety increased as Ben brought the limo to a complete stop next to him. The chauffeur didn't move, however. Instead, the rear door opened and Rebecca Hughes poked her head out. She waved for him to come in. Nick obeyed, settling quickly into a seat opposite her.

'Thanks for being available,' she said. 'I appreciate it.'

Ben slipped into first and whisked them off again.

'What was it you wanted to show me?' Nick asked.

'Let's wait until we get there,' Rebecca said. 'Hopefully traffic won't be too bad at this time of day.'

She had a folder on her lap, which she opened and started to read as if he wasn't there. Nick took a nervous glance at the driver's section, but the divider glass was up and Ben's eyes were fixed on the road.

She looked up from her papers. 'How's the investigation going?'

Nick hesitated. He decided to use the only other card he had. 'I've been looking into Lenora Cox,' he said.

'Oh yes, she's the pop star. Wasn't she claiming we made her take drugs?'

'Uh . . . yes.'

Rebecca gave a derisory snort. 'I didn't think those sorts of people need any help in that department.'

Nick refrained from telling Rebecca he'd interviewed Lenora personally and seen the pain of her struggle in her eyes. 'Well, I'm not sure we can say *why* she did what she did,' he said tentatively.

Rebecca continued reading through her paperwork. 'Everyone has free will, Nick. No one makes you take recreational drugs if you don't want to.'

He studied her for a moment before deciding to spring a related topic on her. 'Hey, Rebecca, do you know anything about regression clubs?'

'What?'

She raised an eyebrow, but Nick got the impression she understood the term.

'It's an underground scene,' he continued. 'Where people go to OD. On your product.'

Rebecca bit her lip and put her folder aside. 'I know what they are,' she said. 'The police break them up from time to time. I've been trying to keep their existence out of the news as much as possible.'

'Well, you've done a good job,' Nick said. 'I had to google a fair bit till I found the right forums and communities. Very niche. Very illegal too.'

'Yes, they are. But why have you been googling them?'

'I only just found out about them,' he said. 'I was curious about what you thought.'

'Well, it won't surprise you to know that we severely disapprove of our product being abused like this,' she said.

'No surprise,' he agreed.

He watched again for any obvious changes in her body language, anything that said she might know more about this underworld he'd stumbled into than she was letting on. But he saw nothing obvious.

They drove in silence for forty minutes. As they passed through Canary Wharf, Nick became nervous again. He looked out through the privacy glass as the financial buildings of the City of London gradually receded into the background. This was a part of London he wasn't hugely familiar with, having no cause to come out this far, except maybe once or twice to City Airport. A sign announced they were entering a place called Silvertown. Part of the Port of London, it was a former industrial district that was characterised by derelict warehouses and factories. Nick had read somewhere that it was supposed to be a huge regeneration area that some had said might even be the new Brooklyn. But the project wasn't quite done yet. That much was clear even as the limo turned right and through the open gates of an expansive construction site that was little more than river sand. Ben steered the vehicle carefully around JCBs and digging equipment, arriving on the north bank of the Thames. They were far enough away that no one else was in sight. Where no one could hear you scream, he thought.

'Rebecca . . .'

'It's okay, Nick. Relax.'

But he didn't feel relaxed. The limo stopped.

Ben got out and opened the door. 'After you, sir,' he said in his controlled cockney voice.

Nick looked at Rebecca, who just stared back at him, waiting for him to comply. He nodded feebly and slid across the seat and out into the fresh morning air. His shoes touched the gravel as two seagulls cawed and sailed above his head. He couldn't help wondering if they would soon be pecking at his dead body. Ben swept a hand in the direction he was expected to walk. Nick obeyed, watching the driver closely, especially the contours of his suit jacket, which he hoped to God were not concealing a pistol. They ambled down towards the riverbank, Nick first, Ben's footsteps following behind. There was a single long barge on the water, too far away for him to call for help.

'Okay, that's far enough,' Rebecca said.

He turned around, only part of him dismissing the visual in his mind of Ben pointing a gun at him. Fortunately, he wasn't. Instead, the man was standing statue-still, hands clasped behind his back.

'I wanted you to see this for yourself,' she said.

'See what?'

She tipped her head to one side. 'All of this. Do you know what this site is going to be?'

'No.'

'A research centre,' she said. 'Lakefront Sciences is donating a hundred million pounds to build the biggest clinical trial hub in Europe. Cancer, mostly. But not just that. We'll be funding trials for new and experimental treatments for Parkinson's, Alzheimer's, cystic fibrosis . . . a whole bunch of horrible diseases. It'll be the biggest venture of its kind for decades.'

Nick stepped back, took in the size of the site they were standing in. 'Impressive,' he said. 'You could have just told me about it, though.'

'I wanted you to see it. Imagine the building, right here. See the thousands of people who are going to come here, many of them to have their lives changed.'

'Okay,' he said. 'Why?'

'Because I want you to know the reason I do this,' she

said. 'I want to make a difference to people who are sick. I want to do some good in this world, Nick.'

'Lakefront Sciences does a lot of good,' Ben said.

His unexpected contribution almost made Nick jump. He was used to Ben being Rebecca's silent lackey whenever she was present. It didn't help either that he kept imagining that big blocky head inside a black bike helmet decorated with silver streaks.

'Thank you, Benjamin, I've got this,' Rebecca said gently. She turned back to Nick. 'I just wanted you to take away a picture of this place. To remind you of what the world might be like without Lakefront Sciences in it.'

He stepped back.

'I'm just trying to show you the company helps a lot of people out there,' she said.

She left the last sentence dangling in the air. Another seagull cried as it glided over them. Nick looked at her, then at Ben, then back again.

'Okay, Rebecca. Point made.'

She smiled. 'Good. And thank you for coming out here. Now, where can we drop you?'

He tucked his hands into his trouser pockets and started towards the gate. 'You know what? It's a nice day. I'm just going to walk to the nearest station, okay?'

'You sure? It's quite a long way.'

'I'm sure,' he said. 'I'll be in touch, okay?'

He thought he felt their eyes burning into his back as he left, but he didn't care. This had creeped him out a little and he needed to get away from whatever lesson Rebecca and her muscled heavy were trying to teach him.

FIFTY-EIGHT

(0)

She was right about the station. Nick ended up ordering an Uber, and even that took its precious time coming. Once he was in the back seat, he closed his eyes and allowed himself to replay what had happened. Was it a warning? Or was he just being paranoid? The familiar melody of his phone played again and he fished it out from inside his jacket.

'Nick,' DI Flynn said. 'You okay?'

'Tracy!'

'You asked me to call you,' she said. 'Is everything all right?'

Nick felt a flush of anger. 'Actually, Tracy, no. I've just been driven to Docklands where I seriously thought I was in for some gangland-style execution from Ben Cooper. Where the fuck was your tail?'

There was silence and for a moment he thought the line might have cut. But then he heard Flynn whispering to colleagues in the background.

'Hi, Nick,' she said when she came back on. 'I'm being

told we did have an officer following Cooper, but he lost the limousine in traffic this morning. Roadworks or something. I'm so sorry. What happened, exactly? Are you okay?'

He felt calmer at her genuinely conciliatory tone. 'I'm a bit freaked out. But don't worry, I'm okay.' He told her what had happened. 'I'm not sure why they drove me out here,' he concluded. 'I think Rebecca Hughes wanted to make a point of some kind.'

Flynn sighed. 'Seems like quite a lot of effort to go to,' she said.

Nick agreed. He leaned his head against the glass, staring at the river while he formulated his next thought. 'You know, there might be another way of linking them all back to Doyle's murder.'

'Like what?' Flynn asked.

'I'd check that warehouse again,' he said. 'In fact, I'd send that officer back down there tonight.'

'Why? What will he find?'

'If I'm right, a regression club.'

'A regression . . . what? You mean those illegal gatherings where people pretend to be children?'

'Uh-huh.'

'And how do you know this?'

Nick took her through the events of the previous night. 'Your officer was right, there was likely no one in it when he checked. Empty and locked up tight. I understand most of them prefer to stay anonymous. The details are usually put online and quickly deleted. A location, a time. And they only take cash too. It's quite a lucrative business. But the place was jam-packed last night.'

'You went inside?' Flynn said.

'What can I say? It was too weird not to investigate. It didn't seem dangerous. And it was kind of open to the public.'

Flynn was quiet for a moment. 'I've heard stories about these events,' she said eventually. 'What was it like?'

'Weird,' he said. 'Adults running around, convinced in their heads that they're little kids. Sounds a bit creepy when I put it like that, huh?'

'Yes, it does,' she agreed. 'Did you happen to see the courier last night? Or the other man?'

'I don't think so,' he said. 'There were a lot of people there. But I can't remember their faces being among them.'

He told her many of the volunteers wore red suits and looked after the paying customers. 'They might have been there and I missed them,' he said. 'But what I'm really wondering is what they were transporting to Davenport-Ross's house that night. And what the hell is inside it? It's listed as an asset of DPR Holdings, so something must be going on there.'

'I agree,' Flynn said. 'But we can't just search the house, sadly. Just because you followed that courier there doesn't mean anything illegal took place inside.'

'But someone in that house clearly knows the people who had Doyle killed,' Nick said.

'Yeah. We have that link now, thanks to you. But without a warrant, there's no getting access to the property.'

'You could start surveillance,' he suggested.

'We could, yeah. But we'd have to be very careful.'

'Why? Wait,' Nick said. 'Is this because Davenport-Ross is a lord?'

She hesitated. 'Accusing someone that high up can be tricky,' she said. 'They often have friends in even higher places. One wrong move and I could end my career.'

'You're scared,' he said.

It was more an observation than an accusation.

Flynn sighed. 'Look, I'm still a long way off from my pension. If this lord is involved in any way with what happened to Doyle, we need to be very careful how we go about all this.'

He couldn't believe what he was hearing. 'You really are worried.'

'I won't lie. I could lose everything if we botched this one up,' Flynn said. 'I'm all for investigating what he has to do with all this. But we need to do it right.'

Nick felt a flash of irritation now. 'Surely what we need to do,' he said, 'is to take a closer look at the activities of m'lud?'

'We will,' Flynn promised. 'But we need to do it by the book. If I were you, I'd forget about the mansion. Get back into Rebecca Hughes's good books if you can. That's the angle that could break this open.'

'But what about Davenport-Ross?' he asked. He was feeling frustrated now at Flynn's unwillingness to take bolder action.

'Look, if he's broken the law, we'll get him,' Flynn said. 'I guarantee you that. But we need solid proof before we make a move against someone of his stature.'

'What bollocks,' Nick said.

'Come on, Nick. Cut me some slack here. I know you've burned some bridges in the past, but this is still just a story for you. For someone like me, there could be very serious consequences. Just let me do this my way, all right?'

'Okay, fine,' he said tightly.

They agreed to talk later. His Uber driver was entering the Blackwall Tunnel, which meant he was halfway home already. He was a little shocked, if he was honest. Whatever else he thought of Flynn, he hadn't taken her for a coward. But the more he mulled it over, the more he sympathised. Flynn was part of the civic tree, only on one of its lower branches. He imagined it was easy for someone like Davenport-Ross to make life difficult for her if he chose to. Nick, on the other hand, had no career to protect. Flynn had been right. It wasn't the same. But she was also right about not being able to get a warrant without proof that something illegal was going on at Dove's House. But how were they supposed to do that? Then an idea struck him. One that he suspected Flynn would strongly disapprove of. But sometimes if evidence didn't come to you, there was no choice but to seek it out yourself.

FIFTY-NINE

(0)

The following morning, Nick sat cross-legged on top of a hill in the middle of a field in Cambridge. The fresh country air only marginally erased his sleepiness. His night had been full of tossing and turning until he had given in and eventually hauled himself out of bed. A cold shower had gradually resulted in a brain that felt vaguely functional. When he'd emerged from it, he discovered to his horror that it was only 4 a.m. He'd paced up and down the living room, throwing back mugs of coffee as he willed the time to pass.

Eventually, streaks of sun broke through into the flat and he was able to slip outside to prepare the Honda. He carefully secured the drone to the back of the bike, double-checking the straps and the weight before setting off. The trip had taken two hours. He'd stopped once, for petrol and a sandwich, before hitting the motorway again. By the time he'd found the field, the sun was high and his stomach was rumbling. Fortunately, the sandwich took care of the latter problem, but all was not right in the world quite yet. The drone sat on the grass, lifeless and awaiting instructions. This was especially disappointing as it was meant to be the easiest drone to operate, a fact he knew because he had declared so himself in the article 'The UK's Top 10 Drones'. The young salesman in the electronic shop had likewise vouched for the model. It wasn't the battery that was the problem because Nick had spent the night charging the unit. Instead, it was finding the remote network he needed to connect to on his phone. The drone continued to lie still as he struggled to locate it. Finally, however, the network name popped up.

'Aha!'

At last, the drone came alive with a strong 5G connection that indicated all systems were go. He clicked on the controls menu on the app and, a second later, four propellers started up.

'Houston, we have lift off!' he cried.

Fortunately, the app itself was designed with an easy interface, but Nick had to cup one hand over the phone screen to see clearly in the sunlight. He moved a graphic slider button which, in turn, caused the drone to whir gently as it rose into the air. The app displayed a monitor window divided into four screens. Each was a bird's-eye view, fed directly off the HD cameras mounted on the corners of the drone. The top right-hand screen currently showed himself looking up at the drone, which had now ascended eighty feet. Nick switched to a feature called map mode, creating a two-dimensional map overlay, a white dot blipping to show the drone's current location. He moved the directional arrow and glanced up. The drone drifted further away from him like a child's lost balloon.

He carefully used the app to steer the drone north, passing high over the oak tree where his bike was parked, then beyond, until it became a pinprick in the distance. Switching views, he rotated the cameras to point downwards. In all four windows, the A1386 coiled like a snake winding through a carpet of green. It was handy having the map overlay. From this high up, Nick barely recognised it as the same road he had followed the white van down. It took him several more minutes, but eventually the small screens showed the rooftop of Dove's House, its wings extending north and south. The grounds surrounding the house were manicured and landscaped, including an impressive hedge maze. Now he was about to enter illegal territory, but he was already committed. He needed to do what Flynn could not, and he was prepared to accept the consequences. In his mind, it was no different from breaking a super-injunction. The means were justified. But what the ends would be, however, remained to be seen. The stats on the bottom of the screen told him the drone was two and a half miles away from his location. He switched off the map mode, keeping the drone high, following a rough route of east–west and back again.

Nick set the cameras to face four different directions around the property. One showed the doors to an expansive garage at the front of the house. They were partly open, but the drone was too high to see inside. A second camera took in the sweep of the mansion's sprawling driveway. The images were incredible. Nick lowered the drone to get a peek into the upper windows. No one appeared to be home. He piloted it higher, letting it hover at a hundred feet. In the left-hand corner screen, a moving dot ambled along the southern end of the property. He saw two more of these, in different screens. One by the main gate, another to the west of the house. *Security maybe?* he wondered, remembering the voices he'd heard behind the wall that night. He zoomed in closer, keeping the drone level. The left corner screen revealed the first dot to be a woman in a suit. She was wearing sunglasses and an earpiece, like the Secret Service bodyguards you saw on TV. Definitely security. The camera was sharp enough to show her face. About thirty-five, hair in a neat bun, mouth turned down. The woman had a puzzled expression and was staring straight up at the camera. Fuck. She'd made the drone.

'Okay, my friend. Mission accomplished. It's time to bring you home.'

He searched for the boomerang button. It was a feature he remembered from his research. A one-touch command that programmed the drone to return to its launch location, essentially performing its flight in reverse. He located it and was about to click 'return' when he caught the glint of something shiny in the corner screen. The security woman had whipped out a gun. A pistol with a long silencer on it. Two brief flashes and the camera winked out. The other three feeds showed the grounds of the mansion rapidly rising up towards them. Nick grimaced at the ensuing heavy thud. His drone had just been shot down.

Though he was over two miles away, Nick did not want to hang around. He ran over to the oak tree where he'd left his Honda. He kick-started the bike's engine, negotiating through tufts of grass and around cowpats until he arrived at the same gate he'd originally come through. There, he dismounted quickly in order to open the latch. Within seconds of being back on the road, he heard the roar of a car approaching fast. His heart skipped as he checked his side mirror. A Peugeot was gaining on him. A sunlit windscreen prevented him from seeing who the vehicle's occupants were, but they were getting closer. He tensed as the car swooshed past. It was just a family out for a drive. Nothing more. He relaxed his hand on the throttle and reminded himself that he had seen no cars on the mansion grounds. They couldn't possibly be out looking for him this soon. But still. He wouldn't feel safe until he was back home.

SIXTY

(0)

'What on earth?'

He heard the shock that tinged Tracy Flynn's voice on the other end of the phone as she watched the footage he had just emailed her.

'What do you make of it?' he asked.

'It's definitely an illegal firearm,' Flynn said. 'On Lord Davenport-Ross's property too. You said you saw more armed people on the grounds?'

'I don't have close-up footage, but yes.'

'This is probable cause, Nick. We can get a warrant and search that mansion with this.'

His shoulders loosened as he leaned back in his kitchen chair.

'But you do know you've broken the law to get it,' she said.

'Data Protection Act,' he confirmed. 'I've probably violated the personal privacy rights of these armed guards.'

'This is serious,' Flynn said. 'The law is the law.'

'I don't care, Tracy,' Nick said. 'We need to know what's going on inside that house. And if I'm fined, hell, if I go to jail, then fuck it. It will be worth it.'

'Well, I suppose it's good you've accepted responsibility.'

'I've been prepared for the consequences since I took on this story,' he said.

'Yes, that hardly surprises me,' Flynn said.

'Any chance you can hold off arresting me until we know what the hell is going on in that house?'

Flynn laughed drily.

'I'll see what I can do,' she said. 'I hate to say this, but this footage might well have been worth it. We'll have a team in there tonight, searching that property. And then we'll see what's what.'

'Great,' he said.

'Sit tight,' Flynn said. 'I'll be in touch.'

After he hung up, he breathed a long sigh of relief. Hopefully, the drone op would break this whole mystery open. He supposed time would tell. It was all down to the police now.

Flynn called him back at three o'clock.

'Bad news,' she said. 'Our warrant got rejected.'

'What?'

'Warrants are issued under section eight of the Police and Criminal Evidence Act,' Flynn said. 'Which means they need to be signed off by a magistrate. Who, in this case, didn't accept it.'

'What? Why?'

'They said the drone footage was obtained illegally and that invalidates the warrant.'

'What the fuck,' Nick said. 'So what do we do now?'

'We can appeal,' Flynn said. 'But it means there's no chance we'll get into that property today.'

'Shit.'

'I'm sorry,' Flynn said. 'I actually thought you'd given us something we could work with. Listen, we *will* appeal. But in the meantime, I've been thinking. Let's not take any chances. I'm sending another security detail to your home to keep watch.'

He gripped the phone tighter. 'You really think that's necessary?'

'I'm afraid I do,' she said. 'We haven't figured out all the connections yet. But at the risk of sounding paranoid, if Lord Davenport-Ross were to somehow hear about our applying for a warrant, then it's possible Gladstone could. And if someone from the property has also reported the drone . . .'

'You think they could link it back to me?' he asked.

'It depends on who *they* are,' Flynn said, 'but if Gladstone knows it was you poking your nose around at the Barrel Inn, it's not a stretch. And if they start panicking what that drone might or might not have seen . . .'

He shut his eyes.

'There's already been one attempt on your life,' she reminded him.

But she didn't need to say it. Though she had promised not to let Ben Cooper out of their sight again, they had lost him before. And now Nick was picturing him dressed in his leathers and a distinctive black-and-silver helmet, beating down his front door. Holding a pistol and silencer.

'I think that's a sensible idea, Tracy,' he said, opening his eyes again.

'And whatever you do, don't pick up the phone if Rebecca Hughes or anyone else at Lakefront calls you, okay? At least till I figure this out.'

'Got it,' he said.

'Good. The car should be with you within thirty minutes. We'll talk again tomorrow, okay? I'll keep you posted.'

'Okay,' he agreed.

'It's just a little setback,' Flynn said. 'Until I can figure something out.'

'I hope so,' he said. 'And thanks, Tracy.'

True to her word, Flynn sent a squad car twenty minutes after their call. Nick spotted it through the window, parking up unsubtly across the street. It looked like it was occupied by Flynn's twelve-year-olds. There was no announcement. The two young men simply switched off the engine and watched the flat as if expecting trouble at any minute. Nick sincerely hoped there wouldn't be any.

SIXTY-ONE

(0)

He slept badly again, ostensibly because of the summer heat, but in reality his preoccupied mind continued to churn. He awoke to discover his bedsheets were soaked with sweat. Slipping out of bed, he trudged towards the window and drew back the curtains. PC Zoomers One and Two were still sitting in the car out on the street. Christ. They must have stayed awake all night. He gave them a wave, which they returned with solemn nods in unison, like weird clockwork automatons. After a much-needed caffeine kick, Nick returned to the bedroom, stripped off the damp sheets and carried them to the kitchen. He was about to shove them into the washing machine when he was interrupted by a call from Flynn.

'No joy,' she said. 'The magistrate heard about our appeal. He wants to respond to our objection, which is his legal right. I'm afraid the warrant will be postponed until next week.'

It was like she had stuck him with an electric shocker, jolting him back to where they had left off yesterday.

'You're kidding me,' he said. 'Can he really do that?'

'English law's a funny thing,' Flynn said. 'Much of it is written to protect the integrity of our justices. If anything makes them even slightly sniffy, they have the full legal right to reply.'

'Fuck.'

Nick had limited knowledge of how the legal system worked, and none at all about police warrants. But he thought he picked up the undercurrent of frustration in Flynn's voice.

'This could ruin our chances,' she said. 'If word about this somehow leaks it's possible there'll be no illegal guns, or illegal anything else, when we eventually search that house.'

'So that's it?' he asked.

'For now,' Flynn said. 'We need to sit tight, wait for the second judgement – and take it from there.'

'And what about me?' he said.

'The patrols are swapping out,' she said. 'There'll be a relief car coming soon. I'm sorry about this, but we'll need to keep a close eye on you from this point on.'

He nodded. 'And Cooper?'

'We still have eyes on him, don't worry. He met with some friends in the pub last night. Nothing out of the ordinary. If he goes anywhere near you, we'll know about it.'

'Thank you,' he said. 'I really appreciate you looking out for me.'

'Try and have a pleasant weekend,' Flynn said.

He let out a cynical laugh.

'I'll be back in touch on Monday,' she said. 'In the meantime, same advice as yesterday. Just sit tight. And no more contact with anyone at Lakefront Sciences.'

'Got it.'

'And Nick?'

'Yes, Tracy?'

'We will find out what those bastards have been covering up, and we will get them, no matter how long it takes.'

'I believe you,' he said.

He returned to the laundry. Now the sheets were in, he figured he might as well do another load. He sought out the heavy wicker basket in the bedroom and pulled out last week's clothes. He emptied the pockets of a pair of jeans from a couple of days ago. A crumpled piece of paper fell out. Confused, he picked it up and discovered it contained a child's crude drawing. He remembered himself and Anuj, colouring with crayons at a long table. Yes. This drawing had been done by his friend. It depicted three stick figures, two boys and a girl. A flashback followed, something Anuj had said to him when they were in Play Ground.

I miss my friends.

Tom. And Will. And Sophia.

While all the characters were drawn with bright colours, it was the last figure, the girl, that he couldn't stop staring at. She had been sketched with bunched hair in two pigtails. On her feet, Anuj had added bright pink boots.

'*Shit,*' Nick said.

Whoever the courier was, and whatever her connections, she was also a regular punter in the club. And Anuj knew who she was. He abandoned the laundry for the laptop. *Anuj.* A regular but not hugely common name. Nick dropped it into the search bar in Facebook. He had to scroll through several misses before he found the Anuj he wanted. Anuj Kashari. Thirty-one years old. An IT director. Nick squinted more closely at the profile picture. That was him all right. Anuj had made a recent video post. Just yesterday, in fact. He clicked play. It opened on what Nick assumed was the inside of Anuj's home. A living room, sparsely furnished, with Scandinavian themes. There was a view of the London cityscape through a large window. A familiar face filled the screen.

'Hello, everyone,' Anuj said.

The video cut, and the face reappeared at a slightly different angle from before.

'This is to say what I want to do,' Anuj said.

His dark brown eyes darted above what Nick assumed was his laptop camera, held for a moment, then stared into the lens again.

'I want to go live overseas,' he said.

His lips curled into a smile, and he giggled. The video chopped again, and Anuj's head returned. His expression had changed, however. Now he looked sombre, almost sad.

'I hate my job,' Anuj said. 'I want to go live somewhere else . . .'

He slowed his speech down as if talking to someone hard of hearing.

'I'm sorry to not say goodbye. But please don't look for me. I am happy and want to go. I'll see you soon, Mummy. And Daddy. And Bindi. And . . . oh yes, and all my friends. I love you and see you soon. Please don't worry.'

There the video ended. Friends of Anuj had posted comments underneath.

Sorry to see you go.

Wait WTF where you off to?

When are you off? Good luck, mate.

There was only one comment, several posts down, that asked: *Are you pissed? LOL.* It was the only one Nick credited with any intelligence. Something was clearly off. He replayed the video, watched Anuj giggle again. He knew that giggle. He'd heard it before, in Play Ground. Anuj was regressed. But why? Why would he announce his intention to emigrate on social media? And why would he do it overdosed on Nostal? He recalled Anuj's anger about the UK's punitive laws when it came to regressing on Nostal. He had not said where he was going. Perhaps a country with more lax drug laws, somewhere that would allow him to regress as often as he wanted. There were contact details in Anuj's bio. Nick used the phone number listed there, hoping to get through. But the network operator announced the number had not been recognised. Either Anuj did not want to be contacted, or else he'd had his phone disconnected already. Or maybe he hadn't left at all, Nick thought. He realised what he really suspected. That maybe, somehow, Anuj Kashari had been *disappeared*.

SIXTY-TWO

(O)

A soft siren blip came from outside. He got up to peer through the kitchen window, only to find the PC Zoomers pulling out as a new squad car took their place. The new couple, a man and woman this time, looked older than their counterparts. They didn't even glance Nick's way. He sighed, returning to the sofa. He still couldn't believe he needed a police escort. More to the point, he couldn't believe that dick of a magistrate. Was he really interested in how the footage had been obtained or was he just trying to protect a lord's reputation? Nick was surprised and somewhat relieved to find his numbness slowly turning to anger. When he interrogated this new feeling, he discovered that it was directed at the unseen forces at play. It was impossible to know what exactly Lord Davenport-Ross was up to in Dove's House. But he'd bet any amount of money that all those security guards patrolling the grounds were guarding whatever it was. And who were they? Were they part of McCreadie's crew, or a separate organisation? Then there was the mystery of the holy trinity. Lord Davenport-Ross, Jeremy Gladstone and Rebecca Hughes. Who knew about what? Who was involved in what? Either in Mark Doyle's murder or whatever the hell they were doing out there in Cambridge. One thing Nick knew for sure. The hands of the police were tied while the appeal process dragged on. He recalled Tracy Flynn's words. 'If word about this somehow leaks, it's possible there'll be no illegal guns, or illegal anything else, when we eventually search that house.'

She was likely right. The longer they waited, the greater the chance his lordship might learn about the warrant. And if that happened, he would certainly pack up whatever shady operation was going on. Nick gritted his teeth, remembering his exposé of Stephen Harvey's shady business with Mohammad Aziz Badawi. Back in his heyday, Harvey didn't have a noble title; he was just your bog-standard corrupt politician. But the principle was the same. Harvey considered himself above the law, believing he could do whatever he liked and that no one could touch him. But Nick had taken *him* down, hadn't he? Maybe it was time for all the guilty parties at Lakefront Sciences to get the same treatment. To have whatever illegal activities they were hiding exposed, even if it meant going up against a high-society lord. He remembered what Sam had said about him. 'I can't think of anyone else who'd have the balls to take them on.'

Sam had been right. Nick had never shied away from exposing the truth. He wasn't about to do so now.

He printed two colour stills from the drone's footage on his hard drive and headed out. Then he rode down to Bond Street, followed again by his escorts in blue, who had been told he needed to run a quick errand. The squad car waited dutifully as he parked up at an extended bay just for motorbikes. Inside the tailor's shop, he showed the photos to the female assistant behind the counter. The first image was of the security woman who had shot down his drone. Fortunately, it was taken moments before she had pulled out her gun. Nick had also saved a second still from the footage, this time from a second camera, that had shown a male security guard from elsewhere in the grounds, wearing the same type of suit. This one was smaller and low res, but together he hoped they would be enough.

'And you need to copy this?' the assistant said.

'If possible,' Nick said.

She looked closer at the photos. 'The suit itself is Cambridge grey. Jacket is single-breasted, sack rather than structured. Notch lapels. Hard to say if the pockets are patch or ticket. Does that matter?'

'As long as they look near enough the same,' Nick said.

'Okay. I can't see buttons, but my best guess is four. It's the standard. They're more likely to be stacked than spaced, but I can't be certain. The back could be vented but if the suit is English, I'd say not.'

'Great. What about the trousers?'

The assistant, whose badge announced her as 'Francesca', simply shrugged. 'Trousers are trousers. You just need to match the colour.'

'Have you got any of this in stock? I really need it today.'

Francesca gave him a tight-lipped smile. 'Of course. What do you want to do about the shoes?'

'I can rustle up a pair myself,' he said. 'And I already have a tie.'

Twenty-eight minutes later, Nick walked out with the right apparel tucked into a portable suit bag. The changing booth inside the store had shown a perfect fit. He was all set to walk into the lion's den, looking like a bona fide lion.

At 5 p.m., he arrived back at the flat, slung the suit bag down onto the sofa, and flopped himself down. He dialled another contact in his phone. After a few rings, a familiar voice answered.

'Hello?'

'Sam, it's Nick,' he said. 'I need a favour.'

'Of course,' Sam said. 'What is it?'

'I think I'm close on the Lakefront story,' Nick said. 'But I might need some insurance, just in case.'

He could sense Sam's concern. 'What are you doing, Nick? You're not in danger, are you?'

'I hope not,' he said. 'But if I do get the evidence I need, I need someone who can do the right thing with it. Tell me, can you keep a close eye on your phone tonight?'

Julia Conway was next on his call list.

'I-is everything okay?' she asked.

'All good,' Nick said soothingly. 'Are you still at your aunt's?'

She confirmed that she was.

'Listen, I don't want to alarm you or anything,' he said. 'But I just wanted to say that if anything happens to me, I want you to call Sam. He'll look out for you, okay?'

'Nick, is everything all right? Why are you talking like this?'

'Let's just say I might be wandering into some dangerous territory,' he said.

'What?'

'Well, if you can call Cambridge dangerous,' he added with a dry laugh.

'Nick, you're scaring me,' Julia said with obvious alarm.

He felt bad. It was the last thing he wanted, but he had to make sure she would know what to do if the worst happened.

'Seriously, don't worry,' he said, 'I'm just being over-cautious. I'll probably be fine. But just remember what I said, okay? Go to Sam.'

'O-okay,' she said.

The last person on his call list was not available. Which was something of a relief to him because he hadn't wanted to worry her either.

'Hi Heather,' he said, after the beep of her voicemail. 'It's me. I just wanted you to know that I totally get why you needed to keep your distance. And I wanted to tell you that even if we never speak to each other again, I wouldn't have changed the week that we had. Take care of yourself, okay?'

He hung up, thinking how morbid his phone calls had been. He really hated the fatalistic tone they all had. But as he'd told Julia, it was only precautionary. If he was careful with his planning, he could be in and out before they even knew he was there.

He spent the next hour going over the drone footage on his laptop one last time. He studied two things in particular. The layout of the grounds and the security staff who were patrolling it. Zooming in and out of the stills, he froze again on the shooter who had brought his drone down. He stared at the grimacing woman again, pointing her gun at the screen. Was he ready to face them? There was no choice but to find out.

He waited until 9 p.m., then switched off the lights in every room. Hopefully, the cops outside would just think he was turning in early. There was no way they could know where he was going. They would only call Flynn. And while she might not be jailing him for flying a drone, she would sure as hell draw the line at actual breaking and entering. The only downside, of course, was that the Honda was parked outside, directly in front of the patrol car. For once, he would have to leave it behind. Nick changed into his new suit, retrieved a pair of pliers from under the sink, and double-checked he hadn't forgotten anything. Satisfied, he slid open the lounge window and slipped out into the narrow side garden. From there, he shuffled down to the back gate, which he was relieved to find unlocked. A minute later, he was standing on the street, hailing an Uber. When it arrived, he clambered into the back, flashing a smile at his driver.

'Hope you're up for a big fare tonight,' he said.

He watched the streets slowly go by as the car crawled its way out of London. Closer, he hoped, towards the truth.

SIXTY-THREE

(O)

By 10 p.m., he was crouching on the same grassy knoll adjacent to the high hedge and wall that bordered Davenport-Ross's mansion. The night was dark, with cloud covering the moon. Crickets were the only sound that pierced the country air. No cars had come or gone from Dove's House's main gate in the half hour he'd been watching. His eyes remained fixed on the main entrance. Still no activity.

It was now or never. He rose slowly to his knees and brushed his suit down. The white shirt he was wearing underneath was already soaked with sweat, but there was little he could do about that. He moved towards the hedge, lining himself up with one of the CCTV cameras that was pointed inside the grounds so his approach wouldn't be detected. He felt along the brickwork. There was no ledge, but he found a foothold on a lower branch and used it to hoist himself up. His fingers brushed the top of the wall. The mounted camera rotated slowly from left to right, sweeping an arc of the garden inside the perimeter. Nick ran his hand along the coiled barbed wire that had also been placed along the wall to deter intruders. He retrieved the pliers from his inside jacket pocket and, standing on tiptoes, began to cut. When he was done, he waited slowly, watching the rotation of the swivelling camera and counting down the seconds in his head. He would need to time it just right.

He fell with a thud when he dropped from the wall into the garden. Everything around him was darkness, the starlight offering him little guidance. He sprang to his haunches and moved swiftly away from the arc of the camera's returning gaze. Nick was confident he was out of its range, but if he wasn't, he had to hope that being dressed as security would fool whoever was watching the monitors. Once the noise of his own heartbeat abated, he moved forward in the darkness, holding his breath and listening carefully. The footage had indicated there had been five guards on patrol. But it was possible whoever was in the mansion had stepped up security since discovering the drone. He would have to be vigilant. The lights of the house were visible up ahead. Despite the inky blackness, he could see patio-style doors in the distance. He continued to adjust his suit as he moved forward, still limping slightly from the drop. One of his wrist cuffs had snagged on the wall, but he was able to cover it up by tugging his jacket sleeve down. He fished a white wireless earphone out of his trouser pocket and placed it carefully in his left ear. It wasn't a real earpiece, but it was a similar shape and colour to the security woman's, so it would probably pass. It was so dark, however, he was hopeful nobody would spot him on the grounds anyway.

He crossed the lawn, the mansion lights getting nearer with every step. No voices carried from inside, but he heard a strange clicking sound nearby. At first he thought it might be the crickets, but then he realised it was sprinklers. Luckily, they were too far away to reach him. His heart pounded as he weaved between low-level opaque shapes that he guessed were potted plants and shrubs and around an outdoor table and chairs. Sweat continued to stream off him as he finally reached the patio and the entrance to the house. Through the glass doors, he saw a sprawling room filled with expensive-looking furniture. A plush Ottoman sofa sat next to an ornate bureau cabinet, while a Persian rug that had the sheen of real silk covered a section of the wooden floor. There was a floor-to-ceiling bookshelf at one end of the room, an open archway at the other. Nobody was inside. Nick drew in a breath. Tried the handle. The door was unlocked. He swung it gently inwards and listened. No sounds came from the rest of the mansion. Feeling emboldened, he stepped inside. His shoes pressed down on the wood flooring, but it didn't squeak. He strained his ears. Still nothing but silence. He released a breath. Everything so far had gone the way he had hoped. But how long could that last?

SIXTY-FOUR

(O)

From the reading room, he moved into an immense hallway with chandeliers hanging from the ceiling. A thick burgundy carpet kept his footsteps whisper-quiet as he approached the base of a grand staircase. The stairs led up to a landing, where they forked in two, twisting back on themselves up to the next floor. An obligatory grandfather clock stood at the bottom of the staircase. Nick stopped for a moment to retrieve his phone. He took a couple of quick pictures, then debated which way to go. He chose the long corridor left of the stairs. Gold-framed portraits lined both walls of the passageway. The painting to his immediate left depicted a tall man dressed in a velvety long coat, waistcoat and breeches, sporting a cravat and carrying a folded hat under one arm. Nick would not have been surprised to see a pack of hunting dogs behind him. The others were in a similar vein – puffy, red-faced cherubic men with patrician noses and sharp half smiles, dressed through the ages. The Davenport-Ross lineage. Only their outfits seemed to change through time. The last portrait was of the current Davenport-Ross, dressed in overwhelming tweed. The gallery suggested that the lord probably lived here at least some of the year. That, or else he just had an elephantine ego. Nick tapped his camera button again, capturing the portraits. He'd barely snapped five of them before a door slammed further up the corridor. A figure emerged, heading towards him. Nick's first instinct was to run, but it was too late. He'd already been spotted. As the figure drew closer, Nick saw it was a man in a butler's uniform.

'Is everything all right?' the butler asked.

He spoke with a thick, central European accent Nick couldn't pin down.

'Er, fine,' he replied, tucking the phone away.

'You people don't normally come inside,' the butler said, examining Nick's suit. 'Is anything wrong?'

'Oh no, no. Just switching up the patrols a bit.' Nick touched his earpiece as if someone was speaking into it.

'Nothing to do with the mayor's visit?' the butler said.

The mayor? he wondered. *What mayor?*

'Yes, yes,' Nick lied. 'The mayor's visit! We're, er, stepping up the security. Can't be too careful.' He grinned, aware that his face was sweating. Aware that he looked ridiculous.

But the butler seemed satisfied. 'His Lordship is still entertain in dining room.' The man thumbed at the area behind his shoulder. 'They still on whiskies so don't expect them to go downstairs for maybe one hour,' he added.

'Okay,' Nick mumbled. 'Um . . . good to know. Carry on.'

The butler nodded and moved off slowly to another part of the house. As Nick watched him go, he let snippets circle in his mind for a bit longer. Whatever other business this house conducted, it was clear Lord Davenport-Ross did use it as a residence. He was even hosting a dinner party here tonight. *Don't expect them to go downstairs.* What was downstairs? The butler had said it with some emphasis too, as though Nick, in his capacity as a security guard, would have known exactly what he meant. Maybe his lordship and his guests retired to the basement to play billiards or whatever people like them liked to do. He took a tentative step forward before he remembered MeaNonCulpa's words on the dark web. *It's time for another package. Can you deliver tonight?* Now Nick pictured a foggy opium den, Lord Davenport-Ross and whatever dignitaries were in that dining room lazing on boudoir sofas with rubber bands around their arms, needles in their veins. Best not let his imagination run away with him. The corridor ahead was empty and Nick was pretty sure it led the way downstairs, to whatever was down there. His instincts told him he needed to find out.

He passed the dining room. Double oak doors kept its occupants from view, but he could hear muffled, gruff laughter and the clinking of glasses. The strong aroma of cigar smoke also seeped under the threshold. He strode on, keen to get away from the doors in case Davenport-Ross or one of his dinner guests should come out and ask him what his business was. He passed a small table with a bouquet of flowers in a vase that was probably Ming dynasty, given the setting. The walls, all dark wood panelling, combined with the corridor's low lighting, made him feel as if he was walking through a dim and hazy dream. A maid burst out of a door to his right, startling him. She was carrying a bottle of malt whisky, its label facing outward as if she was about to present it. Nick looked at her fresh young face and then down at the bottle itself. It was a Chivas Regal Royal Salute.

'Excuse me,' the girl said.

'No, excuse *me*,' he said.

She hurried past him, over to the dining room, and knocked gently on the door. Nick left her behind, moving on quickly and pressing ahead until he reached the end of the corridor. A single door greeted him, this one accessed only by a keypad. *Shit.* He took a picture of it on his phone, then stared at the pad, trying to figure out what to do. Thinking on his feet, he opened his mobile browser. The signal was patchy, but he managed to bring up Davenport-Ross's Wikipedia entry. At the top of the page, it listed the lord's birthday. August 7, 1957. Nick doubted it was that easy, but it was also true he wouldn't know until he tried. His first guess was a two-two-four combination: date, month, full year. Eight keys in total. He punched them in. There was a *buzz-buzz-clunk* noise, followed by a small bulb above the pad flashing red. Fuck. He tried two-two-two. *Buzz-buzz-clunk.* Well, that was pointless, wasn't it? He thought briefly of doing the American date/month inversion but decided against it. What if the keypad was rigged for three-strikes-and-you're-out? He had a sudden vision of his third failed attempt setting off an alarm inside the mansion. He was chewing over his next move when the door made another buzzing sound. This time, it opened out towards him. Standing on the other side was a second maid. She had dark hair, curled into a bun.

She stared at Nick through tired eyes. 'More dressing gowns,' she groaned. 'What on earth do they get up to down there?'

There was nothing for it but to improvise again. 'How would I know?' Nick said. 'Downstairs is . . . downstairs.'

She laughed. 'They don't tell you either, huh? They hate it when any of us go down there. Every time they call for something, someone's there to meet me at the bottom of the stairs.'

'I know,' Nick said, trying to smile. 'What can you do?'

He felt like every bead of sweat his body could produce was manifesting itself on his face right now. But the maid seemed to buy his improv.

'So what do they want you for anyway?' she asked.

'Uh, they didn't say,' he replied. 'And I didn't ask.'

'Yep,' she agreed. 'I guess they do pay us not to, don't they?'

He mumbled something in solidarity while she moved past him and disappeared down the corridor. Nick quickly jammed his shoe to prevent the door closing shut again. And once the maid was out of sight, he quietly slipped through. He found himself at the top of a set of circular stairs, winding around a thick concrete pillar. What the fuck was this? A nuclear bunker? Not seeing any other choice, Nick closed the door behind him and began his descent.

SIXTY-FIVE

(O)

He proceeded carefully, one foot in front of the other, slowly following the staircase around and down. It was even dimmer than it had been in the corridor, only the occasional dull lightbulb to guide his steps. Though it was probably his imagination, it also seemed to get darker with each spiral he made, as though he was descending into some Dantean nightmare. The air tasted strange too, becoming worse the deeper he went. At last he reached the bottom. He was inside a closed antechamber, with a secondary door on the far side. A series of gym-style lockers ran across the wall to his right. To his left was a tall hamper. On closer inspection he saw it was full of the dressing gowns the maid had mentioned.

The far door was not locked. He pushed it open cautiously, peering through the crack. Beyond, the light was still muted by low-wattage bulbs hanging from the ceiling. Together, they were bright enough to illuminate a courtyard-like space that expanded outwards for some distance, possibly beyond the foundations of the mansion itself. On the other side of it, he saw the dark mouths of several stone archways. He was acutely aware that this was no standard basement. This bizarre silo, whatever it was, had been purpose built. No one was within his immediate vision, so he moved through the doorway into the strange new space. The air quality instantly improved, evidence of the immense subterranean structure he was now in. The soles of his shoes sounded loud against the cold flagstone tiles that covered the floor. But no one appeared. With every inch of progress, Nick felt increasing trepidation. And it wasn't just the knowledge that he was trespassing. There was something deeply wrong with this place. He heard distant sounds, too faint to make out, but they sounded oddly melodic. As he approached the rows of archways, he saw each one was an entrance to a long corridor with inner walls that emitted a soft red glow. He picked the first mouth he came to, his senses heightened, his heart beating. Squinting, he tried to make out what was in the passageway ahead. It looked as though there were rooms on either side, with bars across them, like cages in a zoo. Once he was inside the corridor, the impression was confirmed. Rows of jail cells, too many to count, all bathed in soft red light from the regular sconce-like bulbs that were mounted on the walls. They were housed inside wire cages, reminding Nick of a World War Two bomb shelter. At the distant end of the corridor, he could make out glitzy, multicoloured lights. It seemed to be where the melody was coming from. *What the hell is this?* he wondered. A voice startled him. It was barely louder than a whisper.

'Hello? Mister?'

It was a little girl's voice. Nick turned to his right. He drew closer to the sound, to a set of bars.

'Who's there?' he whispered back coarsely.

A light came on. Well, not a light exactly. More like a night light. A small lamp, in the middle of the cell-like room. In its short range, a face was illuminated. A female face, smiling, head bobbing animatedly. Nick half expected the broad smile to be missing some milk teeth, but as the face drew near, it morphed into a grown woman's. She looked around thirty. The woman stepped closer to the bars, still beaming from ear to ear. The light was actually a lamp, he saw now. Handheld and battery powered. A night lamp shaped like a penguin. He remembered his young niece had one just like it.

'Hello, mister!' the woman cried. Her eyes lit up as she saw him. 'Have you come to take me to Fun Land?'

Nick frowned. As he let the question hang in the air, he listened again to the melody from the far end of the passage.

'Fun Land, huh?'

The distant music, he realised, was accordion based. It was carnival music. *Fun Land*. For a moment, he was confused. He scrutinised the woman more closely. She was standing behind the locked gate of her cell, quite obviously a prisoner here. There were no keys that he could see. But it wasn't the locked gate that was drawing his eye. Rather, it was the clothes she was wearing. Blue denim overalls. And pink wellington boots.

It's time for another package. Can you deliver tonight?

He felt something cold touch his spine and creep its way down it. 'Sophia?' he asked tentatively.

'Have you come to let me out?' she said, in a sing-songy voice. 'Have I been good enough to go to Fun Land?'

'How long have you been here, Sophia?'

'What do you mean?'

'How long have you been down here?'

'Down?'

'In this room?'

'My playroom?'

She backed away and gently arced the lamp in a circle around her, showing off the chamber to him. The room consisted of an oversized Wendy house, like the one he'd seen in the regression club, with doors big enough for an adult to pass through. There was a single toilet by the wall. The lamp's light passed over too quickly for Nick to see any more details, but he did notice a black holdall. It was full of brightly coloured clothes.

'This is where I play,' Sophia announced.

Nick removed his phone and took several snaps of the cell and Sophia herself.

'But how long have you been in here?' he repeated.

'Not long enough to go to Fun Land,' she replied.

The smile turned sad and, even in the lamp's feeble light, Nick saw her eyes welling up.

She looked at him accusingly. 'You're not here to take me?'

'I . . .'

'I haven't done enough yet?'

'Enough what?' he asked.

'Enough of the gross stuff,' she said.

'What do you mean, gross stuff?'

'Where you touch my pee-pee. And I touch yours.'

'What?'

'That's what Nanny says to do. If I want to go to Fun Land. I have to make the guests happy.'

Nick felt his throat dry up. He barely swallowed as he tried to ask the next question. 'Which guests, Sophia?'

'The ones who come,' she said. She pointed. 'The Bigs. Like you.'

He stepped back into the darkness and found himself pressed up against a hard shape.

'What—?'

'Well, hello, Nick.'

He stumbled backwards as a bright new light burst out of the murky blackness, blinding him. Torchlight. The silhouette behind it was large and intimidating. For a moment, Nick was confused. There was a familiar quality to the voice that he couldn't quite place. And then he could. It belonged to a stockily built woman who had sat across his kitchen table just days ago.

'Tracy?' he said.

Nick's brain was still doing cartwheels. His initial thought was that Flynn had obtained her warrant after all and she had entered the mansion and had just discovered this . . . whatever this was. But there was something about her gait, her overall familiarity with this place.

'You're in on it,' he said.

He still did not know what *it* was, but he was forming an idea. And he didn't like the shape of it at all.

'Please do be quiet,' she said. 'You'll wake the others.'

Nick looked around at the cells. At least twenty on each side. Forty per corridor, times seven. Two hundred and eighty people, locked away in jails.

'You just couldn't stay away, could you?' Flynn said. 'Just too fucking curious, weren't you?'

Through the dazzling light, Nick discerned the shape of a gun in her right hand.

'What *is* this place?' he asked.

Flynn didn't answer. Instead, she hit a button on the wall with her free hand. A silent alarm, perhaps? He considered making a run for it, but she still had the gun barrel trained on him. So he just stood there stupidly.

'Hey, Nanny!' Sophia cried from behind bars. 'Is it time for a story?'

Without moving her gaze from Nick, Flynn tapped the bars with her torch. 'No, it is not, Sophia,' she said firmly. 'It's way past your bedtime, young lady. Where are your pyjamas? And why aren't you in bed? Do you want Nanny to give you a good hiding?'

Sophia, a grown woman in body but not in mind, burst into tears. 'Please, Nanny! No. I'll be good.'

'Then be a good girl,' Flynn said, 'and get to bed.'

Sophia sniffed into the air, holding steady, apparently

hoping that 'Nanny' would give in. But after a minute, she realised she was not going to and reluctantly got into her bed. Nick watched her with a mixture of both fascination and revulsion. He had so many questions, but he needed to let his brain clear. Flynn had not shot him yet. So maybe he had a chance to get out of here if he played his cards right. Another voice cried out from somewhere nearby.

'Nanny? Is that you? Is it my turn to be nice?'

This voice belonged to a man, but there was that peculiar infantilised quality to it too.

'No, Thomas,' Flynn said. 'It's not your turn tonight. Go to sleep, there's a good boy.'

'Yes, Nanny,' the man said obediently.

Flynn turned her attention back to Nick. 'What a palaver! Do you see the fuss you've caused?'

Before Nick could answer, another figure walked across the stone floor to join the two of them.

'I very much doubt this fellow has the foggiest what trouble he's caused, what?'

The outer reaches of Flynn's torch gave some definition to the new person. Jowly. Late sixties. Dinner jacket. Hands tucked casually into his trouser pockets. Nick recognised Lord Davenport-Ross immediately.

SIXTY-SIX

(O)

'What's going on here, Nanny?' Davenport-Ross asked. 'Why has this chap wandered downstairs without permission? I thought I was very clear.'

'He's not one of your security men, m'lord,' Flynn said. 'He's a journalist.'

'What?'

'I was trying to spare you from ever having to worry about him, m'lord. Had him chasing shadows, or so I thought. But it seems he's found us after all.'

'I see. Has he anything to do with this drone do-dah I keep hearing about?'

'It was his, m'lord, yes. I'm sorry, I didn't realise what he was up to. I really did try to keep him away from this place. But he's persistent if nothing else.'

'Oh,' Lord Davenport-Ross said. 'Oh dear. One doesn't like the sound of that. Tell me, Nanny, does anyone else know he's here?'

'No, m'lord. He's been reporting in to me this whole time.

I've been trying to keep him busy and occupied, but he keeps sticking his nose where it doesn't belong.'

'Well, chap? Is this true?'

Nick swallowed. Davenport-Ross was not armed and, although a heavyset man, he was pretty sure he could take him. Flynn and her gun were a different story, however. She was a trained police officer. He didn't fancy his chances of wrestling the weapon off her.

'Let's put it this way, *m'lord*,' he said, deliberately mocking the title. 'I wouldn't have come here alone if I didn't have backup. If I don't report back in within the next hour, the authorities will be notified.'

He didn't know why he had said that. The threat was as unconvincing as his delivery. There was a snort from Davenport-Ross, which turned into full-blown braying.

'My dear chap,' the lord said. 'Where do you think you are, in some cheap picture film?' He pronounced it *fil-lim*. 'You think authorities frighten me? We have Detective Inspector Flynn from the Met police right here! Perhaps you'd like to address your complaint to her?'

Nick said nothing. He glared at Flynn. All this time, she was just a smokescreen.

'Was there even a warrant?' he asked her.

'I'm afraid not,' Flynn said. 'I was just hoping to put you off the scent. And keep you away from m'lord's business.'

Nick frowned at Flynn. 'Tracy, what the fuck is going on? Why are you here? Surely you're not into this kinky shit too?'

'Don't you dare judge me,' Flynn said angrily. 'You haven't got a clue how the mind of a child works. I know.'

Nick remembered their conversation at his kitchen table all those days ago. 'Funny thing about kids. They can be a lot more grown up than we give them credit for. A lot more.'

He wondered what she had done in her own home. What she had used her position to cover.

'You've done things with your own kids?' Nick asked her.

'Abused them?' He was half choking as he struggled to get the words out.

'Well, I've stopped now, if it makes you feel better,' Flynn said. 'M'lord has helped me see that it's safer to enjoy what we like with this lot.'

'But that's stupid,' Nick said. 'These people are not kids!'

'Oh, but they *are*, chap,' Davenport-Ross said. 'In the most important way there is.'

Sophia, out of bed again, drew up to the bars and pressed her face keenly through them. 'Daddy, is that you?'

Davenport-Ross flashed her an avuncular smile and moved over so that he could kiss her forehead. He caressed the top of her head with his fingers and reached for one of her pigtails. 'So pretty,' he said. 'Don't you think? It's so exciting how the Nostal just wipes their minds of all sexual experience.'

Sophia smiled at him, and he grinned at Nick.

'How old are you, my dear?' Davenport-Ross asked her.

'I'm almost five!' Sophia said proudly.

'See?' he said.

'You people are sick!' Nick said. 'You need to be locked up!'

Davenport-Ross snorted, waving his arms about in an exaggerated flourish. 'Oh, mea culpa! *Mea culpa!*'

'So it was you,' Nick said. 'On the Black Road site. You gave the order to take this woman from the club.'

'There's no taking, you imbecile. The clubs are mine. I own them. And I pay for the people who run them too. That means the regressors are mine.'

Nick heard a noise from one of the other cells. Another woman, gurgling and bawling like a baby.

'Shush now,' Flynn said. 'You'll wake the lot of 'em.'

'Christ, how old is *she* supposed to be?' Nick said.

'Melinda? She's ten months,' Davenport-Ross said. 'He

really is pig-ignorant, isn't he, Nanny? I've had just about enough of him.'

'Me too, m'lord. Shall I shoot him?'

'He certainly deserves it, Nanny.'

Nick was speechless, trying to take in the insanity that was before him. He had to think fast and act now before it was too late to escape this deranged sex dungeon with his life.

SIXTY-SEVEN

(O)

Flynn cocked the gun.

'Nanny, what's the dose precisely?' Lord Davenport-Ross said.

'Minus thirty, m'lord,' she said.

'Well, then two darts ought to do it.'

Shocked and confused, Nick opened his mouth to speak, but nothing came out.

Seeing his puzzled expression, the lord tutted. 'Relax, chap. You'll just be going to sleep. We'll put you in the big cot with Melinda.'

Flynn stepped forward again, finally at the end of her patience.

'Wait!' he cried out.

Too late, he felt a sharp sting in his chest as if bitten by a giant mosquito. He stared down at the dart. Instinctively, he reached down and pulled it out. *Ping!* Another flew out from behind Flynn's torchlight. The sharp end of the dart penetrated his jacket before hitting his phone in the inside pocket. The dart bounced off him and fell to the floor. Flynn hesitated, unsure about what had just happened. Nick used the moment, flinging the first dart at her with as much force as he could. It created just the distraction he needed as it whizzed past Flynn's face, close to her eyes. By the time she cried out and dropped the torch, he was already moving. His shoes hit the stone floor loudly and he sucked in sharp breaths, sprinting down the corridor.

'Nanny . . .' Davenport-Ross cried.

Other voices were stirring now. More regressed child-adults, waking up to the din.

'Don't worry, he won't get far, m'lord,' Flynn said.

She could be right, Nick thought as he reached the end of the corridor. He was already out of breath. He stopped dead, not just because his lungs were burning, but because he was puzzled by what he saw ahead of him – a raised platform, a couple of feet high, accessed by tiered steps that ran all the way along its edge. On the platform were fairground attractions. A carousel with merry-go-round horses. A classic teacup ride. There was a tower in the background too. A helter-skelter, maybe. To the far left, he thought he even saw a full-sized Ferris wheel. He realised why the spiral steps had taken so long to get down. They had dug deep so they could build an underground amusement park. How on earth had they got all this down here? Though no one was in the fairground, Nick heard muted funfair music being piped softly through speakers somewhere—

He felt a sharp stabbing pain in the back of his neck.

'Got him, m'lord!' Flynn cried.

'You rotter!' Davenport-Ross shouted. 'Dose him again, Nanny!'

Nick heard Flynn reload the tranquilliser gun. *Shit.* He scrabbled at his nape, yanking the dart out violently and, panicking, started to run again.

SIXTY-EIGHT

(0)

He sprinted along the neighbouring corridor, doubling back on himself. Cells on either side of him blurred past, full of more sleeping child-people. He still felt the after-sting of the dart. All this time Flynn had been carrying a tranquilliser gun. While a dart was infinitely preferable to a real bullet, he had reason to worry. As a delivery system, it was probably a lot quicker than swallowing a pill. He'd pulled both darts out almost instantly, but who knew how much of an effect they could already be having? It might just be the adrenaline pumping but he felt as though maybe

(-5)

it was starting to work, even now. Ahead, he saw the courtyard and beyond it, the doorway at the bottom of the steps. Would he reach it in time? Flynn was in hot pursuit now, but it would depend on which way she had gone. It was still possible that he might have the jump, just. But if she had doubled back along her own corridor

(-10)

she might head him off at the pass. And then he would be screwed. *My God*, he thought. He was feeling increasingly energetic, convinced his legs could take him faster, and further. It wasn't like a shot of adrenaline, more like a growing, no, *ballooning*, sense of confidence in the vigour of his body. He felt a shift in him, his pace somehow quickening the way it would have if he'd been running on a treadmill several years ago. It was both good and bad

(-15)

that it was working so effectively. He figured it had to be the delivery system. The drug was reaching his bloodstream faster. He was no expert but one thing he knew. Ultimately, this wouldn't be good. Not if the effects were accelerated and he started

(-20)

regressing faster than usual. The courtyard loomed closer as he summoned whatever energy, real or imagined, was inside him, and tried to channel it into his limbs so he could reach

(-25)

it. Flynn appeared out of nowhere, blocking his exit. She had run parallel to him after all, clearly expecting his strategy. Snarling, she aimed the tranq gun at him. *Fuck!*

(-30)

He rolled as the dart plinked against the stone floor. A miss. Up on his feet and back the way he had come. But before he could get away, he felt a sharp pain, this time in his buttocks. *Shit*. He reached around, pulled out the dart even as he kept moving. His muscles burned as he ran back down the passageway, putting as much distance between him and Flynn as possible. He sensed she was falling behind, perhaps hampered by fatigue. At the end of the tunnel, he turned left. He ran past two more archways and towards a stone wall . . . with a new door. *A way out?* he wondered. Nothing to do but try. It was a white door, easy to focus on, becoming ever larger as he neared it. He wondered how long it would be before the new dose would start to take.

(-35)

He reached the door, wriggled the handle. To his relief, it was unlocked. In the corridor behind him, Flynn's heavy footsteps resounded ever louder. Nick flung the door open and stepped inside, slamming it behind him.

(-38)

It was a dead end. Some kind of CCTV monitoring room. Nobody was inside, but there were several rows of monitors in front of a control desk. The screens mostly had views of the corridor exits. Cameras had been mounted on the archways, using night vision. Some were pointed inwards, capturing the closest cell inside the mouth of the tunnels. One monitor showed a woman-child asleep on her bed, cuddling a stuffed rabbit. Another, a grown man in crocodile pyjamas at his cell door, straining to see what the excitement was all about.

(-40)

He spotted Flynn on yet another monitor screen. She had just reached the end of the corridor, the tranq gun clutched in her hand. Nick looked desperately around him. His eye was drawn to a lever on the wall, marked 'RELEASE ALL'.

(-43)

Instinctively, he pulled it, hoping that it might create a distraction. He was rewarded by a loud buzzing noise and the sound of hundreds of metal bars clanking. On the monitors, the gates of cells opened as the bars rolled slowly back. The croc pyjama man stepped cautiously out of his prison. So did another Little, on a different screen. Flynn froze, looking frantically around her as the Littles who were awake began wandering out en masse. He heard Davenport-Ross howl, banshee-like, and command her to do something. *Perfect.* Hopefully that was enough of a distract . . .

(-47)

. . . dis . . . thing that would make the bad people get angry.

(-48)

If they were angry, maybe he could run quick and get away from the Bigs, he thought.

(-49)

He ran out of the room, with no direction in mind. It was hard to do thinkies at all now, to focus his thoughts together. Though only seconds were passing, he was aware on some subconscious level that he was slipping deeper into an abyss inside his own mind. He lunged forward, aiming for the nearest corridor. And discovered that his legs no longer worked.

(-50)

He was on all fours. Crawling. He knew cold from the stones his fingers and knees scuttled across. He started crying. He needed comfort. Needed to cry. He was alone, afraid. A blurry shape hovered ahead. He crawled towards it, hoping desperately it would be his mother. The shape stooped, embraced him. But instead of the bosom-serenity he craved, he felt harsh hands pull him across the stone. He bawled even louder and the blurry shape leaned forward, whispered something fierce in his ear, something that wasn't kind, soft or motherly.

(-55)

And then deeper still. Darker. Only the sound of his own blood pumping through him, instinctively reminding him of that other pulse he knew once, immersed in fluid. A place he was safe, once. No hunger, no needs. A place where he just *was*.

(-60)

Then there was nothing but black. And after that, nothing at all.

PART FOUR

SIXTY-NINE

(O)

A wooden slat was all he saw when he finally opened his eyes. It was close enough to his face that the tip of his nose brushed against its grooves. He sucked in a deep breath. He had access to air, thank God. His leg felt crusty; his trousers were soaked in urine, which had now dried, suggesting he had been gone for some time. But gone where? It felt like he'd been in a coma, with no dreams or memories. His head ached and his mouth was bitter, as though he had drunk a hundred litres of moonshine. As he slowly tried to orientate, he probed his throbbing brain, trying to recall how he had come to be here. And where was here exactly? He was lying on his back, sandwiched between a cold concrete floor and a wooden one above. A short gap between two of the slats afforded him a view of a bright yellow ceiling. He turned his sore head and tried to wriggle his limbs. There was a shuffle, followed by the sound of a door closing quietly above. Then footsteps. An eye appeared through the gap. Large and brown, with earnest intent.

'You're wake!'

Nick recognised the voice. 'Anuj! Can you get me out of here?'

'Wait, wait,' the other man said.

There was more shuffling, and then a strip of light appeared as a slat was lifted up and taken away. Anuj repeated this manoeuvre several times until there was a gap large enough for Nick to sit up in. He rubbed the back of his head and examined his clothes. His shirt and jacket were both torn. Anuj helped him onto the floorboards and he took in his surroundings. He was inside a Wendy house with a lemon-yellow interior. It had been built extra large and included an adult-sized table and chairs in red Formica. It also appeared to have working electricity inside, with lights on the walls and ceiling. Carefully, he staggered over to a chair and sat down. His body felt like a stone.

'What happened?' he asked. 'How'd I get here?'

'There were noises,' Anuj said. 'Bigs shouting. They scared Mistuh Bearbah!'

Nick blinked as he tried to listen. There was something off about Anuj. He was wearing pyjamas with Spiderman printed on them.

'You're regressed,' he said.

'What?'

'You're a Little.'

Anuj giggled. Nick bent forwards, gazed into the other man's eyes. Yes, he recognised that glint. Anuj was in child form, just as he had been when they had first met.

'What happened, Anuj? How did I get in here?'

'I *hid* you!' Anuj cried excitedly. 'I saw you crawling on the floor and I knew baddies were after you.'

'Baddies?'

'Daddy and his friends!'

Anuj's face became sad. 'I hate him,' he declared. 'I hate them all! They said I would see my friends if I came here, but

I haven't. Instead, they come in here at night and want to play their games, which I hate. I don't even *like* Fun Land!' He started to sob.

Nick reached out and touched his arm. 'I'm sorry, mate.'

'I hid you,' Anuj sniffed. 'Under the floor. They caught all the Littles and looked in their rooms. They looked for a long time, but they didn't find you!' He grinned suddenly as if he'd already forgotten his tears. 'Mistuh Bearbah and me were too clever for them! Ha ha!'

Nick got up and moved over to the Wendy house's only window. A pair of Avengers-themed curtains had been left open, giving him a clear view outside, into Anuj's cell. It was identical to Sophia's in every respect, down to the queen-sized bed in the centre of the room. The window was pane-less, and he heard muffled sounds from behind the brick walls, presumably from Anuj's captive neighbours. Feeling a little more like himself, Nick attempted to walk around inside the room. He felt a mild wave of nausea, but it was passing. Anuj, meanwhile, diligently replaced the wooden floor slats.

'It's a good hidey!' he was saying. 'I found it all by myself.'

Nick tried to do some basic maths. The lights were on inside Anuj's cell. His best guess was he had been hidden here overnight. Enough time for the Nostal's effects to wear off completely. He remembered more now, his consciousness rewinding itself so fast that it had terrified him. The sensation of crawling, the rapid infantilisation. Most disturbing of all, the black oblivion that had consumed him like a blanket. He shivered. If it wasn't for Anuj, he may never have come back.

'Thank you for rescuing me, Anuj,' he said. 'You did ever so well, mate. I must have been heavy to drag.'

'You were sleeping,' Anuj said, giggling again. 'And you were a fatty boom-boom. Boom-boom! Ha ha.'

Nick remembered the CCTV cameras. His heart froze. Had Flynn checked the footage? If so, why hadn't she found him already? The cameras were mounted on the archways, so she would have at least seen which corridor he had entered. Or would she? He had been on all fours at one point, hadn't he? The camera had been at a fixed angle, which meant he'd probably crawled right under its nose.

'There!' Anuj said. 'All back now.' He turned to Nick, his smile gone again. 'But you must get out and run fast,' he said, 'or they will catch you.'

Nick glanced back at the window. 'How do I get out, Anuj? Is your room always locked?'

Anuj frowned. This question was evidently a tough one for him. He plodded back over to the plastic table set and sat down to scratch his chin. 'They'll come by soon. You can run out when the door is open!'

Nick felt a pang of adrenaline as he became aware again of the danger he was still in.

'You must be fast,' Anuj said. 'Sometimes I see the others run. But they use their guns.'

'What?'

There was a loud clang, the sound of cell doors rolling back. The same sound Nick had caused when he'd pulled the master lever in the monitoring room.

'They're here already,' Anuj cried. 'Hide, hide!'

A loud female voice carried through the corridor outside, broadcast by a tannoy system. 'Breakfast time, children!'

It was booming. Authoritative. Yet it also had an ostensibly friendly tone.

'*Who's* hungry?' it teased.

The question was quickly answered by a medley of strange, warped cries that echoed around the stone corridor. Mature voices that belonged to grown men and women, but all laced with a disturbing childish shrill. It sent another judder down Nick. The excited howls were followed by a clanging sound, this one closer and more local. A metallic baton tap-tapping against the bars of the cells.

'Stand by your beds. There's porridge coming!'

The announcement, from a man who sounded nearby, was met by a few boos.

'There are children in this world who have no breakfast this morning. You can't always get the fun cereals.'

More boos came from the cells.

'You are very lucky to have porridge,' the man insisted. 'So you'll eat up and be grateful, or have your treats taken away. Including time in Fun Land. Is that understood?'

A mixture of sniffles, whimpers and some enthusiastic acquiescing echoed around the floor.

'Good,' the man said. 'That's better.'

'Stand by your beds!' said the female voice on the tannoy. 'And if anyone needs help with the toilet, put your hand up.'

Anuj swallowed and ran quickly to the window, drawing the curtains shut. He turned back to face Nick.

'Don't get found!' he whispered.

With that, he toddled out awkwardly through the front door of the Wendy house and back into his cell. Nick crept back to the curtains, peering through the narrow gap that remained – nervous, watchful.

SEVENTY

(O)

Minutes passed. The cell door was wide open but Anuj stood faithfully by his mattress like a barracks soldier waiting for an inspection. This was clearly a drill that he had done before, perhaps the first morning after he'd been brought here. Nick heard people going into the adjoining cubicles, accompanied by the sound of clinking plates and cutlery. Eventually, a hulk of a man entered Anuj's cell. In one hand, he carried a metal dish containing a dollop of gloopy porridge. In the other, he held a tranquilliser gun. Nick recognised the fat, stocky face. Greg. The bouncer from Play Ground. Greg tucked the gun into his belt, placed the plate on the mattress, and then picked something up from Anuj's bed. It looked like an oversized baby bottle.

'Why is this still full?' Greg said. 'You're supposed to drink it in the night.'

'I wasn't thirsty,' Anuj said defiantly.

'Well, don't worry, I got you covered.'

Greg dipped in his pocket and extracted a small glass vial

with a powder inside. He carefully unscrewed the vial and sprinkled the powder onto the porridge.

'Right then, young man,' he said. 'Come get this down you.'

The powder has to be Nostal, Nick thought. It was probably in the bottle too. These must be the main ways they kept their prisoners constantly regressed. He guessed the tranq guns were likely just backup, in case any of the prisoners tried anything, or their doses wore off earlier than expected. A bandolier stuffed with spare darts was strapped across Greg's chest, suggesting the guns were still used relatively often. Anuj took his breakfast dish but made a big show of dropping the spoon Greg handed to him. The utensil rolled under the bed. Cursing, Greg knelt down and fumbled for it, at which point Anuj waved frantically in Nick's direction. Nick took the hint, slipping through the front door of the Wendy house. He crept softly around the front of the bed towards the open doorway. But he wasn't quiet enough.

Greg snapped his head around. 'Hey, it's you! What the fuck?'

Nick froze.

'It was you who broke in here, wasn't it? They said you escaped! Everyone's been scouring the fucking mansion lookin' for you. Wait till his lordship finds out I got you!'

Greg was on his haunches now, one fat hand reaching for the gun. But Nick had already bolted out of the cell and, for the second time in twelve hours, sprinted down the stony corridor.

'Stop him!' Greg shouted.

A woman appeared from another open cell to Nick's right, carrying an empty breakfast dish. He slammed into her, causing them both to tumble. Greg puffed his way out of Anuj's cell, tranq gun at the ready. On impulse, Nick grabbed the woman's porridge dish and threw it, hitting Greg squarely in the face.

'You fucker!' he screamed, dropping his weapon as he clasped his hands over his nose.

Nick rolled towards him, scooped up the gun and shot Greg square in the chest. The hefty bouncer threw his hands open, looking down at the dart in disbelief. But before he could react, Nick was on his feet, smashing Greg's nose with the barrel of the weapon. The chunky man collapsed onto one knee. Nick took that as his cue to wrestle the bandolier off him. It came off easier than he expected, his stunned opponent still too dazed to offer resistance as Nick yanked it over one fat shoulder. He stepped back, pulling a dart from one of the bandolier's slots. It was transparent, filled with ground liquified Nostal, with a red fletching at the end to help it fly. He examined the gun. Pneumatically powered, with a simple bolt that flicked the barrel mechanism back. Sensing Greg stir, Nick quickly loaded the dart into the gun's barrel – and fired again. Greg groaned and fell onto his back. Nick spun around to face the woman, who had managed to stagger to her feet. She stared in horror as he nimbly loaded another dart and pointed the tranq gun at her.

'I don't mean this as a compliment,' he said, 'but you don't look a day over twenty-five . . . . so if these are minus thirties, I'll only need the one.'

The woman raised her hands slowly. 'Please,' she said. 'Don't.'

A snore erupted from behind them. Greg.

'That was quick,' Nick said. 'Sleeping like a baby already.' He smiled. 'Sorry,' he said and shot her.

She screamed and ran at him, but he sidestepped her. She tripped over Greg's immobile body and into another open cell, landing face first on the floor. The scene was watched in awe by the cell's occupier, a twenty-something woman wearing a tiara and a Disney princess dress. Nick's attacker spasmed by her feet. It wouldn't be long until the Nostal took. By some miracle, no one had appeared to investigate all the commotion, but he knew that wouldn't last long. The young woman in the Disney dress stared wide-eyed at him in confusion and wonder.

'Relax, honey,' Nick said. 'She won't hurt you. No one will again.'

With his free hand, he slung the bandolier over his shoulder and reached inside his jacket. His phone was still there. The screen was cracked, but the camera still worked. He started recording the video.

'My name is Nick Winters,' he said, 'and I'm a journalist.'

He spoke loudly and enunciated each word, rotating his body so the phone's camera took in the entire sweep of the corridor with its rows of open cell doors.

'What I'm about to show you defies belief,' he continued. 'But I promise you, this is one hundred per cent real.'

SEVENTY-ONE

(O)

Nick was halfway through recording his report when they finally emerged. One by one they came, drawn by his loud, pronounced voice. Before long, they had crowded the exit points at both ends of the corridor. Employees, he guessed, paid to keep the great kinky dungeon running. There were about twenty of them. He zoomed in on one randomly.

'Oh, and who do we have here?' Nick asked. 'Would you like to state your name for the record, sir?'

The man automatically shot a palm up over his face.

'Come on,' Nick teased. 'One comment, on the record.'

He tutted. 'Anyone care to comment about what's been going on here?'

It was strange, the psychological effect he had. They were more afraid of the phone camera than the tranq gun. When he stepped forward, they stepped back like it was a dance. Some hid their faces, others turned and ran when they saw what he was doing. He walked towards the end of the corridor that opened out onto Fun Land. The crazy construction would make for gripping visuals when the video went public. Who was going to believe the oddity of a fun fair buried deep underground? Predictably, the staffers blocking his exit backed away as he approached. He recognised one of the group as Brenda, Greg's counterpart from Play Ground.

'Hey, Brenda! Don't you want to answer some of *my* questions for a change? I've got plenty!'

'Fuck off,' Brenda said.

She turned her back, shuffling shamefully away with the others like anxious cattle collectively sensing a predator. But they were the real predators. And Nick was going to make sure the world knew it.

'There you are! You are one slippery fish!'

He looked up at the raised stage and at Fun Land's bright, glitzy lights in time to see Tracy Flynn step out from behind a carousel of merry-go-round horses.

'You had us worried,' she said. 'We've been searching every inch of this house for you. We've even had our men out on the roads! Where've you been hiding?'

Nick held his phone up firmly at her as she approached.

'What are you going to do with that?' she sneered. 'Post it on Facebook?'

Nick saw she was armed with her tranq gun. He walked towards the stage, keeping his phone held steady. A short flight of steps brought him up onto the dais, where he and Flynn became level. All the while, his other hand remained behind his back, hiding his own gun from sight.

'I have a friend waiting,' Nick said, 'ready to press the button on this. He's been standing by.'

'I see,' Flynn said. 'And how are you going to send it to him, exactly?'

Nick was disappointed to see that, unlike the others who had freaked out at being recorded, she knew the obvious: that there was no cellular signal down here. There was only one chance now. As Flynn closed in, his thumb flicked his phone over to its still camera setting. 'Smile!' he yelled, and pressed the flash.

Momentarily blinded, Flynn covered her eyes. Nick shot a dart into her. She cried out, clasping at her shoulder blade where the tip had penetrated. Flynn lunged forward just as Nick moved out of the way, but not before the ball of her fist smashed the weapon from his hand. *Fuck.* There was no time to go back for it. He was already running towards the carousel, weaving his way around the colourful horses, adrenaline pumping through him again. Flynn looked about forty-ish, which meant if he could only hold out long enough, her mental state would reduce to that of a ten-year-old girl. But that was still one beefy ten-year-old. Would she still be able to take him down? He stepped off the merry-go-round and frantically surveyed where to go next. A dart flew past his eyes. Somehow, Flynn had found her way around the outside of the ride and was closing in.

'Bad man,' she said, in a weirder, younger voice. 'You won't stop me 'cos you were naughty.'

Nick ducked to the right, into the open archway of a new amusement. An assortment of mirrors greeted him, mounted on frames with wheels. They were all different sizes and lengths, positioned together to form a maze. He moved swiftly through the labyrinth of glass panes, distorted clones of himself surrounding him as he ran.

'You can't hide, baddy man!' Flynn shouted after him.

He thought he heard her move in and, for a moment, imagined they would have a dramatic showdown in this house of mirrors like they did in the movies. But then he realised she was simply waiting for him to come out. He hoped to God there was a back entrance. But, after some wandering, he realised there was nothing behind the collection of mirrors but a solid wall. His stomach sank. He'd trapped himself again. The only way out was the way in.

'Hey, why don't you come in here?' Nick teased. 'I'm not getting any younger.'

No response.

'That was a joke,' he said. 'I guess maybe you're not old enough to get it.'

Why was he joking? Nothing about this was remotely funny. He slipped closer to the entrance. Think, *think*. He paused by one of the mirrors, staring at its trolley wheels. With the right positioning . . . He wriggled a second mirror, so that the first caught the fullness of his reflection . . . then gave the frame a gentle push. The mirror glided out of the doorway. Flynn instinctively fired her gun at his reflection, the dart clinking redundantly on the glass. Not quite believing he'd fooled her, Nick surged forward, using the wheeled mirror as a shield. The mirror rammed into her bulk, sending her flying backwards into a teacup seat on the ride behind. She gasped for breath as Nick ran over to fetch his gun from the floor. He reloaded it and quickly shot her in the neck. Flynn glared at him, but her crumpled position prevented her from leaping up. He shot her with a second dose, more than enough to infantilise her.

'Nanny!' a horribly familiar voice cried out.

Lord Davenport-Ross emerged from one of the corridor archways. He was wearing a beige linen suit and carried a rifle in his arms – a hunting weapon perhaps. Behind him trailed four security guards carrying silenced pistols.

'No regression for you now, chap,' Davenport-Ross said. 'I'm afraid you've forced us to do things the old-fashioned way. You can't say you weren't given a chance.'

Nick stiffened as the lord and his armed entourage stepped towards him. He panicked, glanced behind him. His only chance was to retreat deeper into their indoor amusement park, pursued by five armed men. He couldn't say he liked the odds.

SEVENTY-TWO

(O)

He ran into Fun Land's teacup ride first, stepping over Flynn's limp body. Loud pings of metal hitting metal followed as bullets ricocheted off the colourful carriages.

'That's it, chaps!' Davenport-Ross cried.

Nick remained stooped as he carved a path through the cup-shaped seats. His fingers trembled as they tried to reload his next dart. He didn't imagine he could take all five of them out, but he couldn't give up, not yet. If he had any chance of surviving, he had to take advantage of each moment. On the other side of the attraction, he had two choices. A looming bouncy castle, over to his right. It wasn't your standard inflatable castle. This one had multiple doorways and, presumably, rooms inside. Places to hide, but also places where you could find yourself cornered. The alternative was the Ferris wheel, straight ahead. He chose the wheel, sprinting to an entry gate and up the short exit stairs. There was a control booth at the bottom with an open door. He briefly considered starting the wheel up, for a distraction. But the plethora of buttons looked far too complicated. Instead, he ran to the first gondola and leapt up, grabbing the roof, and pulling himself up the side. From there, he hoisted himself up onto the spokes. Only then did he dare to look behind him. None of his pursuers were in sight yet, but he heard them crashing through the covered teacup ride. They must have thought he was hiding somewhere inside it. Nick pushed on, climbing up the spoke hand over hand, levering himself slowly up until he was able to drop down onto the roof of the next gondola. From there, he had an excellent vantage point. High enough to be hidden but with a bird's-eye view below. He watched the first of the security men emerge, pistol poised as he looked sharply left and right. Nick leaned over the roof, shot the guy in the back, and rolled quickly out of sight.

'Shit!' he heard the man shout.

'Where is he?' said another voice from below.

'Never mind that. I've been shot!'

'It's just Nostal, you tit. It won't kill you.'

More footsteps approached.

'Chaps, chaps,' Davenport-Ross said. 'Do you see him?'

'He fuckin' shot me!'

'Where? Show me the angle . . . oh, you fool. You've taken the dart out. Where did it come from?'

'Over there, I think,' the man said.

Nick shut his eyes and felt his heart pound loudly in his chest. He hoped to God the man wasn't pointing upwards at the gondola.

'The bouncy castle?' Davenport-Ross said.

Nick felt relief flow back through him as he heard their footsteps hurry over to the inflatable castle. When he felt brave enough, he rolled back over and snuck a peek. Davenport-Ross and three of the men were entering the castle. The last security guy, however, was only just exiting the teacup ride. Nick froze. The man spotted him and whipped up his gun. Time stopped. There was no chance to react, only to wait for the inevitable bullet in his forehead. But before the gunman could fire, another figure burst into view and jumped onto the man's back.

'He's my friend! Leave him alone!'

Anuj wrapped both arms around the man's neck and pulled him backwards. Nick was grateful. Not just for Anuj's bravery, but for the reality of his biology, which was heavy enough to bring the security man down. Nick tried to aim the tranq gun, but the men were too enmeshed in their struggle to be easily distinguished from one another. Instead, he slid quickly across the gondola's roof, dropped onto the spoke, and propelled himself off. He wasn't quite powerful enough to land on top of them, but he was close. He rolled to his left, swinging the butt of the tranq gun across, bringing it down hard on the gunman's head. The man cried out, holding the back of his skull as Anuj kicked him backwards. Nick shot the man in the face, reloaded and shot again, injecting him with the full dose of minus sixty. Then, he swapped his tranq gun for the pistol that had fallen on the floor. Anuj's strong arms wrapped around him. He patted his friend affectionately on the back.

'Thank you, Anuj,' he said. 'You saved me again. Now . . . mind out, okay?'

Nick gently steered Anuj aside as he aimed the pistol at the bouncy castle in the distance. He had never fired a real gun before, had no idea what he was doing. He pulled the trigger, not even stopping to consider whether there was a safety switch he needed to turn off first. The gun recoiled. A bullet hit the side of the inflatable castle, puncturing its rubbery skin. He fired off another round, then another. Holes appeared in one corner of the castle, black dots in the PVC, followed by the loud hiss of escaping air. Nick pressed the trigger again, but discovered he'd already emptied the chamber. Muffled angry voices came from deep inside as

Davenport-Ross and his remaining cronies tried to work out what was going on. The corner would soon start imploding, an inverse mushroom that would eventually collapse. If he was lucky, they would all be trapped inside it. Nick threw the gun on the floor and grabbed Anuj's hand.

'Come with me,' he said. 'We're getting out of here!'

SEVENTY-THREE

(0)

Though his legs were as long as Nick's own, Anuj toddled like a young child, impeding their progress. Nick wished he had the strength to pick him up and run.

'Come on, Anuj! Faster!'

'But I am fast!'

Nick leapt off the dais and onto the stone floor, turning around to take Anuj by the armpits as he flopped forward. The sheer weight of his body was absurd, and Nick grunted with the strain as he staggered backwards.

'Hurry, please, Anuj,' he said. 'The *baddies* are coming after us!'

Thankfully, that didn't seem to be the case yet. But it wouldn't be long. He grabbed Anuj's arm again. The pair sprinted down the stone corridor, the cell doors all shut again, the prisoners back inside their cages. Fortunately, their escape route looked clear. At last, they crossed the great courtyard and reached the exit door at the bottom of the steps. Nick stooped over to catch his breath, a stitch forming in his chest. This only made Anuj laugh.

'You're tired already? Haha! Fatty boom-boom!'

Although he had run with unnaturally small steps, Anuj was apparently convinced he had a child's stamina. Nick wished he believed the same. They started up again, Nick grabbing the rail, praying they didn't encounter anyone on the steps on the way up. The climb was hard but necessary; there was no other option but to push through. He hoped to God that the keypad at the top was entrance-only. Luckily, he needn't have worried. When they finally made it to the top, both now panting and gasping, he discovered the door could be opened from the inside. Cautiously, he ventured into the corridor. Anuj followed, clutching his free hand.

'You ready to run some more?' Nick asked him.

Anuj nodded. They ran down the passageway towards the staircase and the grand hallway, past the kitchen and the dining room. Their feet hit rich red carpet as freedom came ever nearer. But halfway towards their goal, a wooden panel in the wall ahead of them slid open, and Davenport-Ross stepped out into the corridor. Nick could only assume it was a secret lift, another way down to the sex dungeon. The lord stood poised with his hunting rifle as his posse of remaining assassins stumbled out behind.

'*Chap!*' Davenport-Ross screamed.

'Back, *back!*' Nick yelled at Anuj.

He pivoted them one hundred and eighty degrees and they ran back the way they had come. A butler appeared from the kitchen, perhaps curious about the commotion. Nick tore past him, kicked the kitchen door open, and he and Anuj ducked through into an immaculate white-tiled galley and ran between the stainless steel units to a door on the far side. Nick pushed it open. The pungent smell of motor oil filled his nostrils. They were inside an immense garage. Nick recalled seeing its doors on the drone camera footage. Several classic cars were parked in neat rows on the long concrete floor, including a Rolls-Royce and a Bentley. In the centre of the garage was the incongruous sight of a man kneeling in front of a motorbike. The bike was suspended upside down, one loose wheel lying beside it. The man was holding a spanner and was doing some kind of maintenance work. Nick recognised him from the pictures he'd seen online. Adam McCreadie. A familiar helmet lay next to the bike. *Black, with silver streaks.* He let go of Anuj and charged forwards. McCreadie turned his head, looking confused at the sight of a grown man in pyjamas and another, bloodied and bruised, in front of him. Nick saw his brain trying to process what was happening. But it was already too late. Filled with righteous anger, he scooped up the distinctive helmet and smacked McCreadie across the face. McCreadie grunted and collapsed, and Nick kicked the upended bike onto him for good measure.

'Hurry, Anuj! Come on!'

He dashed back to grab the man-boy's hand once more and they made for the open garage door, not stopping until they were out in the broad daylight of the normal world that both flooded and blinded them.

Across the pebbled circle of the driveway and around the stone fountain in its centre. Now it was Nick's turn to try to keep up with Anuj. Whether it was because he was finally free of his subterranean cage or his toddler energy had increased, he'd clearly got his second wind. There was no stopping him.

'Run to the gate!' Nick shouted after him.

He wasn't sure Anuj heard him as he sprinted along the manicured lawn. The bright sunshine continued to dazzle like an unwelcome stage spotlight, forcing Nick to run with one hand shielding his eyes. There was an almighty crack, like booming thunder, and for a moment Nick was disorientated, his ears reverberating. By the time he had worked out that it was Davenport-Ross's hunting rifle, a second shot rang out, missing him by inches but hitting Anuj squarely in the back of his calf, bringing him down. Nick felt the butt of a rifle land hard in the small of his back and he tumbled forwards all too quickly, hitting the side of his head on the ground. Face down, his bleeding lips tasted freshly cut grass. A hard boot kicked the side of his torso, rolling him onto his back. His head spun. The world had flipped upside down. Sounds echoed all around him as pain shot across his head, neck and then parts of his arms and legs. He heard Anuj's anguished cries. The susurration of sprinklers. Then, worryingly, the clinking of metal as Davenport-Ross reloaded his rifle.

'I'll show you, you uppity little *do-dah*.'

Nick blinked up into the glare and witnessed the business end of Davenport-Ross's weapon. He gurgled blood, which he hoped was coming from a cut in his mouth and nowhere else. A ruddy face came into focus for a moment, and Nick saw the tight hatred in it. Groggily, he attempted to reach into his inner jacket pocket.

The lord crunched a boot down on Nick's arm, crushing the biceps. 'Don't even think of reaching for your gun, chap.'

Nick grinned. 'Too late,' he spat weakly. 'I've already pressed send.'

Confused, the lord momentarily released his heel, allowing Nick to slide out his phone from the fabric of his suit. There was a full bar on display, confirming that his video file had successfully gone.

'It's too late, *m'lud*,' Nick said. 'It's all out there now. My friend Sam will expose you. No more hiding, you sick bastard.'

Davenport-Ross's eyes widened with horror. He staggered backwards, cocking the rifle as he aimed for Nick's head. Nick closed his eyes. He wasn't aware he was holding his breath until he heard a loud crashing, metallic sound. It was followed immediately by a rumbling and a scream. Daring to open his eyelids, Nick saw that the lord was no longer looming over him. In the same spot where he had just been standing, however, was a black stretch limo.

SEVENTY-FOUR

(O)

It was hard to follow the order of events as they unfolded. Nick just about had the strength to prop himself up on his elbows as his brain tried to piece together what had happened. He concluded the metallic clang had been the mansion's front gates breaking. They had come off instantly as the stretch limo had careered through them, the evidence of which was its mangled bonnet and smashed windscreen. The driver of the limo, Ben Cooper, was unharmed and already clambering out of the door. Ben wasted no time, walking boldly up to Lord Davenport-Ross's body sprawled out on the pebble drive. He snatched up the lord's rifle just as a wave of security men closed in on their position. Ben fired two shots, dispatching two of the men expertly. By the time the third man registered the impressive marksmanship, Ben had thrown the weapon at his head. It caught the business end of his face and he fell backwards, disorientated. Ben ran up to him and karate-chopped the gun from his hands. A precise strike to the neck, and then all four enemies were down. Nick watched in amazement as he stooped down, only to rise again with a silenced pistol in each hand like the hero in some crazy action movie.

Ben turned back to check on Rebecca Hughes, who was only just emerging from the back of the limo. 'You okay, ma'am?' he called out.

'I'm good,' she said.

'Okay. I'm going to check the house.'

He gave her a solemn nod and ran on towards the open garage, weapons at the ready.

'Afghanistan,' Rebecca reminded Nick.

She extended a hand. Nick took it and used his other arm to shunt himself up onto his knees. From there, he worked on staggering to his feet.

'Davenport-Ross?' he said. ' Is he . . . ?'

They both turned. The lord was stirring faintly. Still alive. But not likely to be getting up any time soon. Behind them, agonised cries rose in the air as a figure writhed animatedly on the grass.

'Anuj! Hang on!' Nick limped over to his friend, who was rocking back and forth on his back, cradling his shin.

'It hurts!' he wailed.

'I know, I know. *Shh*. We'll get a doctor, okay? He'll know what to do.'

'The baddies shot me!' Anuj cried.

With some effort, Nick knelt down and reached out to him, but he recoiled at his touch.

'Let me take a look,' Rebecca said, crouching next to him.

'*Owww!*'

'The wound doesn't look deep, but we need to stop the bleeding,' Rebecca said.

Nick removed his jacket and handed it to her. Rebecca twisted it and wrapped it around Anuj's calf.

She pressed down hard, beckoning Nick to help her. Then both of them held the jacket firmly over the wound.

'We need to call an ambulance,' Rebecca said.

Gunshots echoed from inside the house, and Nick snapped his head back. He had the feeling they all originated from Ben.

'Maybe we should call a couple,' he said.

He picked up his phone with his free hand and dialled 999.

They waited.

'How did you know I was here?' Nick asked.

'You can thank Benjamin,' Rebecca said. 'After you left us, he told me he was concerned that you looked really scared. He said he'd only ever seen fear like that in a man's eyes when his life was in danger. I didn't think any more of it at the time, but then we found Julia.'

'Julia?' he repeated, dumbly.

'I was notified that a junior employer from the legal department had taken sudden leave just after our IT sweep, and we put two and two together. She wasn't answering her phone, so I called her parents, suggested legal action if they didn't tell me where she was. Long story short, they gave up the aunt's address and Ben and I drove over there last night.'

Nick closed his eyes. So much for getting Julia away from all this.

'The poor girl was distraught,' Rebecca continued. 'I honestly believe she thought we were there to harm her. She was obviously upset and she kept asking if we had, and I quote, *done* anything to you. We were honestly baffled, but she insisted you were in danger, just as Benjamin had suspected.'

Nick shook his head, trying to piece it all together. 'But . . . you came *here*,' he said.

'Yes, well. Eventually, she calmed down and told us about a call you made where you apparently said something about

Cambridge being a danger zone. Then I remembered that you'd asked me about Lord Davenport-Ross's Cambridge mansion.'

She stopped short as Anuj let out another blood-curdling scream.

'Hang on a minute.'

She pressed down on the wound again. Anuj groaned, and she stroked his forehead gently.

'You weren't answering your phone either, so I asked Benjamin what he thought we should do. He said you could be in some kind of danger and perhaps we should drive up here and check. Next thing you know, we're at the gates and he starts shouting that he can see you're being shot at. You're lucky we got here in time.'

'So you have no idea about any of it?' Nick said. 'What they're doing here?'

'No,' she said, taking a moment to look around. 'But it's obviously something dubious.'

Nick turned to Anuj, who had swapped out his pain-filled sobs for soft whimpers. The ambulances were taking their time. Ben eventually reappeared on the front steps, still carrying his weapons. He walked solemnly back to meet them.

'You all right, Benjamin?' Rebecca asked him. 'What on earth is going on?'

Behind him, emerging through the front door of the mansion, came a stream of adults, mostly dressed in pyjamas. Some were carrying cuddly toys, looking frightened and lost.

'They've been abducting them,' Nick said. 'From the regression clubs. Taking them while they're pumped up on Nostal. To bring them here.'

'What for?' she asked.

He didn't answer. Ben reached them and fell onto his buttocks. He looked weary, as though being inside the mansion had added ten years to his life.

'So, you found the basement, huh?' Nick said.

'Sick fucks,' Ben said, quietly.

The zombie horde of bewildered regressors shuffled along the lawn, looking around as if expecting guardians to suddenly appear and help them. God only knew how many of Davenport-Ross's employees Ben had shot, but the smarter ones would have fled when the gunfire had started. He swallowed as the adult-kids circled listlessly. Some talked amongst themselves, others looked pleadingly at the three of them. He thought he heard a man ask whether it was okay for him to be out of his room. A child-woman spotted Davenport-Ross and ran over to his semi-conscious body.

'Daddy? Are you okay?'

'Stay away from him!' Nick shouted. 'Stay away from Daddy. He's a bad man and the police are coming for him.'

The woman stared back in wide-eyed disbelief.

The sound of distant sirens filled the air. Nick turned back to Rebecca. She was shaking her head in bewilderment, taking in the chaos that surrounded them.

'What on earth's been going on here, Nick?' she asked.

At the driveway, the first ambulance appeared, navigating around the mangled gate. A police car followed behind, its siren flashing blue.

'Something evil,' he said. 'Something that should never have been allowed to happen.'

He sighed, feeling the weight of the last twenty-four hours bear down on his body. 'Something your drug unfortunately made possible,' he said.

PART FIVE

SEVENTY-FIVE

(O)

It was a cooler, cloudier September morning when Nick once again entered the lobby of Lakefront Sciences and announced himself at reception. After signing in, he was given a day pass and escorted to one of the lifts. He emerged in the restaurant, where the views over London were as impressive as he remembered. Rebecca Hughes and Jeremy Gladstone were at the same corner table where he'd first had lunch with them. The pair greeted him.

'Thanks for making the time for this,' Nick said.

He took his seat and ordered a cappuccino. When the waiter had brought it, Nick removed his phone from his pocket and emailed both of them his copy. A week had passed since the events at Dove's House. Thanks to Sam Goddard being on standby, the *Sunday Record* had broken the story first, though it was quickly picked up by every other media outlet in the country. These were only reports on the basic facts, however, so Sam had officially commissioned Nick to write a feature, an in-depth piece that would tell the entire story. With the revelations that had now come to light, the newspaper's legal team also launched a counter-challenge to the super-injunction, which the High Court had immediately granted. Nick had not been surprised to learn that the judge who had initially rubber-stamped the super-injunction was himself under investigation for being a member of Davenport-Ross's private underground club. Now that he was free to report on everything, Nick wanted to invite comments or corrections before he went live, which he preferred to do face to face. He waited patiently as Rebecca and Jeremy Gladstone diligently read through his draft on their devices, neither saying a word until they had reached the final paragraph. Rebecca was first to finish, marking the act with a deep sigh and pushing her phone away along the table as if she could distance herself from the story itself.

'I hope it's not that bad,' Nick said.

'Well, that all depends on your definition,' Gladstone said.

His discomfort was clear by the pinched way his hands were holding his tablet. The CEO shook his head. 'So much of it was happening right under my own nose,' he said. 'Davenport-Ross even had accomplices inside the company. Perverts, like himself, in our manufacturing and distribution departments, helping him siphon off the supply to keep their little clubs and whatnot going. A few missing invoices here and there, so who's to notice? I didn't even know.'

Nick nodded sympathetically. 'I don't think anyone knew.'

'Don't worry,' Gladstone said with what sounded like summoned resolve. 'Now it's all out in the open, justice will be served. I imagine everyone involved will be going to jail for a very long time.'

'If they ever track them all down,' Nick said. 'The police say it goes even deeper than anyone thought. There were hundreds of secret members, apparently. Judges, lawyers, local politicians.'

'Indeed.' Gladstone sighed. 'A regular deep-state paedophile ring, by all accounts. Well, of a kind I suppose.'

'Who'd have thought full-grown adults would have appealed to these degenerates?' Rebecca said.

'They got off on their innocence,' Nick said. 'That's what their doped-up victims had in common with real kids. Plus, I guess it doesn't hurt that adults were a lot easier to make disappear. Less of a media circus.'

'Especially if you also have help from police who are in on it,' Rebecca said.

Nick nodded glumly. 'The anti-corruption cops who interviewed me said they think Flynn had up to a hundred officers working with her. As well as criminals.'

'You really had no idea she was a part of it?' Gladstone asked.

'None,' Nick said. 'She said she needed my help, but all she did was send me off in wrong directions.'

'Why didn't she just try and get rid of you?' Gladstone said. 'Like they did with Doyle?'

'I'm sure she wanted to. But she also knew she had to be very careful. When journalists vanish, people tend to ask questions. She didn't want that kind of heat.'

'But that bit about you getting chased,' Rebecca said. 'It wasn't her that sent that guy to kill you?'

'You mean Adam McCreadie? No, Flynn didn't sign off on that. The investigating officers told me she claims McCreadie acted on his own.'

He told them how Flynn's network had first alerted her the moment Nick contacted Doyle at Pentonville prison.

'Apparently, the first thing Flynn did was ask McCreadie to keep an eye on me,' he said. 'She probably expected him just to report back on what I was up to. But when he saw me go into his local, where his own boys hang out, he took matters into his own hands. Flynn thought it a reckless move and told McCreadie to back off. That she'd handle me a different way.'

Nick took another sip of his coffee and looked at Gladstone. 'The problem she faced was she knew full well I wouldn't just let my investigation go,' he said. 'So at first she spun me some yarn about how *you* were their prime suspect and how they were on the case. But then she finds out about your job offer and figures it's the perfect way to keep me onside, chasing dead ends until she could figure out what to do with me. Of course, by the time I broke into the mansion and exposed them, disappearing me was the only option she had left.'

'I bet by then she wished that this McCreadie fellow *had* killed you that night,' Gladstone said.

'I'm so glad he's been caught too,' Rebecca said. 'He sounded like a very unhinged man.'

'Makes you wonder why Flynn ever got involved with a loose cannon like that in the first place,' Gladstone said.

'That one's simple,' Nick said. 'There was a quid pro quo between McCreadie and Flynn. A few promises to turn a blind eye to his organisation's activities in return for their services. His guys ran the regression clubs, provided security. And, of course, delivered the, er, packages.'

At the mention of the packages, the table went quiet for a second.

Gladstone cleared his throat. 'Well,' he said, softly, 'it's good that you exposed them. You have our thanks.'

'Really?'

Nick wasn't sure he'd heard Gladstone correctly.

'It all would have come out sooner or later,' the CEO said. 'So, yes.'

Nick looked across at Rebecca, then at Gladstone. 'I was hoping you could clear one detail for me, though,' he said. 'The super-injunction. Was that originally Davenport-Ross's idea?'

Rebecca glanced at her boss.

'He pushed for it hard as soon as we knew about the Doyle case,' Gladstone said. 'And him being our biggest stakeholder, his voice carried the most weight. Of course, we didn't know what he was up to. All he told us was that he wanted to stop the negative stories spreading that could affect our share price.'

'Which I have to say I agreed with at the time,' Rebecca said. 'The super-injunction made sense from a PR point of view too.'

'Yet what he really cared about was the trial,' Nick said. 'And the negative publicity. People everywhere questioning whether Nostal was safe. The risk of a public outcry, maybe even pressure groups. Enough of a public outcry and you guys might have had to take Nostal off the market altogether.' Nick shook his head. 'And that was his lordship's biggest risk,' he said. 'No more Nostal would mean no more pretend kids for him and his friends.'

Gladstone sighed. 'All that effort, and they still decided to have Doyle killed. What a waste.'

'Not necessarily,' Nick said. 'I think he knew full well what could have happened. Super-injunctions are not perfect. Sometimes the story leaks in another country. Occasionally, there are people like me who don't care about what'll happen if they publish it. There was never any solid guarantee he could keep the trial a secret. Better to make double sure, and have no trial proceedings to report on at all.'

The trio were silent for a moment. Gladstone regarded him with what Nick took to be a look of either pity or kindness.

'Any other comments?' Nick said. 'Anything you want to go on record before we go to print?'

'Not from me,' Gladstone said.

Rebecca shook her head.

'Then I have something I want to say,' Nick said. 'For the

record. I'm glad you guys weren't the total bad guys I feared you were. And I'm pleased you had nothing to do with this.'

'Thanks, Nick,' Rebecca said quietly. 'If that's all, let me see you out.'

Nick nodded, shook Gladstone's hand, and rose from his chair.

But before he made for the exit, he turned back to the CEO one last time. 'Can I ask you something?' he said.

'Of course,' Gladstone said.

'The whole time you wanted me to investigate those claimants. You kept insisting they must be making it up. That Nostal was perfectly safe.'

'I did indeed,' Gladstone said.

'Well, what I want to know is whether you still believe that? Do you still think Mark Doyle did what he did in control of himself? And what about all those people? Do you wonder whether there really was something dangerous about Nostal, all this time?'

The CEO shrugged. 'I still don't believe there's anything to it,' he said. 'But belief is not proof. Maybe all the tests and safeguards missed something. It wouldn't have been the first time it's happened in the history of medicine. But as to whether that's the truth of it . . . ?' He shook his head and stared out of the window. 'What the hell does that even matter anymore?' he said.

SEVENTY-SIX

(O)

Rebecca seemed pensive as they made their way down the corridor towards the lifts. She opened her mouth as if to speak, then closed it again, shaking her head.

'What?' he asked her. 'Just say it.'

She shrugged. 'You really did think I would be involved in something illegal,' she said.

'Sorry,' he said.

He was too.

The lift doors pinged open, and they entered the car. Rebecca punched the lobby button and they started their descent.

She turned to face him. 'I resigned this morning,' she said.

'What?' he said. 'Why?'

'Well, for one, I'm the head of PR. I wouldn't exactly say I've been particularly successful at protecting Lakefront's reputation, would you?'

'I'm not sure that any of that is your fault,' he said.

She smiled. 'Nice of you to say. But the captain goes down with the ship.'

'Isn't Gladstone the captain?'

'Don't worry, he'll be out of a job too soon enough,' she said. 'I can't see our remaining shareholders being especially happy that we've lost Lakefront's most profitable drug for good.'

Nick nodded. 'There's no way you think the government will reconsider the ban?'

'No government anywhere in the world will,' she said. 'Not after this. All anyone thinks about Nostal now is that it's the go-to drug for kidnapping and rape. It's become the new Rohypnol overnight. Even worse maybe.'

They rode in silence for a while.

'What will you do?'

'I don't know yet,' she said. 'But I'll land on my feet, somehow.'

'What about Ben?' he asked.

'He'll be fine. He's gone over to work for Jeremy now. I suspect when he moves on, he'll take him with him.'

'I still feel bad that I ever suspected him of trying to murder me.'

'I'm sure he's over it,' Rebecca said.

'Will you be okay?' he asked.

'I'll be fine, honestly. I don't care about the job. I mean, I loved it. Don't get me wrong. But there's a lot more to worry about than money. With Nostal gone, I mean.'

'There is?' he said.

Her eyes took on a haunted look. She glanced down at the pendant necklace, then back at Nick. She bit her lip, then opened the pendant, revealing a small photo of a young woman's face. A brunette, with cheekbones that Nick saw had more than a passing resemblance.

'My sister,' Rebecca said. 'She died three years ago. A sudden heart attack. It was a rare, genetic fluke.'

'I'm so sorry,' Nick said.

She shook her head. 'I'll live,' she said. 'Unlike Chloe. But Nostal's success was helping to fund so much medical research. Projects that could have potentially saved other people's lives in the future.'

'I'm sorry,' he said again. 'I'm sure your sister would have been very proud of you.'

'I miss her so much,' Rebecca sighed. 'But the Nostal used to help with that too.'

Seeing his puzzled expression, she tapped her handbag. 'I was taking minus five to help me deal with my grief,' she said. 'It took me straight back to how I felt before I had the news. And you know what? It really worked. Better than therapy, even.'

She closed the necklace. 'I won't be the only one,' she said. 'For a lot of people out there, when their existing supply runs out, there'll be a lot of harsh realities to face.'

Nick nodded, his thoughts returning closer to home. The lift reached the lobby, and they made their way to the revolving doors.

'Goodbye, Rebecca,' he said. 'Take care of yourself, okay?'

'You too, Nick,' she said.

SEVENTY-SEVEN

(0)

'It's perfect,' Julia Conway said, reading Nick's article on her phone.

They were sitting in a café opposite the Lakefront building.

'I kept your name out of it too, like I promised.'

'Yes, thank you,' she said. 'Though I suppose it didn't matter because they found me out anyway.'

'I'm sorry, that was my fault,' Nick said. 'I told Flynn I had a source inside Lakefront. She told Davenport-Ross, who insisted Jeremy Gladstone do the IT sweep. I wish I hadn't said anything, but I thought I could trust her. She tried to be subtle whenever she asked about you. But she must have been secretly pissed off that I wouldn't give up your name.'

'Well, it doesn't really matter now, does it?' Julia said. 'All's well that ends well, right? So when does it come out?'

'It's in tomorrow's edition,' Nick said.

'A proper paper too,' she said, sipping her tea. 'Not your website, like you said.'

'Proper,' he agreed.

She put her cup down.

'So what now?' he asked her. 'You're going back to work as usual?'

'For now,' Julia said. 'Now I know my employer isn't out to kill me, I've no reason not to carry on as normal.'

'And do you want to carry on?' he asked.

'Now that Nostal is being recalled, I don't see why not.'

He nodded. 'You did a brave thing,' he said. 'You should be proud of it. I hope you know that.'

She blushed again. 'Thank you.'

He patted her on the shoulder, an awkward avuncular gesture that he knew was inadequate, but he hoped expressed his admiration for her. He was deeply grateful too. After all, she had ended up saving his life. And she hadn't been the only one.

SEVENTY-EIGHT

(O)

It took him a long time to reach St James's Park and almost as long to find somewhere to park the bike. Anuj was waiting for him at a table outside the busy café. He was sitting in a wheelchair, one leg in a plaster cast, facing the pond. The afternoon was still cloudy, but there was no rain yet. It was weird seeing his friend again, especially when they were both adults. The two sat, enjoying the views of the water. The sounds of children shrieking and laughing carried across from a nearby play area.

'It's good,' Anuj said, finishing the article.

'You sure you don't mind that you're mentioned by name?' Nick asked.

Anuj shook his head. 'It's important your readers know this happened to real people.'

It had, in fact, been one of the more harrowing aspects of the story for Nick to write. He had interviewed Anuj in the days after their escape and still didn't like to think about it. The official investigation found that Littles abducted from the underground clubs would be asked, in their dosed state, to sign letters or send emails. Whatever they figured would help family and friends buy their stories about moving away. It wasn't always abroad either. Sometimes it would just be from one part of the country to another. As long as it was far enough. At the end of the day, no one could say they were not adults, capable of making their own decisions. It was enough to put proper police off the scent. Nick still remembered Anuj describing how he was literally given Smarties to say his lines on the goodbye video Nick had watched. 'It's okay,' his friend had said. 'I wasn't in that hellhole for long. Not like some of the others. And I don't remember much of it, thank God.'

'You know, I never thanked you properly,' Anuj said now. 'For saving me.'

'No need,' Nick said. 'You saved me too. I'm just glad you're okay.'

'You heard about the ban, right?'

'I did,' Nick said.

Anuj tilted his head towards the play area. Nick followed his gaze until it fell on a young boy of about four, sitting on top of a slide. He slid down, chuckling merrily as his mother scooped him up. A little girl followed, squealing with delight as soon as she let go of the slide's handles.

'Look at them,' Anuj said. 'Not a care in the world. That was us that night.'

'I remember,' Nick said.

'It was magical,' Anuj said. 'And now a little magic has gone out of the world.'

Nick bit his lip thoughtfully. 'Maybe we're better off,' he said. 'It wasn't real, what the Nostal did. The only magic is that it was all an illusion.'

Anuj shrugged. 'All I know is that I won't ever feel like that again.' He pointed at the toddler boy.

Nick saw he had already found his way to the top of the slide and was gliding all the way down again, squealing with unadulterated delight. A random memory of Charles Mills popped into Nick's mind. The old man in a photograph, proudly holding up a marlin fish. His face had seemed so happy. He remembered Lenora Cox, too, smoking as she gushed about the purity of heart behind her music. And then he thought again of the night that he had made love to Heather and cried afterwards. How, in that moment, it had felt as though the fairy tale lived again. But that was the thing about fairy tales. They were designed for children. Sometimes, you were better off growing up.

SEVENTY-NINE

(-30/0)

They stood on Brighton pier, gazing at the sunset as it cast sparkles on the ocean. Their hands were clasped together, their hearts beating with youthful giddiness. Nick stared at Heather, thinking about all they had once been, everything they had once felt. She had spent a long time convincing him to ingest one more pill. He had wrestled with it but, in the end, he concluded that if millions of people around the world were finishing up their last doses, two more probably wouldn't make much difference. But he'd also been clear with her it had to be a one-time thing. She'd said that was exactly the point. 'It's important that we feel it go,' she had told him. It was the only fitting way to try to start a new chapter. Nick hadn't been so sure, but he had really wanted to try – and was just happy that she had changed her mind. And now they were back, having popped one last little green pill. For the last three hours, they had been nineteen again. In love again. But he was starting to feel the effects dissipate. He could tell she was experiencing the same by the sad way she looked at him. He squeezed her hand harder, and they stared into each other's eyes. Eventually, her pupils shrank from their dilated state.

'Anything?' she asked, after a while.

'Nope,' he said. 'It's all gone.'

It felt wrong, holding her hand. *She* felt wrong. But still they held on to each other. He watched her face, sensing it dissolve from his college sweetheart to the near fifty-year-old woman who stood before him.

'My name's Heather,' she said. 'I used to like Nirvana and grunge when I was young. Nowadays, I mostly listen to Radio Four.'

He nodded, recalling what she'd once said to him. *The truth is, at our age, we're very different people now anyway.*

'I'm Nick,' he said. 'I used to hate the way whisky tasted when I was young. Now I love it.'

'Pleased to meet you,' she said. 'How would you like to buy me a coffee, Nick?'

'Sure,' he said. 'Where would you like to go?'

'Just take me somewhere that wasn't here back then,' she said.

'A coffee shop that wasn't here in the nineties? We'll be spoilt for choice.'

He smiled and walked with her back down the pier, towards the town.

'Who knows where it'll lead?' she'd told him. 'Maybe nowhere. But maybe also somewhere new.'

Nick wasn't sure what *somewhere new* would look like. Or if they would even find it. But he was happy that they were both here, walking towards the unknown. Whatever happened now, at least they were going forward.

ENJOYED THIS BOOK?

If you liked *Back*, I'd be very grateful if you'd consider leaving a review on Amazon (it can be as short as you like). It makes a huge difference for an author like me and helps readers find my books more easily.

FANCY A FREE EBOOK?

Get a thrilling ebook for free when you sign up to receive my occasional newsletter. I promise I'll never spam you. And you can opt out any time.

To get your free copy, just go to **dmsearle.com/ebook**

ACKNOWLEDGEMENTS

My deep thanks to the beta readers who offered valuable feedback on earlier drafts. A special mention to Stuart Bache, who did an amazing job on the cover and my editor, Lesley Jones. This novel wouldn't be possible without all those who helped shape it.

www.ingramcontent.com/pod-product-compliance
Lightning Source LLC
Chambersburg PA
CBHW011128190726
48289CB00012B/2954